FORBIDDEN FLAME

Forbidden Flame

Lacey Carlyle

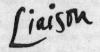

Publisher's message

This novel creates an imaginary sexual world. In the real world,
readers are advised to practise safe sex.

Copyright © 1999 Lacey Carlyle

The right of Lacey Carlyle to be identified as the Author
of the Work has been asserted by her in accordance with
the Copyright, Designs and Patents Act 1988.

First published in 1999
by HEADLINE BOOK PUBLISHING

A HEADLINE LIAISON paperback

10 9 8 7 6 5 4 3 2 1

ISBN 0 7472 6134 2

Typeset by CBS, Martlesham Heath, Ipswich, Suffolk
Printed and bound in Great Britain by
Mackays of Chatham plc, Chatham, Kent

HEADLINE BOOK PUBLISHING
A division of Hodder Headline PLC
338 Euston Road, London NW1 3BH

Forbidden Flame

Chapter One

'I'm sorry, Jasper – I really have to go,' said Jonquil, glancing at her watch for the third time in a minute. 'I've got a meeting and I should have left a quarter of an hour ago.'

'Why didn't you say?' replied Jasper, obviously unaware of the urgency with which she was trying to get him off the phone.

'I did,' she reminded him before adding, 'we'll meet for lunch one day next week – okay?'

'I suppose so. Better get back to work or my boss will be breathing down my neck as usual. Do you know what he said, yesterday? That I—'

'Tell me about it when I see you. Goodbye.'

Jonquil hastily put the phone down and grabbed her briefcase from the chair before dashing out of her apartment. She didn't like being late and always allowed herself plenty of time to get to a meeting – particularly one as important as this.

She was fond of her brother, but if there was something he wanted to talk about, it was virtually impossible to stop him. It had been bad luck that she'd decided to pick up the phone rather than allowing her answering machine to click into operation.

The journey by tube seemed endless. When she arrived at Piccadilly she raced up the escalator and then hurried along as fast as her high-heeled shoes and the congested pavements would let her. Once she reached the production company, she ran up two flights of stairs towards the conference room, her shoulder-length, red-gold hair flying.

Jonquil was a freelance writer who specialised in scripts for promotional corporate videos and training films. This was the third time she'd been asked to work for this particular company, which had a prestigious client list.

A new client wanted a series of films to promote his business in the international market. The project would last for several months and offer her some much needed financial security – at least for the immediate future. This meeting was very important and her heart sank as she stepped into the conference room and saw that it had already begun.

'Sorry I'm late,' she announced, going swiftly around to the empty chair on the far side of the table and sinking into it.

'We've only just started,' Hal, the producer, reassured her. 'I think you know everyone except our new client, Boyd—'

'We've met,' came a cool voice from across the table. 'How are you, Jonquil?'

Jonquil had half-risen so she could lean across to shake his hand but, at the sound of that familiar deep voice, the very ground beneath her feet seemed to shift and she had to cling onto the edge of the table to stop herself from keeling over.

There was a buzzing in her ears which blocked out all sound except her own breathing as she gazed into the deep blue eyes of the man she'd crossed an ocean to escape from, seven years ago.

'*B . . . Boyd*,' she stuttered.

An aeon seemed to pass as she fought for self-control. She noticed that he looked much the same, except for a few lines around the eyes and just the faintest touch of premature grey in his dark hair. His strong nose and thick brows still dominated his hard-boned face and, right at that moment, his faintly derisive smile chilled her to her very core.

It was as if they were alone in the room as he repeated, 'How are you, Jonquil?'

'I . . . I'm fine,' she faltered, mentally cursing herself for her lack of poise. He leant casually back in his chair, the spread of his shoulders in the jacket of a well-cut, charcoal-grey suit just as impressive as she remembered.

She became aware that everyone in the room was watching them with interest and she busied herself by taking a notebook and pen from her briefcase.

Hal, a big bear of a man casually dressed in a creased cotton jacket and jeans, cleared his throat, threw her a quizzical glance and said, 'We're looking at six different videos, each of which highlights some aspect of the company's operation. The first one will . . .'

Her head spinning and working purely on automatic pilot, Jonquil took notes while she wondered why, of all the men in the world, she'd been thrown into unwelcome contact with the one she'd have given almost *anything* to avoid.

Coffee was passed around and she glanced up as she took her cup to see that Boyd was looking at her, his eyes wandering over the delicate lines of her face with its small, straight nose sprinkled with freckles. His gaze lingered for a moment on her lips, before travelling down to the swell of her breasts beneath the jacket of her severely tailored crimson suit.

She felt warm colour gather in her pale cheeks then sweep inexorably downwards, suffusing her with heat which made the room feel suddenly stuffy and airless. To her embarrassment, she felt her nipples hardening beneath her clothing, reminding her that Boyd was the only man she'd ever known who could get her into a state of red-hot arousal just by looking at her.

Already a wanton flame of lust was licking disturbingly at her sex, while heady unwelcome images of him striding round the table, laying her across it and screwing her in front of the others flitted across her mind.

She was furious with herself for reacting in such a way to someone who'd treated her so abysmally. Surely seven years was long enough to make her immune to him?

At last, after what seemed an eternity, it was lunchtime and everyone began to disperse. Jonquil turned to exchange a few words with Natalie, the director, hoping that Boyd would leave the room before she did. But he was talking to Hal and, when Natalie moved away, Jonquil had no option but to rise to her feet and walk around the table towards the door.

With unhurried grace, Boyd rose to his feet and blocked the doorway, towering over her even though she was five foot six and wearing high heels. She'd forgotten how *big* he was. At six foot two, he was easily the tallest man in the room.

'How about having lunch together?' he asked her, the polite words at odds with the hostility she could see in his eyes. 'We could catch up on old times.'

'Whatever makes you think I'd want to do that?' she asked

3

sweetly, hanging onto her poise by a thread. 'Excuse me – may I get past you, please?'

She thought for a minute he was going to continue blocking the doorway, but Natalie came up at that moment and he moved reluctantly to one side. Natalie paused to say to Jonquil, 'Hal and I were thinking of taking Boyd to Gino's – would you like to join us?'

'Sorry – I . . . I've got several errands to run,' she excused herself. Natalie went off down the corridor and, as Jonquil brushed past Boyd, he seized her wrist.

'I want to talk to you,' he said in a low voice.

'Well, I don't want to talk to you,' she hissed, jerking free and striding away.

She took refuge in a nearby café bar and ordered a sandwich and, as an afterthought, a glass of dry white wine. She rarely drank at lunchtime, but her head was still reeling from the shock she'd sustained that morning and she felt as though she needed a drink.

As she nibbled without appetite at her mozzarella and tomato on ciabatta bread, she thought that enough time should have passed for her to get over Boyd. Until today, she'd told herself that he was nothing more than a dim and distant memory; but suddenly, like a thunderbolt, he was back in her life without any warning at all.

The worst of it was that she'd be working alongside him for months, having to see him regularly at production meetings, and she didn't think she'd be able to stand it. Just being in the same room made her smoulder with a combination of lust and loathing.

She'd have to tell Hal that she couldn't write the scripts after all. But she had no other work in the pipeline and bills still plopped through her letter box whether she was working or not.

Jonquil bit her lip and put her sandwich back on her plate only half-eaten. How could she afford to give up a lucrative commission without any certainty of finding other work in the immediate future?

In New York, she'd worked full-time for a production

4

company and had earned a good salary, but on returning to London she'd discovered that most writers in her field operated on a freelance basis and there were no permanent positions going. She'd had little alternative but to strike out on her own and hadn't done too badly, but work wasn't exactly thick on the ground. No, she had to see this job through – whatever it cost her.

When she'd first known Boyd, she'd been young, wide-eyed and very naive. Now she'd grown up and was every inch the well-groomed, hard-working professional woman. He'd caught her off guard that morning, but she'd make sure it didn't happen again. In all their future encounters, she'd be cool, poised and very distant. She'd never let him guess just how fragile her defences were where he was concerned.

Once had been enough.

She strode back into the building and dashed forward to catch the old-fashioned lift just as the doors were closing. In her preoccupied state, she didn't notice that it had stopped about three inches above ground level. She tripped and went sprawling into it, her briefcase flying out of her hand.

For one sickening moment she thought she was going to crash to the floor, but the lift's only occupant leapt forward to catch her and she felt herself being hauled upright and held tightly against a hard chest by arms which tightened around her like steel bands.

It didn't take more than a moment for her to identify her rescuer. The faint whiff of the light cologne he wore would have been enough to tell her – it was the one he used to wear all those years ago. But she didn't even need that to let her know who was holding her so closely; something deep inside her would have known it was Boyd under any circumstances.

She struggled to regain her footing, but she'd lost one of her shoes and couldn't get her balance, forcing her to cling to him. The wool of his jacket was smooth beneath her cheek and the virile length of his body was pressed against hers so intimately that at once she felt a treacherous response high up in her sex.

She looked up into his face and almost quailed at the expression on his face, a curious mix of hostility and desire.

She tried to push him away, but he didn't relinquish his hold on her. The lift doors closed on them and it began to ascend, then stopped as he pressed one of the buttons on the control panel.

She managed to get her foot back in her shoe and snapped, 'Let me go!'

'You don't sound very grateful, considering I've just saved you from a fall,' he retorted, moving away from her.

'Thank you,' she muttered crossly.

'Maybe you shouldn't drink at lunchtime if it makes you unsteady on your feet.'

Outrage washed over her – he made it sound as if she'd downed at least half a bottle of wine all by herself.

'I only had one glass,' she protested, then bit her lip with annoyance for feeling she had to defend herself. She glared at him, her grey eyes stormy. 'And would you mind setting the lift going again? I don't particularly want to spend a second longer than necessary trapped in here with you.'

'Afraid of being alone with me?' he smirked. 'I want to talk to you and, as you refused my invitation to lunch, this looks like the best opportunity I'm going to get.'

'If you want to discuss the scripts, we can do that in the conference room in front of the others.'

'I don't. I want to talk about us.'

'Us?' she spat. 'There is no *us* and hasn't been for seven years.'

'I think we should clear the air between us,' he insisted.

'Clear the air?' she blazed. 'It would take more than a conversation to do that.'

'We're going to be working closely together for several months and I don't want there to be any awkwardness between us.'

Awkwardness? He'd behaved despicably, turned her life upside down and broken her heart, yet he didn't want there to be any *awkwardness* between them.

'Hal tells me you're very good at your job,' he continued. 'And these promotional videos are important to my company. I think it's in both our interests to try to get along and forget the past.'

6

Easy for him to say. It hadn't been him who'd had to leave family and friends behind to start a new life in New York in an attempt to banish a broken affair from her mind.

'Is that it?' she asked in a honeyed tone.

He ran his hand through his crisp dark hair, looking suddenly at a loss.

'No, that isn't it – but something tells me I'm not going to get the answers I want from you, however hard I try.'

Answers? Now what was he talking about? Not that she cared.

'My only interest is in doing a good job,' she said crisply. 'I'll listen to anything you have to say about the scripts, but that's as far as it goes. Whenever we have to spend time together, I'll treat you with the professional courtesy I'd accord any client. Other than that – stay away from me.'

'Did the time we spent together mean nothing to you?' he asked in a low voice.

'I was seeing a lot of men around then,' she said flippantly. 'They all sort of blur, if you get the picture.'

'Yes,' he replied, his voice taut with anger. 'I get the picture. But I don't believe for one moment that you responded to anyone else the way you responded to me.'

'Believe it,' she retorted, keeping her fury in check with difficulty.

He dragged her into his arms and his mouth swooped on hers as he buried his hand under the fall of red-gold hair on the back of her neck. The intervening years definitely hadn't affected his capacity to arouse her, because every nerve-ending in her body clamoured in chaotic response, suffusing her with wayward heat.

His lips were hard against hers at first, moving with lethal intent, then they gentled and became persuasive as he explored the warm velvet of her mouth. The blood was rioting through her body like quicksilver as his tongue found hers. She could tell that her nipples had hardened and there was a moist heat in her female core which was intensifying by the second.

She made a small sound, somewhere between a mew and a moan, and tried weakly to disengage her mouth, but she was ensnared by the red-hot flame of his sexual expertise. She knew without a shadow of à doubt that if she didn't stop him right

7

now, she wouldn't be able to and they'd end up screwing in the lift.

Mustering her last shreds of self-control, she pushed him violently away. 'Let me go!'

He leant back against the wall and subjected her to a thorough visual survey. She felt seared by the heat of his gaze as he looked her over, taking in the way the fine wool of her suit clung to her slender curves. The skirt ended a modest three inches above the knee but the way he studied her legs made her feel as if it were the skimpiest of mini skirts.

She resisted the temptation to fold her arms defensively and instead gazed steadily back at him, a challenging light in her dark grey eyes.

'You're even more beautiful and sexy than I remembered you,' he remarked at last.

Determined to pay him back in kind, she took a deep breath and retorted, 'I can barely remember what you looked like then, so I'm afraid I can't return the compliment.'

'Where did you go?' he asked. 'I spent months trying to find you.'

'New York. And I can't imagine why you bothered to look for me, after the way you behaved.'

'Wasn't I entitled to an opportunity to explain?' he demanded, his face hardening.

'What would have been the point? Anyway, as far as I was concerned, it would have been over once I left university. Now if you don't mind, I'd like to continue up to the second floor.'

She was taken by surprise when he took her firmly by the upper arms and pushed her back against the wall, holding her there and glaring down at her.

'What do you mean, it would have been over once you left university?'

'I was planning to end the relationship myself but you just got in before me,' she lied.

She shrank from the fury on his face, then let out a muffled exclamation of protest as his mouth descended on hers again. His hand slid inside her blouse and found her breasts, caressing them into aching peaks of desire. Shards of sheer erotic sensation lanced down to her sex, provoking a tickling trickle

8

of moisture which made her black lace panties damp within seconds.

She could feel the hard ridge of his manhood digging into her side, and dizzily recalled how wonderful it had felt embedded deep inside her. One hand slid down her backside to the hem of her skirt and peeled it upwards so he could stroke the curvaceous globes of her bottom.

She knew this was madness and that she should call a halt before it went any further, but even as she tried to get a grip on herself, her thighs parted to invite a more intimate caress.

He pushed his fingers inside her panties from behind and delved into the slick furrow of her sex-flesh, emitting a faint sound of satisfaction as he realised how wet she was.

His mouth left hers and trailed hard kisses down her neck as he pushed two fingers slowly into her sex, swivelling them around in a lengthy exploration.

Jonquil had already lost the ability to think rationally and could only react instinctively, bearing down against the delicious invasion, her hips undulating with need.

When he withdrew his fingers, she wanted nothing more than for him to replace them with the swollen column of his manhood. Instead, he caressed his way over her hips and belly and then brushed over the smooth skin of her inner thighs, just above her stocking-tops.

She was on fire for him and couldn't stop herself leaning weakly against the lift wall; her pelvis thrust demandingly forward as he teased her by massaging her vulva with the palm of his hand until the crotch of her briefs had wedged itself into the sticky furrows of her labia.

He dragged the flimsy scrap of lace roughly downwards and she moaned as he took the aching bud of her clit and stroked it with the maddeningly deft touch she remembered so well. She forgot she was in a lift in an office building in Soho, forgot that she detested the man touching her with such casual expertise, forgot everything except her overwhelming need for release.

The smoky heat in her loins transmitted itself throughout her body as she ascended higher and higher up the spiral of arousal. He increased the pressure of his fingers, moving them faster over the plump sliver of flesh.

'*Aaaaaah!*' she cried again as, in a crashing wave of heat, she came, her body shuddering with the intensity of the spasms rippling through it. She sagged against the wall, her eyes closed, as she slowly came back to reality. The pleasure she'd experienced at her climax ebbed swiftly away, to be replaced by shame.

Without looking at him, she straightened her clothing, her cheeks flaming with mortification. How could she have let him bring her to an orgasm within hours of making an unwelcome reappearance in her life? She took refuge in anger.

'What on earth do you think you're doing?' she hissed. 'How dare you trap me in here then grope me against my will?'

'I was just making a point,' he said, smiling so smugly that she longed to slap him.

She saw that his blue eyes were glittering with triumph, provoking her to retaliate. 'If . . . if you must know, I was thinking about my current lover and pretending you were him,' she blurted out.

She saw contempt on his face as he reached past her for the control panel saying, 'You certainly have changed. The old Jonquil would never have lied to me.'

At that moment, the lift shuddered to a halt and the doors clattered open. She stumbled out and hurried off to take refuge in the ladies' until she'd got herself under some sort of control.

The afternoon passed in a daze until at last, around four, the meeting broke up and Hal took Boyd to go over the budgets.

'Where do you know our gorgeous new client from?' asked Natalie as soon as he'd left the room. She was a slim brunette who wore horn-rimmed glasses which gave her an intellectual air. Even dressed in her usual clothing, which today consisted of Doc Martens, baggy camouflage trousers and a long-sleeved, lovat-green t-shirt, she was an attractive woman.

'He did some part-time lecturing at the university I attended,' Jonquil mumbled in reply. 'But I haven't seen him since then.'

It was true as far as it went. She didn't want anyone to know how much Boyd had once meant to her.

10

'I wonder if he's married,' said Natalie. 'Gorgeous *and* rich – what a lethal combination.'

'As far as I know, he is,' Jonquil replied, keeping her tone casual with an effort.

'This is going to be a great project to work on.' Natalie began loading papers into the rucksack she used instead of a briefcase. 'Big budgets, long deadlines – a production company's dream. There's even the possibility of some foreign locations.'

Jonquil had been so fazed by the events of the day and the painful memories which had been dredged up, that she hadn't given any thought to the fact that to be the head of a software company planning to commission a series of films, Boyd must be extremely successful.

Seven years ago his operation had consisted of only a dozen people, but it had already been doing well. Now it must be huge.

'I'm afraid I don't know much about the company,' she admitted. When Hal had called her, he'd mentioned that the scripts were for a leading software firm, but the name hadn't meant anything to her – Boyd must have changed it at some stage.

'You've been living in New York, haven't you? Or you'd have read about it when it floated, a couple of years ago – it was one of the most successful flotations on record.'

Natalie glanced at her watch and picked up her rucksack. 'I'm due in the editing suite. I hope I manage to get out before eight when I'm supposed to be meeting my partner for a meal – I was an hour late on Tuesday and he hasn't stopped going on about it since. Are you still seeing Damon?'

'Yes, he's coming round this evening.'

'How's it going with him?'

'Fine.' Realising that this sounded abrupt when Natalie was just being her usual friendly self, Jonquil continued with an effort, 'He wants me to attend a dinner with the partners in his firm on Friday. We're going to *La Maison*, which I've heard has a reputation for the most sublime food.'

'It's wonderful. I've only been once but it was one of the best meals I've ever eaten. Must dash – see you.'

'Bye, Natalie.'

Chapter Two

Despite a long soak in the bath and a glass of Soave, Jonquil was still reeling as she thought about the traumatic day she'd just had. How *could* she have been so lacking in self-control that she'd allowed Boyd to touch her so intimately? She must have taken leave of her senses. Just the memory of it brought a hot flush of humiliation to her cheeks.

As if it wasn't bad enough that fate had tossed him casually back into her life, to let herself fall into his sexual thrall again like that was completely unforgivable.

Had he been as shocked as she'd been to have someone from the past reappear so unexpectedly? Had he felt guilty when he'd remembered how he'd treated her? If that *had* been the case, he'd certainly given no sign of it – in fact, if anything, he'd acted as if she'd been the one who'd treated *him* badly. She towelled herself dry and then went into her bedroom to dress, still furious with herself.

Her apartment was on the top floor of a large Edwardian semi-detached house in Muswell Hill and consisted of a bathroom, kitchen, two large airy rooms overlooking the garden and a smaller one she used as an office.

She slipped into a lacy bra and panties, then pulled on a loose-fitting silk shirt in hyacinth-blue with a pair of beige trousers, trying not to think about the way Boyd had caressed her and her own embarrassingly eager response. She willed herself to put him out of her mind as she went into her office to get down to some work.

When she opened the door of her apartment to Damon, a couple of hours later, she looked at him with affection. He might not make her pulses race the way that Boyd did but, in the few weeks she'd been seeing him, he'd shown himself to be solid and reliable – just what she needed in her life, at the moment.

He had light brown hair, hazel eyes and a moustache. Too many expense-account lunches were just beginning to show and he'd told her that he planned to take up jogging.

He bent to kiss her; then, as she took the boxes of pizza from him, he asked, 'How did the meeting go?'

'OK,' she replied, going into the kitchen, 'but the head of the company rubbed me up the wrong way.'

'You've worked with difficult clients before,' he said, crossing to the fridge and helping himself to a can of beer.

'I knew him, actually – he was a part-time lecturer in computer studies at university when I was there.' She'd considered telling Damon the whole story but decided against it; it would only complicate the issue.

'I wish I'd bought shares in the company when it floated,' he commented, taking a gulp of his beer. 'I'd have made a killing.' He dabbled in the stock market and he'd been impressed when Jonquil had told him about the commission.

'I'm not looking forward to having to work with him,' she admitted.

'I'm sure you'll manage to get along with him OK, once you get into the project. Who knows where it might lead to – he's a very influential man. Are you still OK for Friday?'

The dinner with the partners of the software distribution firm he worked for sounded just the sort of formal occasion that Jonquil disliked, but he'd seemed keen that she should go, so she'd accepted the invitation, thinking that at least the food would be good.

'I certainly am,' she said, trying to smile brightly, hoping it wouldn't be too much of an ordeal.

They chatted over the meal and then watched a film on TV. By the time it was only half over, she was stifling yawns; it seemed to have been a long day and she was more than ready for bed. When the credits came up, she was about to mention how tired she was in the hope that Damon would take the hint and leave, but he took her in his arms and kissed her.

She was horrified when her first impulse was to recoil. Annoyed with herself, she tried to respond, but somehow it

14

was Boyd's face she saw and not his.

She took his hand, saying, 'Let's go into the bedroom. I'm feeling a bit tense and I need to relax.' She thought if he gave her a massage with scented oil it might help her get into the mood.

She slipped out of her clothes, but when she picked up the bottle from the bedside table and turned towards him, she saw that he'd already stripped off his own garments to reveal his semi-tumescent member.

Before she could speak, he removed the oil from her hand and said, 'No need for that – your mouth's all I want to feel on my cock at the moment.'

He pushed her to her knees but before she could protest that fellating him hadn't been what she'd had in mind, the end of his phallus was nudging between her lips. Somewhat unenthusiastically, she ran her tongue over the glans and then commenced a rhythmic sucking, her hand clasping the shaft, just the way he liked her to.

It hardened to full tumescence under her ministrations but, as she continued to pleasure him, her wayward thoughts returned to Boyd again. What was it about him that provoked such a response from her? It couldn't just be that he was the best lover she'd ever had. It was more than that – there was something primitive in the way her body reacted to his, something that made her uncomfortable because it was beyond her control.

The memory of the confident way he'd slid his hand into her panties earlier that day made her shiver and her clit tingled as if he were about to touch it now. Of all her lovers, he'd been the only one who could bring her to a climax so swiftly and easily – with Damon, she often didn't come at all.

Just the thought of their encounter made her feel hot and moist so, when Damon drew her to her feet and then onto the bed, at least she was in a state of arousal. He stroked her breasts, and she had to suppress a brief flare of irritation when he twiddled her nipples as if tuning in a radio. She'd told him a couple of times that it was uncomfortable, but he seemed to have forgotten again.

He thrust his hand between her legs and, when he felt how

15

wet she was, grunted, 'See – I knew that having my dick in your mouth would do the trick.'

He rolled on top of her and entered her with no further foreplay, but thinking about Boyd had got her libido up and running and she pushed her pelvis upwards to meet each thrust. Gradually, her arousal began to mount and she clutched his shoulders, her movements imbued with a sense of urgency as she strove for release before he came and lost interest in the proceedings.

She could feel her climax hovering just out of reach and, to spur herself on, she imagined it was Boyd's hard muscled body moving over hers, his hands on her breasts, driving her inexorably towards satisfaction. She gasped as her slim frame was racked by a lengthy spasm of pleasure – not a moment too soon, as Damon made several last staccato thrusts and erupted into her.

He rolled off her and fell asleep immediately, leaving her to slide out of bed and go and take a quick shower, wondering why she felt so unfulfilled, despite the fact she'd come.

When she arrived at *La Maison* on Friday evening it was to find the elegantly appointed bar thronging with several groups of people, but Damon and his party hadn't arrived.

There was a single vacant bar stool and, although she'd rather have sat at one of the tables, they were all taken. Her dress was a simple style in midnight blue silk with a scooped neck that skimmed her collarbones at the front and plunged to the waist at the back. It was also rather tight-fitting, so climbing onto the bar stool while trying not to show too much thigh was difficult.

'What can I get you?' asked the barman.

'Dry sherry, please.'

'Make that a bottle of champagne,' said a deep voice just to her right.

A frisson of alarm feathered down her spine and the tiny hairs on the back of her neck stood on end as she realised that Boyd had materialised next to her and was now standing much too close and looking mockingly down at her.

Mentally cursing the perfidy of fate that had just thrown

them together for the second time in a week, Jonquil summoned a bright smile and said, 'Sherry's fine for me, thanks.'

'Moët,' he continued, unperturbed, 'and two glasses.'

To Jonquil's annoyance, the barman ignored her and hastened to open a bottle of champagne with just the discreetest of pops. A tiny wisp of aromatic vapour escaped from the neck as he tilted it and filled two tulip-shaped glasses.

'To the past,' said Boyd, raising his glass.

'Forgive me if I don't join you in that particular toast,' she retorted, lifting her eyes to his face for the first time – then wishing she hadn't as her stomach lurched.

How had he become even more attractive in the intervening years? She'd have welcomed some sign of degeneration – receding hair, sagging jowls or a thickening waistline. But instead he was as darkly handsome as ever. He still made her female core quicken just by standing next to her.

'Then what about drinking to the future?' he asked, his glass still held aloft. 'To a successful project.'

Grudgingly, she reminded herself that he *was* the client and took a sip of her champagne, feeling the bubbles explode in her mouth, filling it with the deliciously dry, golden taste of the wine.

She became aware that he was studying her dress and bare back with unconcealed interest, bringing a faint flush to her cheeks and making her wish she hadn't already removed her jacket. Without thinking, she took a gulp of her champagne and then had to stop herself coughing as the effervescent liquid tickled the back of her throat.

'Who are you meeting, or are you planning to dine alone?' he continued.

Biting back the words, 'Mind your own business,' which had sprung unbidden to her lips, she managed to smile coolly and reply, 'Some friends.'

Wishing he wasn't standing so close to her, because it was distinctly unsettling to feel a slow smouldering heat growing in her quim, she looked around to see if she could spot Damon. Where the hell was he? It was with a sense of enormous relief that she saw him entering the restaurant with several other people.

17

'Sorry I'm late,' he greeted her, kissing her on the cheek. 'It took a while to get everyone into cabs and over here.'

'That's okay,' she said, summoning a smile. 'I've just been enjoying a drink.' She slid off her bar stool, hoping to avoid introducing Boyd, but he was too quick for her.

'I've been keeping Jonquil company while she waited,' he said, proffering his hand. Damon's face lit up when she reluctantly performed the introduction and he realised who her companion was.

He pumped Boyd's hand enthusiastically, saying, 'Jonquil mentioned she was working on a project for your company. She's very excited about it.'

'Believe me – not as excited as I am.' Boyd was smiling blandly as he uttered the words, but the fleeting glance he shot at Jonquil was laden with hidden meaning.

'Let me introduce my colleagues,' said Damon, turning to where they were standing. It was obvious that they too knew who Boyd was and Jonquil got the impression that Damon's stock had just risen considerably for having such a well-connected girlfriend.

'Won't you join us for dinner, Boyd?' asked Kevin, the senior partner, a plump balding man with shrewd eyes who was accompanied by his wife, a frosty-faced woman in her forties.

'Thank you, but I'm meeting someone.'

It had already crossed Jonquil's mind that he might be meeting the detestable Julie, and she didn't know how she was going to be civil to her.

'Perhaps we could have coffee and cognac together after dinner,' suggested Kevin.

'Possibly,' Boyd returned pleasantly.

The waiter came up at that moment to show them to their table and Jonquil was able to say, 'Goodbye – thank you for the champagne,' as if they were the most casual of acquaintances.

Throughout dinner she smiled mechanically and joined politely in the conversation, but she kept imagining that Boyd's eyes were boring into her back. When he was eventually shown to his table, she was conscious of a feeling of relief as she saw that

18

his dinner companion was another man. Probably his wife was at home with the children – they must surely have some by now.

She was so wound up that she barely noticed what the food was like. The meal seemed interminable and she could have kicked Damon when the conversation returned to Boyd again and Damon volunteered the information that not only was she currently working for him, but that she'd known him at college.

'Did you know him well?' Kevin wanted to know.

'He was a part-time tutor on the computer studies course.'

'You must have been close, to have kept in touch for all these years,' continued Kevin. 'How often do you see him?'

Wondering why on earth he was asking that, Jonquil accepted the dessert menu from the waiter and studied it attentively, even though she didn't want one.

'We didn't keep in touch and, before this week, I hadn't seen him for years,' she retorted, trying not to let her discomfort show.

She knew that Boyd was a financial force to be reckoned with these days and she was sure that Kevin's firm would undoubtedly be interested in doing business with him, but that was nothing to do with her.

'Presumably you'll be working with him very closely for a while?' Kevin was obviously going to be like a dog with a bone.

Rising to her feet, Jonquil murmured, 'Excuse me,' and left the table. In the opulently appointed white-and-gold powder-room, she splashed some cold water on her flushed face and heartily wished that she'd refused Damon's invitation to join them for dinner. She lingered as long as she dared, touching up her lipstick and combing her hair, then returned reluctantly to the table.

Halfway across the restaurant she saw to her horror that Boyd was now ensconced with their party and everyone had moved on to brandy and coffee. An extra chair had been drawn up between her seat and Kevin's and he was leaning towards Boyd and saying something.

'How was your meal?' Boyd asked. His smile was pleasant, but there was a gleam in his eyes which alarmed her.

19

'Fine, thanks,' she murmured.

'I ordered you a Remy to have with your coffee,' Damon told her.

'Thank you.'

Jonquil didn't actually like brandy, but she picked up the glass and took a sip, thinking she needed something to help her through the next half hour.

Boyd's muscular thigh made electrifying contact with hers, setting off a rapid pulse in her sex that itched unbearably. She jerked her leg away, but then it made contact with Kevin's. He gave her a lecherous look and returned the pressure under the cover of the starched tablecloth.

She hastily withdrew and immediately felt the hard length of Boyd's thigh again. He shot her an amused sidelong glance which made it clear that he knew what was going on and was enjoying her discomfort, prompting her to push her chair back so she wasn't touching anyone.

She willed the evening to come to an end, but no one seemed in a hurry to leave. Eventually, unable to stand it a moment longer, she caught Damon's eye and said, 'I'm tired. Do you think we could go?'

Before Damon had the chance to reply, Kevin said jovially, 'The night's only young. Let's all have another cognac.'

'I'm just about to get off,' said Boyd, 'so I'll drive you home, if your friend isn't ready to leave.'

His unwelcome offer threw her into a quandary. He was the person she most wanted to get away from, but it would be difficult to refuse in front of everyone else. She cast an appealing glance at Damon, but he merely smiled cheerfully at her.

'That's OK – I can get a taxi,' she managed to say.

'I wouldn't hear of it.' Boyd rose lithely to his feet and smiled around the table. 'It was good to meet you all.' Kevin rose too and shook his hand vigorously. Unable to believe that Damon wasn't about to rescue her, Jonquil made one last attempt.

'Damon – won't you come too?'

'OK, if you—'

'Damon and I have some business to discuss, but I'm sure that Boyd will see you safely back.' Kevin's interjection made

20

Damon, who'd risen to his feet, sit back down again.

Fuming, but outmanoeuvred, Jonquil allowed Damon to kiss her goodnight. 'I'll call you tomorrow,' he promised her.

'I managed to find a parking place only a couple of streets away,' Boyd told her as they stepped outside into the crisp autumn night air.

'I'm surprised a man in your position doesn't have a chauffeured limousine,' she said with needle-sharp sweetness.

'I do,' he returned unperturbed, 'but I enjoy driving, so I don't use it all the time.' There was a silence as they crossed the road and then he continued, 'How long have you been seeing Eamon?'

Marvelling that everyone was suddenly interested in her private life, she said, 'His name's Damon and I've been seeing him for a while.' Let him make of that what he could.

'He isn't right for you.'

The calm way in which he spoke infuriated her as much as his actual words. She stopped short and turned to face him.

'What an arrogant thing to say. You don't know him or anything about him.'

'Perhaps not, but I know you.' His eyes glittered in the light of a street lamp.

'Correction,' she spat. 'You *used* to know me.'

She turned on her heel and began to walk away. He followed her, caught her up in three long strides and took her arm.

'The car's this way.'

'Then I suggest you go and find it. I'll flag down a cab.'

He didn't relinquish his grip on her arm. 'I wouldn't hear of letting you wander the streets on your own at night. I owe it to Eamon to take good care of you.'

She still planned to get a cab as soon as they reached the main road, but unfortunately they came to Boyd's car just before the junction and she hesitated, uncertain what to do.

'Jonquil – get in. We're going to be spending plenty of time with one another over the coming months, so you may as well get used to the idea.'

Being alone with him was the last thing on her agenda, but there didn't seem to be any way out of it. Unwillingly, she slid into the low front seat.

21

'Where to?' he asked, getting in next to her.

'Muswell Hill.'

'We're practically neighbours. I live in Hampstead.'

She didn't reply, determined to sit in cold, aloof silence for the duration of the drive.

He pulled out into the traffic before continuing, 'Eamon must be very trusting, letting another man drive you home, particularly when you're looking so . . . inviting.'

Stung, she snapped, '*Damon* has no reason to be otherwise.'

'Doesn't he know that you're usually seeing a lot of men all at the same time?'

She recognised the words she'd used to taunt him with earlier in the week, now thrown back at her.

'I must say that Kevin seemed quite smitten, too,' he went on. 'Will you be adding him to your current dating list?' His jibes were delivered with deadly amicability, as if talking about the weather.

'Hardly – he's married,' she pointed out, hoping Boyd would take the none-too-subtle hint.

'You mean that's where you draw the line? I'm sure that will be a great comfort to Eamon when he discovers he's just one of a crowd.'

She scowled into the darkness, determined not to rise to the bait or – even more tempting – to fling Julie, the woman he'd left her for, in his face. She shifted restlessly on her seat, aware of a tingling sensation deep inside and told herself to keep a firm grip and not allow herself to be rattled.

Why on earth had he insisted on giving her a lift? It didn't make sense that he would go out of his way to spend time with her now, after ditching her so ruthlessly all those years ago. The journey seemed to take forever but, at long last, he pulled up in her driveway and, alarmingly, switched the engine off. She scrambled hastily from the car, fumbling for her keys.

'Thanks for the lift,' she said ungraciously, only to find that he'd got out, too. 'I wasn't thinking of inviting you in,' she added.

'It wouldn't be very gentlemanly of me not to escort you to your door. Surely Eamon always makes sure you get inside safely?'

'I usually invite *Damon* in,' she countered. He appropriated her keys with a swift movement which took her by surprise. Not prepared to behave in an undignified manner by trying to snatch them back, she had to wait until he unlocked the front door.

'Thank you,' she said icily, stepping inside then turning to reach for the keys, but he followed her into the hall and closed the door. 'Perhaps I didn't make the situation clear enough,' she continued. 'When I said I wasn't thinking of inviting you in, what was it you thought I meant?'

'I just wanted to see you safely into your own flat – anyone could be lurking on the stairs. Which floor is it on?' A touch of injured innocence in his voice made her feel fleetingly guilty; then she reminded herself that this was Boyd and the guilt evaporated instantly.

'The top floor but, as the front door's always locked, it's unlikely anyone could get in.'

'You never know. One of the other occupants may have buzzed a friend in and someone hiding in the shadows might have slipped in behind them.'

'Thanks for making me uneasy – I've always felt safe once I was inside. But if you want to trail up two steep flights of stairs behind me, be my guest.'

Jonquil began to ascend the stairs, conscious of Boyd right behind her, knowing his eyes were on her backside and legs. On the top landing she turned, intending to demand her keys back, but at the sight of the expression on his face, the words dried in her mouth.

A laser blast of sheer sexuality made her tremble and feel dizzy, just as it always had before, letting her know she was no more immune to him now than she was then.

He backed her up against her front door, not actually touching her but with his potency wreathing itself around her like a seductive drug. Reaching past her, he unlocked it and followed her into the apartment. She swallowed and tried to speak, to demand that he leave, but nothing came out.

'Take your jacket off,' he ordered her, folding his arms and watching her intently. Not sure why she seemed incapable of telling him to piss off, Jonquil found herself removing it and letting it slide to the floor.

23

'And the dress.'

Like an automaton programmed to respond to a specific voice pattern, she drew it slowly down at the front to expose her naked breasts. His dark blue eyes wandered over them, searing her with carnal heat, sending the blood surging wantonly through her veins and making her nipples jut out like chunks of coral.

The dress slithered to the carpet, revealing her pearl-grey satin suspender belt, matching panties and sheer stockings. He took in the curve of her hips and the length of her legs while she stood motionless in front of him.

'Just as beautiful as I remember,' he said hoarsely. Jonquil found her eyes drawn to his groin and the unmistakable bulge which indicated the level of his own arousal. 'Stroke your breasts,' he continued, in a tone of voice which brooked no refusal.

Slowly, her hand drifted to her creamy orbs and she allowed her fingers to trail over the swollen peaks of her nipples. She toyed with them languorously, touching them in the way that gave her most pleasure. She could feel the stealthy trickle of her own juices gathering in her vulva, ready to soak into the crotch of her panties. Somehow, she wasn't sure how, one of her hands glided down to the top of her panties, then fell to cup her mound.

'You know what I want to see,' he croaked, his eyes riveted to the flimsy satin covering her hidden delta. She did know. Boyd had always liked to watch her masturbate and would sit and observe her delicate manipulation of her own clitoris with intense concentration; then, when she'd brought herself to a climax, would make love to her until she was drained and sated.

The first time he'd asked her to pleasure herself in front of him, she'd felt too inhibited to comply and had refused, pink-cheeked. But, then as now, he'd been determined that she should and she'd found herself parting her thighs and coaxing her tiny bud from its hiding place among the petals of her labia.

With no strength to refuse him, she drew her briefs down her legs and stepped out of them, aware that her burnished fleece was damp where it curled over her outer sex-lips. Her legs were unsteady and she sank onto a hard-backed chair, parting her thighs.

Her hand slid into the furrow of her sex and she traced the folds of her vulva, working her way slowly inwards until she reached the throbbing nub of sensitive flesh which was the centre of her pleasure.

Inflamed by his scrutiny, she stroked it softly, aware that her fingers were making a tiny squelching sound as they moved over the drenched point. She meant to take her time and make him wait, but her own urgency overtook her and, within a couple of minutes, her hand was moving faster and faster.

A faint film of perspiration gathered on her cleavage as a wave of heat washed over her, to be followed by a climax which convulsed her entire body with racking spasms.

Her head fell back on her shoulders and her eyes fluttered closed, then flew open again as she heard him clear his throat. It was no good; she knew he was about to sweep her into his arms and carry her into the bedroom, then remind her in the most telling way possible that, whatever she might like to think to the contrary, she was still in his sexual thrall.

Instead, she was astonished to hear the sound of the door opening. He paused on the threshold to regard her sombrely.

'You shouldn't have run away,' he told her, then slammed the door behind him.

Chapter Three

'Kevin really liked you,' said Damon, leaning back against the work surface in Jonquil's kitchen with his arms folded, watching her dice a green pepper.

She wished she could return the compliment but, as she hadn't taken to him, she merely smiled mechanically and looked around for her stir-fry pan. It was behind Damon and she had to reach round him as he continued, 'He said you were a real asset, pretty *and* smart.'

She was obviously supposed to be gratified by this but couldn't think of anything to say which wouldn't sound sarcastic. She moved over to the cooker to put the pan to heat, but Damon was now standing in front of it and didn't budge until she murmured, 'Excuse me.'

He moved to prop himself up against the fridge-freezer while she drizzled some olive oil into the pan and coated the sides.

'He said we should all get together very soon.' Jonquil looked around for the bean sprouts and remembered that after washing them earlier she'd put them back into the fridge and had to say, 'Excuse me,' again as Damon was now in front of that.

In a burst of uncharacteristic irritation, she wished he'd go and read the paper or watch TV or something. The kitchen was definitely only big enough for one person, but he seemed oblivious to the fact that he was in her way as she tried to prepare a meal.

'Would you set the table, please?' she asked, throwing a handful of bean sprouts into the pan and stirring them.

'What? Oh, yes . . . sure,' he returned, looking vaguely around as if he expected the cutlery to come dancing out of the drawer, a piece at a time.

27

'That drawer there – to the left of the door,' she reminded him.

'Kevin thought perhaps a party would be a good idea,' he went on, making no move towards the cutlery drawer. She tried to remember whether she'd already added the garlic, but Damon's conversation was distracting her and she couldn't concentrate. 'So he said that if it was OK with you, next Friday evening would—'

She looked around for the ginger and saw that Damon was tossing the tin absently up and down. She was just about to ask him to pass it to her when he dropped it. The lid shot off as it hit the floor, and the entire contents were disgorged onto the terracotta tiles.

'For goodness' sake!' she exploded. 'Will you please get out of the kitchen and go and set the table? Can't you see you're in my way?'

He'd bent down to pick up the empty tin and was trying ineffectually to scoop up some of the spilt powder but, at the annoyance in her tone he straightened up, a hurt expression on his face.

'I was only trying to—'

'Well, don't!' she snapped. He turned to leave the room and she wrenched open the drawer and thrust a handful of cutlery at him. 'Just go and set the table, please.'

It was Saturday evening and they'd opted for a quiet evening in with a bottle of wine, but Jonquil was now wishing she'd made an excuse not to see him.

She'd slept badly the night before, following the one-woman show she'd put on for Boyd. She still couldn't believe what she'd done. What was the matter with her, that she acquiesced to his every desire like a wind-up doll with no mind of her own?

She couldn't quite decide which was worse. The fact that she'd brought herself to a climax while he'd watched, or that afterwards he'd left abruptly without making love to her. At the time she'd felt hurt and rejected but, in retrospect, she was deeply relieved that they hadn't ended up screwing – she *never* got involved with married men.

After going to bed, she'd tossed and turned, plagued by

unwelcome but arousing memories until at last she'd drifted into a fitful sleep.

But even sleep brought no respite, because she dreamt that she was backstage at a fashion show, being helped into her midnight-blue silk dress. All around her were stunningly gorgeous, completely naked models waiting to be allocated one of the dazzling creations hanging from a rail.

Jonquil had never seen so many lovely women without their clothes on in one room before and, to her surprise, felt herself becoming aroused. As the dresser fussed with her hair, she turned to a dark-eyed brunette next to her and swallowed at the sight of her creamy orbs, tipped with prominent nipples the colour of milk chocolate.

Jonquil reached out and stroked the tempting peaks, marvelling at the crumpled velvet of the areolae. Unable to help herself, she bent her head, took one crinkled nub between her lips and circled it with her tongue. She felt it hardening even more and sucked softly at it, sliding her arm around the other woman's waist to draw her closer.

The model's skin was so smooth and soft that Jonquil couldn't resist running her hand down her spine to the pert swell of her bottom, clasping one of the firm globes and enjoying the feeling of touching another woman.

She looked down at the brunette's sable fleece, wondering if it could possibly be as silky as it looked. Tentatively, she covered it with her hand and then stroked it gently, the way she might a kitten. A man appeared in front of them and although she wasn't able to see his face, Jonquil knew by his height and the spread of his shoulders that it was Boyd.

'You wanton little slut!' he ground out from between clenched teeth. Startled, she jerked her hand away, then gasped as he seized her wrist and glared down at her. 'You just can't resist it, can you?' he snarled. 'Men, women, it's all the same to you, isn't it?'

He gripped the neckline of her dress with both hands and ripped it down the front, leaving her clad in only her sheer stockings, a wisp of a suspender belt and a matching thong.

Compared to the models she was still over-dressed – or at least she'd thought so – but, looking at the other women, she saw that mysteriously, they were all now wearing sumptuous outfits. Boyd picked up a pair of scissors and she froze in fear as he moved behind her and the cold steel made contact with the warm skin of her derrière.

Holding her breath and not daring to move, she felt him slide the scissors down the cleft between her buttocks. With a decisive movement, he cut through her thong, then snipped it again at the waist. The scrap of material fluttered to the floor, leaving her mound on full display, while he walked away and through the curtain.

A round of applause from the audience indicated that the fashion show was about to begin. The models formed a loose line, then each of them sashayed onto the catwalk in turn, to the accompaniment of a commentary from Boyd.

At least no one was looking at her; but then the dresser took her arm and led her to where the last model was awaiting her turn.

'You're on after her,' the dresser informed Jonquil, who, horrified, indicated her near nudity.

'L . . . like this?' she faltered, but the dresser had already vanished. The final model stalked onto the catwalk with a hip-swinging walk, but it seemed only moments before she returned and gave Jonquil a push, so she found herself on the other side of the curtain, the focus of attention.

She couldn't make out much for the lights dazzling her and the flashes as dozens of photos were taken. She felt that her wooden movements were a clumsy parody of the models' as she made her way to the end of the catwalk, turned and held the position, one hand on her hip. She could feel hundreds of pairs of eyes devouring her body as Boyd spoke into the microphone.

'Jonquil's speciality isn't modelling clothes, but bringing herself to a climax – the more people watching, the better. Show the audience your beautiful quim, Jonquil.'

She couldn't help herself, thrusting her pelvis forwards she parted her thighs lewdly to display her vulva. Turning the other way she repeated the gesture, then drew her outer sex-lips apart to reveal the intricate folds of her sex more fully.

'Jonquil now has three minutes to masturbate herself to

orgasm. If she doesn't succeed, I'll invite members of the audience to assist her.'

He indicated a clock on the wall saying, 'Your time starts ... now.'

Appalled by the idea of strangers touching her intimately in front of so many people, Jonquil slid her hand between her thighs and frantically felt for her clit. But it had shrunk to a tiny triangle of flesh and she had difficulty in easing it from between her inner labia.

She squeezed it gently between her finger and thumb, willing herself to respond to her own touch. Boyd was regarding her with a mocking expression on his face, obviously hoping she'd fail. She stroked it gently, not encouraged by the lack of moisture in the area. The thought gave her an idea.

Ceasing her movements, she beckoned imperiously to him. 'I'm not wet enough – lick me.'

Amazingly, he strolled towards her, then dropped to his knees and probed between her thighs with his tongue. Instantly she felt herself quiver with response and, when he wound his tongue lazily around her tiny nub, her legs trembled so much she could barely stand.

He licked, lapped and sucked at her until she was in ecstasy, feeling her climax growing by the moment. Glancing up at the clock, she could see she only had thirty seconds to go before her time was up. He must have sensed her movement because he tried to remove his face from where it was buried in her dripping delta.

The faint whooshing in her ears and numbness around her wrists signified she was about to come. With all her strength, she thrust his head back into position and ground her groin against his face.

She cried out as she shuddered into a long drawn-out orgasm, just as the clock indicated that she'd made it. Holding onto him to stop herself from falling, she didn't let him disengage himself until the last pleasurable wave had passed.

Then everything went hazy and she awoke to find herself in her own bed, her hand between her thighs.

Following her erotic dream, she'd been listless and heavy-eyed all day and the last thing she felt like doing was listening to Damon talking about his career. It had always formed a major part of his conversation and it had never previously bothered her, but today she wished he'd drop the subject – she had no desire whatsoever to think about last night.

When she'd finished the stir-fry, she took it through to find him hunched on the sofa watching a football match on TV.

'It's ready,' she said, trying to sound good-humoured, then returned to the kitchen for the rice and plates. When she came back, he'd seated himself at the table so he could still see the screen and barely took his eyes off the game as he helped himself to food.

Jonquil sighed to herself – now he was sulking. But she didn't feel up to the effort of apologising and coaxing him out of his bad mood – at least, not yet – so she poured herself a glass of wine and made no attempt to start a conversation.

As soon as he'd finished eating, Damon returned to the sofa while she sat at the table, toying with the remains of her food and wishing fervently that Boyd had remained where she wanted him to be – in her past.

As she didn't seem able to trust herself with him, it looked like she'd have to take whatever steps were necessary to avoid ever being alone with him again. She'd avoid him altogether if she could but, considering she was working for him, she didn't think it would be possible.

When the match was over, Damon started watching a sitcom. She began to clear the table and he rose to help her, still not meeting her eyes.

'I'm sorry I snapped at you,' she ventured as he stacked the dishes next to the sink. 'I . . . I slept badly last night, then I was finding it difficult to concentrate while I was cooking and this kitchen isn't really big enough for two.'

His face cleared. 'That's OK. I should have waited until we were eating, but this could be quite a big deal for us and I'm excited about it. How would next Friday suit you?'

Next Friday? What was he talking about? She recalled with an effort that he'd said something about a party.

'Friday's fine,' she told him. 'I haven't got anything else on.'

'Terrific! Kevin will be pleased.' He rubbed his hands together, his hazel eyes gleaming. 'You needn't go to a lot of trouble: just a few snacks and nibbles to eat and plenty of drink. I'll bring a few bottles myself.'

Jonquil looked at him, totally confused. 'What do you mean, I needn't go to a lot of trouble? Am I supposed to take some food to the party? That's OK. It won't be any trouble – I'll just get something from M&S or the deli.'

It was Damon's turn to look confused. 'If you're giving a party next Friday, you'll need to provide something in the way of food, but it needn't be anything elaborate.'

'*I'm* not giving a party next Friday,' she protested, bewildered by the turn the conversation had taken.

'You just said you were.'

'I thought you were asking me if I wanted to go to one.'

'Weren't you listening? Kevin wants you to give a party and invite Boyd so he can get to know him better.'

With a huge effort Jonquil managed to bite back an angry exclamation. How *dare* Kevin get Damon to ask her to give a party to further *his* business interests? His wretched company was nothing to do with her – let him phone Boyd and suggest a meeting, if he wanted to persuade him into doing business. She became aware that Damon was watching her anxiously.

'You will do it, won't you, Jonquil? If Kevin manages to get even a small slice of the distribution for Boyd's company, it would secure my position with the firm. I might even get offered a partnership, and you know how much that would mean to me.'

He looked at her so appealingly that she hesitated. Her immediate reaction was to tell him in no uncertain terms that it was out of the question, but she wasn't sure she'd be able to bear his disappointment.

He obviously had no idea what he was asking of her and she couldn't blame him for that. She hadn't told him about her past relationship with Boyd and now she wondered if perhaps she should have done.

And what if Boyd brought Julie to the party? It was bad enough having to spend time with him, but seeing him with the woman who now shared his life would make it worse. Why had things suddenly got so complicated?

Damon took her hand. 'Please,' he begged.

Unable to resist the entreaty in his eyes and despite her own feelings, Jonquil found herself wavering.

'All right,' she said reluctantly.

'Thank you, darling.' Damon kissed her hand fervently. 'You might want to invite one or two of your own friends as well, and maybe Jasper would like to come.' Jonquil could tell he was making a big effort to be pleasant, because Damon couldn't stand her brother. 'How about an early night?' he continued.

Although she didn't particularly feel like it, she tried to be receptive to his caresses. But he entered her too soon and came quickly before her climax had even started to build, and then didn't appear to notice that she hadn't achieved her own satisfaction.

Later, as she lay next to him listening to his noisy breathing, Jonquil wondered what on earth she'd let herself in for.

Jasper was waiting for her in the wine bar he'd suggested for their lunch together, leaning against the bar looking handsome and elegant as he made eye contact with an attractive brunette sitting at a table by the wall.

Tall and slender, Jasper had silky fair hair which constantly fell forward onto his forehead, making him appear boyish despite the fact he was nearly thirty. With his aquiline nose and pale grey eyes, he came across like an archetypal upper-class Englishman, a part he played up to the full, despite the fact that their father had been an architect and their mother a teacher.

Today he was wearing a bomber jacket in supple brown leather with a pair of olive-green chinos. Around his neck was a fringed white silk scarf which made him look like an aristocratic Second World War fighter pilot.

'Hi, what can I get you to drink?' He kissed her casually on the cheek and Jonquil didn't miss the disappointed expression on the face of the woman he'd been looking at – she obviously thought they were a couple.

'A glass of dry white wine, please.'

He beckoned to the barman. 'A bottle of Chablis, please, in an ice bucket.'

'That's a bit extravagant,' she protested. 'I'd be quite happy with the house dry white.'

'Only the best is good enough for my sister. Shall we go and sit down?' He picked up a couple of menus and led her to a table on a dais at the end of the room. 'How's it going?' he asked, pouring them both a glass of wine.

'Fine, thanks. How's the new job?'

Jasper seemed to change jobs with unnerving regularity and had recently joined a company which sold medical equipment. He was a good salesman, possessed of abundant charm and perfect manners, but he had a low boredom threshold and was constantly on the look out for a better position.

He pulled a face. 'Fine, but a bit limiting. I'm thinking of moving on.'

'But you've only been there five months,' she pointed out.

He shifted restlessly in his seat. 'I feel under-appreciated. My boss goes through my expenses claims as if it were his own money he was saving by querying every penny. He refused to cough up over half of last month's claim – which has left me a bit short.'

Jonquil hastily feigned deep interest in her menu, hoping he wasn't going to ask for a loan.

'What are you having?' she asked.

'Sorry? Oh, the mussels and the lamb casserole. Anyway, as I was saying, I'm having a few temporary financial problems, so I was wondering if you could lend me a few quid until I'm straight again.'

She'd made him several loans over the years but he often took his time before letting her have the money back. As yet, he hadn't repaid the last loan. Until this moment, she hadn't thought of asking for it but maybe she should, considering that she might have to pull out of her current project if she found she couldn't cope with having to see Boyd on a regular basis.

Putting the menu down, she took a deep breath and looked at him levelly. 'Jasper, you haven't repaid the last money I lent you. Don't you think you should do that, instead of wanting to borrow more?'

He flushed and examined his nails. 'I will as soon as I get a job that pays me what I'm worth, but at the moment I can't find the rent this month.'

She sighed and almost reached for her cheque book, but then she remembered how little she had in her own bank account after buying her apartment.

'Had you thought of leasing a less expensive car than your BMW?' she suggested after a pause. 'It must be costing you a fortune every month.'

A look of irritation flitted across his face. 'Oh, sure, I could buy a bike instead – that *would* impress the clients.'

'There must be some part of your expenditure you could cut back on.'

'Jonquil, what I need is five hundred pounds, not a lecture. Are you going to lend me the money or not?'

'I'll think about it,' she prevaricated, unwilling to say yes, but unable to say no.

'Don't think too long, I need it by the weekend. Here comes the waitress again – shall we order?'

For the rest of the meal, he exerted himself to be a charming, amusing companion, telling her a wryly witty story about a recent sale he'd made. Shortly after their coffee had been served, he glanced at his watch and let out an exclamation. 'I'm due at a meeting in fifteen minutes – damn, I'd better fly.'

'I could do to be getting back myself. Oh, by the way, I'm giving a party on Friday – do come and bring someone if you want to.'

'I'll be there,' he promised and hurried off, leaving her to pay the bill.

On Thursday they had a meeting to discuss the script and Jonquil was aware that this was her last opportunity to invite Boyd – and everyone else working on the project – to her party. Despite her steely determination to remain immune to him, her stomach still lurched as he strode through the door, impeccably dressed in a beautifully tailored dark blue suit.

She'd taken even more care with her own appearance than usual and tried on and rejected three outfits before opting for a cream wool suit worn over a plain round-necked black top.

She'd told herself that she always made the effort to look smart and well turned-out for meetings but, as she'd studied herself in her bedroom mirror, she'd been annoyed to find she was asking herself whether he'd find her attractive in this particular outfit.

What was the matter with her? How could she be concerned by what he thought about her, when he'd behaved unforgivably? She had to admit that she was dreading seeing him, after Friday evening, but was determined that under no circumstances was she going to let him faze her.

Boyd greeted the others before coming over to speak to her, his eyes flickering over her slim figure.

'How's Eamon?' he asked, a bland smile on his face.

'Who?' she retaliated, matching his smile with a determinedly sweet one of her own.

'Surely even you don't have so many men in your life that you can't remember their names?'

Jonquil glanced swiftly around to see if anyone had overheard his jibe, but the production team were clustered at the other end of the conference table, discussing the production schedule.

'I'm sorry,' she said feigning puzzlement. 'I don't remember an Eamon.'

'Let me jog your memory. Moustache . . . putting on weight . . . last Friday evening at *La Maison*.'

'Sorry,' she returned, determined not to be drawn into his game. 'The name still doesn't ring any bells.'

He raised his eyebrows. 'Does that mean Eamon's history?'

At that moment Natalie came to join them saying, 'Are you ready to start?' and Jonquil was able to busy herself arranging her papers in front of her on the table.

As the meeting drew to an end it occurred to her, rather belatedly, that asking Boyd to a party after their exchange of words might be difficult. She was very tempted to forget about it and phone Damon later to say she'd changed her mind. But she'd promised him she'd give a party and she wasn't someone who went back on her word. Boyd was moving towards the door with Hal, so it was now or never.

Taking a deep breath she said, 'By the way, everyone, I'm having a party tomorrow evening and you're all very welcome to come. Sorry it's such short notice.'

There were various murmured acceptances and a couple of people excused themselves on the grounds of prior

37

engagements. She deliberately didn't look at Boyd, devoutly hoping that he wouldn't come and that Kevin's aspirations in that direction were doomed to failure – it would serve him right.

But at least she'd have done what she could to help Damon's career and it wouldn't be her fault if nothing came of it.

As everyone drifted out of the conference room, Boyd came over to her.

'What's the occasion?' he asked.

'I'm sorry?'

'The occasion for the party. I know it's not your birthday so I just wondered if you were celebrating something else.'

'It was Damon's idea,' she heard herself saying and then could have kicked herself. It was none of Boyd's business.

'Damon! That's his name! How could I have made a mistake like that? Is it Damon's birthday?'

'No,' she replied ungraciously, wishing he'd move out of her way.

'His wedding anniversary perhaps? No, it was Kevin who was the married one among your numerous admirers.'

Goaded by his taunts she dug her nails into the palm of her hand, itching to slap him.

Summoning a radiant smile she said, 'We're celebrating our three-month anniversary.'

There was a flash of anger in his eyes before he replied, 'Then I'll be sure and bring something to toast the happy couple.'

He turned on his heel and strode out of the building, his tie blown over his shoulder by the blustery wind.

38

Chapter Four

'Why on earth did I ever agree to this?' Jonquil muttered darkly to herself. It was Friday evening and she'd spent several hours in the afternoon cleaning the apartment and making preparations for the party.

She'd pushed the low-backed cream sofa and armchair against the wall and rearranged all the other furniture so there was enough space to circulate in the centre of the room. A dozen ivory candles stood in holders, ready for lighting later, and a vase of creamy freesias on the mantelpiece added their delicate scent to the air.

Damon came out of the kitchen, where he'd been setting out the glasses he'd borrowed from his local wine merchant.

'Everything ready?' he asked.

'Just about.'

The buzzer went at that moment. It was Kevin, bringing a bottle of cheap wine and his wife, who looked as though she was there under sufferance. He kissed Jonquil heartily and squeezed her hip in a way that made her long to slap him.

'You look gorgeous,' he complimented her. 'Damon's a lucky man to have you on his team.'

She'd taken a lot of time over her appearance and had opted for a figure-skimming dress in jade-green silk which left her shoulders and arms bare. She'd pinned her red-gold hair up so it fell in wavy tendrils over the nape of her slim neck.

'Can I get you a drink, Kevin?' asked Damon.

'Scotch, and my wife will have a glass of white wine.'

'I haven't any Scotch, I'm afraid, although there's lots of wine,' said Jonquil.

'Of course we've some Scotch, darling,' returned Damon, opening one of the kitchen cupboards to reveal a bottle of

39

Glenfiddich she hadn't seen before. He poured Kevin a generous measure and then returned the bottle to the cupboard. Kevin, meanwhile, prowled around the small apartment and Jonquil had the distinct impression that he was evaluating her financial status.

'What time's Boyd coming?' he asked abruptly, glancing at his watch.

'I've no idea,' she returned airily. 'I'm not even sure he'll make it – he has a lot of commitments.'

Other people started to arrive and, within a very short time, her flat was overflowing. As Jonquil moved among the guests, sipping a glass of dry white wine and making sure she talked to everyone at some stage, she just couldn't seem to relax. Every time the buzzer went she found herself watching the door to see if Boyd had arrived. The thought of seeing him with Julie made her feel jittery and she was annoyed with herself for it.

The door opened again, this time to admit her brother, who – much to her surprise – was alone. Jonquil had expected him to bring someone – he never seemed to lack female company. He was beautifully dressed, as always, this evening in a silver-grey suit which Jonquil suspected was either silk, or a silk mix and must have cost the earth.

'Hi, Jonquil.' He took her arm and steered her towards the kitchen. 'I want a huge drink and then I need to talk to you.'

Knowing her brother's weakness for single malt, Jonquil poured him a large Glenfiddich and then left the whisky out with the other drinks. Why should Kevin have his own specially designated bottle?

'Can we go somewhere private?' Jasper asked, taking an appreciative gulp. As the party had now overflowed from the sitting room into her office and bedroom, she looked at him in amazement.

'Where did you have in mind – the bathroom?'

He looked around, a hunted expression on his face, before saying, 'How about my car?'

'I'm not leaving my own party to go and sit in your car. Why don't you just go ahead and say whatever it is you want to say? No one could possibly hear us over the noise.'

'The landing, then. I don't want to have to bellow out my problems and have the record suddenly come to an end and everyone hear.'

Reluctantly, she followed him. 'What is it?'

He averted his gaze and lit a cigarette. 'Have you thought about lending me that five hundred?'

She took a deep breath – this wasn't going to be easy. 'I have, but to be frank I think it's time you got your financial affairs under control rather than keep coming to me. Your landlord can't just evict you – it's illegal. Offer to pay the arrears in instalments or something.'

He drew on his cigarette and stared into space. When she made a move to return to the party he put out a hand to stop her.

'I have to have that money,' he blurted out.

'I've just said that—'

'It isn't my landlord I owe it to.'

'Who is it?' she asked, puzzled.

'You don't need to know that.'

'I do if you're asking me to lend it to you.'

He hesitated, then cast her a sidelong look. 'I did something stupid.'

'What?'

'I bet on a horse belonging to one of my clients – it would have been difficult not to, because he was with me at the time and he said it was a dead cert, but it lost.'

Jonquil looked at him in dismay. 'That *was* stupid,' she agreed.

'Yeah, well, I've learnt my lesson; but I have to have the money because unpleasant things happen to people who don't pay bookies.'

'W . . . what do you mean?'

'What do you think I mean? I'll be found down a back alley with two broken legs or worse.'

The colour drained from Jonquil's face and she leant back against the wall for support.

'They . . . they wouldn't.'

'If it gets around that a bookie's let someone get away without paying a debt, they'd be out of business in weeks.'

'Jasper . . . the other times I lent you money – were those loans to pay gambling debts too?'

He wouldn't meet her eyes. 'I can't remember.'

She felt quite ill. Why had she never suspected it before? He'd occasionally mentioned that he'd been to the races, but somehow she'd never thought he'd be foolish enough to bet more than a fiver once in a while. No wonder he was always short of money if he gambled. She'd thought it was just his expensive lifestyle, but this was much worse. She could only hope he'd meant it when he'd said he'd learnt his lesson and that he wouldn't make the same mistake again.

'If I give you a cheque now, it will be on condition that you never bet on horses again,' she said at last. 'And I want your word on that.'

'All right,' he said immediately.

'Promise me.'

'I promise I'll never bet on horses again. Now would you just write me the cheque, so I can breathe again.'

Silently she went back into her crowded, noisy apartment, found her bag and wrote the cheque. She took it out to him and he pocketed it muttering, 'Thanks, I'll see you,' and hurried off down the stairs.

It was just before eleven when Boyd arrived. Jonquil was standing opposite the door when he walked in and felt her stomach lurch. About to go and greet him, she was pre-empted by Kevin, who leapt forward and pumped his hand, then attempted to drape an arm around his shoulders – difficult because Boyd was at least a head taller than him.

But Boyd turned away and it was only then that Jonquil realised he'd brought someone with him, and it definitely wasn't Julie, whom she remembered as being a petite brunette.

The woman on his arm looked about five foot eight and had a fall of thick, ice-blonde hair which framed a beautiful haughty face dominated by eyes the colour of gooseberries.

Boyd was obviously introducing her to Kevin, whose hot little eyes took in every luscious curve of the woman's body, which was encased in an expensive looking silver sheath dress. Jonquil immediately felt dowdy and insignificant in contrast,

42

and noticed that everyone in the room was staring at the new arrivals.

They certainly made a striking couple; Boyd's dark good looks set off her blonde loveliness to perfection. Summoning a smile that felt as though it could split her face in two, Jonquil made her way across the room.

'Hi, Boyd, I'm delighted you could make it,' she said, her facial muscles already aching from the effort of keeping the corners of her lips turned upwards.

'This is Saskia, my business manager – she handles my corporate affairs as well as a few other things. Saskia, this is Jonquil.'

Swiftly suppressing the unworthy suspicion that Saskia handled more than Boyd's business, Jonquil smiled at her and said, 'Hi, glad you could come.'

Close up Saskia was even more stunning. Her nose tilted deliciously upwards with a sensual little flare around the nostrils and her lashes were long and thick. She was so dazzlingly blonde that she looked Swedish but, when she spoke her voice was pure Home Counties.

'Hello. I hope you don't mind Boyd bringing me along.'

'Not at all, would you—'

'Would you like a drink?' Kevin interrupted eagerly.

'Champagne, please.'

'I'm sorry, but I'm afraid there isn't any, but there's—' began Jonquil.

'I've brought some, as promised,' said Boyd.

It was only then that she noticed the man in the chauffeur's uniform just behind the couple and saw that he was carrying a large box containing a dozen bottles of champagne. Boyd extracted one and handed it to Kevin.

'There you go,' he said amiably. 'If you'll open that, we'll all have a glass.'

Kevin was obviously unused to playing the part of waiter and handed the bottle to Damon, who was hovering just behind him, saying, 'Do the honours, would you?' He turned back to Boyd. 'I'm glad that I've bumped into you again because I have a proposition that might interest you.'

'What sort of proposition?'

43

'A business proposition.'

'I didn't imagine it was a personal one,' returned Boyd, lazily draping an arm around Saskia's slim shoulders. 'Saskia's the one to talk to – she knows more about my business than I do.' He flashed her a smile and she responded by moving closer to him and slipping her arm around his waist, while raising her glass to her lips with a scarlet-nailed hand.

Jonquil felt another stab of pure unadulterated jealousy at the casually possessive way in which she touched him and wondered whether Julie knew she had a rival.

'I'm sure Saskia's great at throwing press launches and organising outings to Ascot,' continued Kevin jovially, 'but I want to talk about a distribution deal which—'

Boyd yawned and cut across him. 'Then she's definitely the one you should talk to. She's got a Master's degree in Business Administration and . . . remind me again, Saskia, what was your first degree?'

'Marketing,' she retorted, giving Kevin a look of such icy disdain it would have frozen coffee poured straight from the percolator.

'Yes, but I'd rather—'

'Boyd, shall we dance?' purred Saskia, putting her empty glass down.

'Good idea,' he said, taking her hand as they moved into the centre of the room. Jonquil was torn between amusement at the look of chagrin on Kevin's face and pain at the sight of the striking couple in each other's arms, dancing to the slow record currently playing. Briefly, she considered changing it to something much faster so they'd have to separate, but instantly dismissed the idea as petty.

Damon drew her to one side. His face was flushed and he'd obviously had a lot to drink, because he swayed slightly as he spoke to her. 'Kevin didn't get very far with Boyd. At the next record I'm going to ask that gorgeous blonde he's brought with him to dance, so the boss can have another go.'

She picked up a bottle of wine and began to top up people's glasses. If Kevin wanted to risk another snub, let him, but she wasn't having anything to do with it.

Damon tapped Saskia on the shoulder. 'Would you like to

dance?' he asked, his eyes riveted to the deep honey-gold valley of her cleavage.

'No, thanks.' She turned to Jonquil. 'Where's your bathroom?'

'Over there and to the right.'

Without another glance at Damon, Saskia undulated across the room, followed by a dozen pairs of male eyes. Kevin joined them and raised his glass of champagne.

'Not a bad drop of fizz,' he said to Boyd, 'but I must introduce you to my wine merchant – he's keeps some vintage Moët in reserve for special clients and I'm sure I could persuade with him to part with a case or two, if I twist his arm. Now, as I was saying before, I think it would be beneficial to both our companies if we got together and—'

'Talk to Saskia. Jonquil, will you dance with me?'

About to refuse on the grounds that she had guests to see to, Jonquil was startled to have Damon remove the wine bottle from her hand and give her a little push in Boyd's direction.

'She'd love to – wouldn't you, darling?' Before she could say anything, Boyd enfolded her in a light embrace and she found herself automatically moving to the soft, seductive music. Such was the force of her response to his close physical proximity that she felt as though she'd been plugged into an electric socket.

She felt his warm breath on her hair as he murmured, 'Drinking straight from the bottle isn't very ladylike – why don't you try a glass? You could always use a tumbler if a goblet doesn't hold enough.'

Her whole body zinged with an erotic tingling sensation and she was very aware of how her slim frame had automatically fitted itself against the lean length of his but, at his teasing words, she stiffened and retorted, 'I was topping up glasses.'

He laughed softly and she cursed herself for rising to the bait. The arms around her tightened and she felt the hard pressure of his chest against her breasts. He moved a hand over her back in a lazy caress that had flames leaping in her belly and made her legs go weak.

'What a beautiful dress,' he said softly. 'Jade-green suits you

– you have good taste in clothes. If only I could say the same about your party guests.'

'He's Damon's boss,' she said defensively, then wished she'd ignored the jibe. She actually agreed with Boyd, which made it all the more galling.

She'd been too busy talking to people to have had much to drink, but she suddenly felt as though she'd downed at least a full bottle of champagne. Her mind had emptied of everything except Boyd's intoxicating nearness, the faint scent of his cologne and the sensation of his hands moving over her back.

Of their own volition, her eyes closed and she leant a little closer to him, savouring the intimacy of their contact. Her breathing had become ragged and she had to fight an urge to wind her arms around his neck and kiss him. She ached for the feel of his lips on hers, the sensation of their bodies moving together, his manhood buried deep inside her sex, filling her completely.

She lost sight of everything except her wayward desires – they might have been alone instead of in a crowded room surrounded by dozens of other people. Slowly, sensually, she undulated her pelvis against his and heard a faint groan escape from his lips, then she felt the strength of his response pressing into her.

His hand slipped between them and found her mound, caressing it intimately, unseen by anyone in the crush of bodies. His touch aroused her the way no one else's ever had, making flames leap in her sex. She wanted him to push her back against the wall, lift her skirt, drag her panties down and take her right there, regardless of everyone else.

She burned for him and, as his probing fingers slid between her thighs over the slippery silk of her briefs, she had to fight an urge to drag his zip down and draw out his shaft.

He knew her body almost as well as she did and was aware of exactly how to touch her. He massaged the prominent bump of her clit in a way that had her gasping and panting, wanting more than he was giving her.

She felt her climax gathering on the periphery of her consciousness and pressed herself against him, craving that dazzling explosion of release. But just as she hovered on the brink, a heavy hand fell on her shoulder.

'Have you seen the whisky anywhere, darling?' asked Damon.

She leapt away from Boyd as if burnt, brought back to reality with an unwelcome jolt. What the hell was she thinking of? Boyd had betrayed her trust in the most callous way and yet here she was acting as if she could barely wait to rip his clothes off and drag him to bed.

'No . . . I have to . . . I have to see to something,' she stuttered and fled towards the bathroom. She reached it just as Saskia was coming out.

The other woman bestowed a distant smile on her as she glided past. Kevin emerged from the sitting room at that moment.

'Saskia!' he exclaimed, rubbing his hands together, 'Just the little lady I wanted to talk to. Why don't we get together for a cosy dinner and I'll explain to you just what my company can do for yours.'

'Call my PA's secretary,' she said, her green eyes glacial, then she vanished into the crowd.

A muted hum of conversation drifted into the reception area of the casino as Jasper signed in. He exchanged a few flirtatious words with the girl on the desk before saying, 'Is Nadine in tonight?'

'She's on the roulette table,' she told him helpfully.

'Thanks.'

He strolled through the heavy double doors and went into the bar, where he ordered a whisky. He was exchanging nods with a couple of acquaintances, when the sound of a throat being cleared immediately to his right made him glance sideways to see the assistant manager was next to him.

'Hi, Jake – how's it going?' Jasper greeted him.

'A bit quiet this evening, but it's early yet. We haven't seen you for a couple of weeks.'

'No, I've been busy.'

'Are you planning to play tonight?'

'Probably just a little flutter.'

Jake cleared his throat again. 'I'm afraid you've already

47

exceeded your agreed limit. We've written to you about it, but you've not been in touch.'

Jasper signalled to the barman to refill his glass. 'What? I haven't exceeded it by much, have I?'

'By several hundred pounds. We'd like you to pay at least half of it off within the next few days and I'm afraid that, if you want to play tonight, it'll have to be cash.'

Jasper's faintly bored expression hid his annoyance as he took out his cigarettes and offered the packet to the man, who shook his head. s

'What if I increase my limit?'

'Not unless you pay off what you owe.'

Jasper lit his cigarette and inhaled deeply, a faintly aggrieved expression on his handsome, boyish face. 'Don't you value my custom?'

'Of course we do. But when you let your account mount up and don't make any attempt to settle it despite two requests, it raises questions about your ability to pay it.'

'I can pay it,' returned Jasper, concealing his irritation with difficulty. 'I just haven't got round to it yet.'

'Perhaps you'd get round to it by the middle of next week – say, Wednesday.' Jake's tone was scrupulously polite, but Jasper didn't miss the veiled threat in his words.

'I'll see what I can do.' He put his empty glass down and sauntered away.

Briefly he considered going into the restaurant to get something to eat, but decided against it. Complimentary sandwiches were provided for those playing the tables – he'd have some of those and save the money.

A brief grin flitted across his face at the thought that he was following Jonquil's advice about living less expensively, but he doubted if she'd see it that way.

He hated having to borrow money off her, but he was desperate. At least her five hundred would get the bookies off his back for a while and give him the chance to raise the other couple of grand he owed. What a run of bad luck he'd had lately, but it had to change soon – it just had to.

He took twenty pounds out of his wallet and exchanged it for a handful of chips, then made his way to the roulette table.

Nadine had just set the wheel in motion and smiled at him as he joined the handful of people avidly watching it.

She was wearing a low-cut ruby-red evening gown with shoe-string shoulder straps and he felt a stirring of excitement as he took in the full effect of her splendid cleavage. A voluptuous brunette with sly, sloe-dark eyes, Nadine always had that effect on him.

The small silver ball rattled to a stop in twenty-seven and she deftly pushed the correct number of chips towards a Chinese man who was the only winner and then raked the rest back.

'What time does your shift finish?' Jasper asked in an undertone as he placed his bet.

'Midnight,' she murmured in reply.

'I'll meet you outside.' She shot him a provocative smile and turned her attention back to the game.

At ten past twelve she left through the back entrance and joined him in the BMW. They kissed, his hands cupping her full, high breasts and such was his sense or urgency that he almost lifted her astride him and had her there and then. But a couple walked past and he released her reluctantly and started the engine.

'Your place?' he asked.

'OK.'

'How much did you lose tonight?' she enquired as they drove over the river.

He pulled a face into the darkness. 'Only twenty pounds.'

'It's a mug's game, Jasper. There's only one winner.'

'That's rich, coming from a casino employee.'

'*They* pay *me*, not the other way round,' she pointed out.

'You sound just like my sister.'

She looked at him in surprise. 'I didn't know you had a sister, but she obviously has more sense than you have. Take some sound advice and find yourself another hobby.'

He laid his hand on her nylon-clad knee and slid her skirt up her thighs until her stocking-tops were exposed. 'I *have* another hobby.'

She laughed, took a small perfume spray from her bag and spritzed her neck, immediately filling the interior of the car with the seductive scent of Chloe.

'So you have,' she agreed.

They enjoyed a pleasantly casual relationship based almost exclusively on mutual physical attraction. Jasper knew that he wasn't the only man in her life and she certainly wasn't the only woman in his, but they had fun together, even if she didn't approve of his gambling.

She had a small apartment in Streatham and, as he followed her up the stairs, he was mesmerised by the swaying of her curvaceous bottom under the clinging silken fabric of her dress. Once through her front door, he shed his jacket and pulled her into his arms, backing her up against the wall as he kissed her.

Her body felt soft and yielding against his and he wound a hand in her dark hair, tipping her head back so he could press kisses on the soft white skin of her throat.

She moaned and his other hand found one breast and caressed it lingeringly over the low-cut front of her gown, before sliding inside to toy with the taut point of her nipple.

His own arousal was mounting with increasing urgency as he drew her shoulder straps down her arms to leave her naked from the waist up.

'You're beautiful,' he breathed, scooping her into his arms and carrying her over to the sofa. He eased her dress down her hips until she lay before him in just her black stockings, suspender belt and French knickers. As he drew the flimsy undergarment downwards, she raised her backside to help him and he trailed a series of kisses across the smooth plains of her belly.

He stripped off his own clothes and joined her, parting her thighs with his knee. He took his time over arousing her, caressing her breasts until her nipples had darkened to the same ruby-red as her dress and then dropping to his knees beside the sofa and kissing her full on her outer sex-lips.

She moaned and opened her thighs even more widely, her hand in his silky fair hair as he thrust his tongue strongly into the whorled entrance to her hidden channel. Inside, she was wet and velvety as he probed her, then swirled his tongue around to catch every last drop of moisture.

She had a faint sea-taste that he loved and he lapped and

licked enthusiastically, burying his face deep in her vulva until it was streaming with her juices. He located the plump triangle of her clit with his tongue and stabbed at it in a lazy rhythm that had her writhing ecstatically.

One thing that Jasper particularly liked about Nadine was that she climaxed easily, and it only took a couple of minutes before she cried out, her back arched and she shuddered into a lengthy orgasm.

She was more than ready for him as he entered her in one smooth stroke, winding her arms around his neck and thrusting her hips demandingly upwards, her eyes fluttering closed.

He continued to caress her as he moved above her, pacing himself and enjoying the feeling of her velvety sheath flexing around his member, making it hard for him to stay in control.

He thrust harder, penetrating her to her very core, riding her until she reached a second climax, then letting go in a surge of gasping release that made him forget – at least for the moment – everything except the pliant body of the woman in his arms.

Chapter Five

On the Saturday morning following Jonquil's party, Damon woke up with a hangover and spent most of the day moaning and demanding both her undivided attention and a series of hot drinks and snacks.

She eventually lost patience in the late afternoon and insisted he went home, saying she had to work. Thankfully alone at last, she found she was unable to settle at her desk and kept wandering restlessly around the apartment, before eventually going for a walk and returning just as it got dark.

Her inability to remain indifferent to Boyd irked her and made her annoyed with herself. He only had to take her in his arms and she found herself on fire, despite the fact that she detested him.

She'd dreaded him bringing Julie to the party, but then been confounded when he'd turned up with the gorgeous Saskia instead. Exactly how did she fit into the picture? Were she and Boyd having an affair? If so, she *almost* felt sorry for Julie. Perhaps she lived in the country with their children and Boyd only returned at weekends while during the week he amused himself with other women.

And then there was Jasper. Did he gamble regularly and was that why he was always so hard up? And if that were the case, would he stop now, or had he got the gambling bug and would continue to back horses despite his promise to her?

It all continued to go round and round in her head until she went to bed early, tired out from thinking about it all.

The offices and administrative centre of Boyd's company were situated in Docklands. A tour had been arranged for Tuesday and Jonquil had no alternative but to go. It turned out to be a cold October day with torrential rain pouring down from a dark, lowering sky and, although she rang for a mini cab, she was told it would be at least two hours before one was available.

She had no alternative but to make her way to Highgate tube station on foot, a twenty minute walk she usually enjoyed in pleasant weather but, with a strong wind blowing the rain down in virtually horizontal sheets, she was drenched before she'd gone a hundred yards.

She'd washed her hair that morning and carefully blown it into a smooth gleaming bob, but within a couple of minutes of leaving her apartment it was tangled around her face in wild wet strands.

By the time she arrived in Soho, all she wanted to do was go home and lie in a hot bath – she was chilled to the bone. As she scrambled into the car Boyd had sent for them, she envied Natalie her practical clothing – today she was wearing a parka with a fur-lined hood over a pair of thick trousers and a fisherman's sweater.

'Terrific party on Friday,' Hal said as the car headed towards Docklands.

'Thanks,' murmured Jonquil, mopping at her face with a handful of tissues which immediately disintegrated into damp shreds.

'I noticed that Boyd brought the ice queen with him,' said Natalie. 'I couldn't get a word of sense out of my boyfriend once the lovely Saskia had arrived.'

'Had you met her before?' Jonquil enquired, keen to gather all the information she could but without wanting to seem too interested.

Natalie pulled a wry face. 'A couple of times. She's terrifyingly efficient and makes me feel hopelessly inadequate on about a dozen different levels.'

'She scares me senseless,' admitted Hal cheerfully. 'One glance and I feel reduced to scruffy schoolboy status.'

'Do you think she'll be there today?' asked Jonquil.

'Probably,' replied Natalie, 'but hopefully she'll be too busy to have any time to spare for us.'

Jonquil didn't like Docklands, she found the area bleak and gloomy – particularly on such a foul day – but she had to admit that the building which housed Boyd's company was very impressive. Designed by a leading architect, it was a triumph of modern construction with floor-to-ceiling windows in dark reflective glass.

Stringent security was obviously a priority, because the reception area was manned by four security guards. Their identities were checked and they were issued with passes before being allowed any further into the building.

'Good morning, everyone – it's good to see you.' Saskia's words were welcoming enough as she approached them, but her tone was cool. 'Let's go to my office.'

Jonquil's heart sank as she took in the other woman's immaculate appearance. Her thick blonde hair had been gathered back in a sleek chignon which drew attention to her perfectly sculpted features and her exquisite sea-green suit bore all the hallmarks of an exclusive design house.

The other woman's flawless grooming made Jonquil feel even more acutely self-conscious about her own disreputable appearance. With every step she took in her wet shoes, she was horribly conscious of the squishing noise she was making. Even worse, they passed a mirror and she saw that she looked even more bedraggled than she'd thought.

Her hair was a wild mass of wet rats' tails, her trench coat was damp and crumpled and her mascara had run, making her look as though she hadn't washed her face in days.

'Saskia, is there a ladies' I could use?' she asked. 'I got drenched on the way to the tube station and I'd like to dry off a bit.'

'There's a bathroom off my office,' she replied to Jonquil's relief. At least she'd get the chance to remove the mascara streaks before she encountered Boyd.

But, to her horror, he was sprawled on a sofa in Saskia's office in his shirt-sleeves, studying some papers. He rose to his feet when they came in and grinned at them.

'Hi – glad you could make it. How about some coffee?' His gaze lighted on Jonquil and she was annoyed to find herself stepping to one side to hide behind Hal. She might detest Boyd, but she didn't like him seeing her looking so unattractive.

'What happened to you?' he asked bluntly.

'I got caught in the rain,' she admitted. 'Is that the bathroom?' she asked hastily, turning to Saskia and nodding towards a door on one wall.

'Yes, do go ahead and clean up.'

Jonquil darted hastily across the room and shut herself in with relief. The full-length mirror showed that the glimpse she'd had of herself had only told half the tale and she only just stopped herself letting out a shriek of horror.

She repaired her appearance as best she could, lingering in the cocooned warmth of the luxurious room, reluctant to return to the office to face her ex-lover. When she went back in, the others were drinking coffee and discussing dates for touring the rest of the company's sites.

'Coffee?' Boyd asked her, as she took a seat on the sofa next to Natalie.

'Please.'

'You still look frozen. I'll get my driver to take you home after he's dropped your colleagues off in Soho.'

'There's no need,' she murmured, wishing he'd stop studying her and imagining that he was wondering what he'd ever seen in her.

He, on the other hand, was looking annoyingly sexy in a blue-and-grey striped tie worn with a crisp white Oxford cotton shirt tucked into pin-striped suit trousers. There was a just a glimpse of dark curling hair at his throat and the sight made her swallow and her mouth go dry.

'There's every need – you look like a half-drowned kitten.' He handed her a cup of steaming coffee, while Natalie and Hal left their seats to go and look at something Saskia was showing them on her computer screen. 'Thanks for inviting me to your party, by the way,' he continued. 'What time did it end?'

'About two.'

'Did Eamon . . . Damon enjoy himself?'

'I think so,' she muttered.

'I hope he realises how lucky he is to have such a loyal and supportive girlfriend,' he commented lazily.

Something in his tone of voice made her wonder if he suspected that Damon had put her up to having the party. Her suspicions were confirmed as he went on, 'He seems very ambitious – he should go far.'

'Boyd – would you come and look at this?' Much to Jonquil's relief, Saskia's low-pitched voice interrupted their conversation. He rose lithely to his feet and went to join her by the computer screen.

There was so much to take in during the next couple of hours that Jonquil's head was spinning as she scribbled page after page of notes.

They broke for lunch at one and joined the queue at the self-service counter in the staff restaurant, then took a window table with a view over Docklands.

Saskia came in shortly afterwards and joined them. She gestured imperiously to one of the restaurant staff and when the woman came over said, 'I'll have a prawn salad with a sparkling mineral water please.'

'I don't think prawn salad's on the menu today,' replied the woman, peering doubtfully towards the day's menu on a board by the counter.

'Then get them to make me one,' retorted Saskia impatiently, putting her hand on Boyd's arm. 'Good news on the export front,' she told him. 'The position's even better than anticipated, but we need to discuss a problem with the French distributors.'

'Sure, I'll drop by your office later.'

'And I got us dinner reservations at Latimer's.'

'Great.' He grinned at her and Jonquil was ashamed to find herself hoping that they'd both choke on their respective meals.

'Hello, Jasper, is it still raining out?' asked Penny, his boss Duncan's secretary.

'Tossing it down,' he returned, smiling at her and pushing his fair hair back from where it had fallen over his forehead. Penny was plain and mousy, but she had an enormous bosom which he found so riveting that it was always an effort to look her in the eye when speaking to her. She was besotted by Jasper and never missed an opportunity to talk to him.

'Where the bloody hell have you been until this time?'

Duncan appeared in the doorway of his office, just as Jasper was sauntering past on the way to his desk. He stopped and turned to face the man.

'Lunch,' he replied affably, trying not to wince at the sight of Duncan's bright pink-and-white striped shirt worn with a luminous yellow tie, both of which clashed not only with each other, but with his sandy hair.

'It's ten past three,' Duncan snapped. 'Lunch in this company is taken between twelve and one or one and two, as well you know. I'm getting tired of your attitude. You seem to think that you can swan in and out as you please and the rules that apply to everyone else don't apply to you. You've been with us several months now but, despite a lot of promises, your sales record is poor, verging on abysmal. Come into my office.'

Reluctantly, Jasper followed him into the stuffy room and sank gracefully onto the chair opposite the desk while Duncan moved behind it and folded his arms over his barrel chest.

'I've had just about enough of you,' he announced. 'Your time keeping's non-existent, your sales sheets are always late and you spend most of your time – when you *are* here – chatting up the female staff.'

'Come on, Duncan,' Jasper protested. 'I've been knocking myself out laying the groundwork and it's just about to pay off – you'll see.'

'No, *you'll* see. If you haven't exceeded your set targets by at least fifty per cent by the end of next month, you're out, excuses or no excuses. Have I made myself clear?'

'Perfectly,' said Jasper, rising to his feet.

'Good, because I've got a meeting in Acton and, by the time I get back, I want you to have fixed up at least half a dozen appointments.'

Jasper pretended not to see Penny's commiserating expression as he left the office and headed for his desk. What was it with Duncan, always on his case and wanting him to clock in and out like some office junior? The sooner he found another job, the better.

Penny touched his shoulder and placed a cup of coffee in front of him.

'He's gone,' she told him in a sympathetic voice. 'Would

you like a biscuit?' She brandished a pack of custard creams, but Jasper only had eyes for her breasts, which he suddenly had an overpowering desire to see naked. Taking her by the wrist he led her into Duncan's office and slammed the door.

'What are we doing in here?' she asked.

He slipped his arms around her waist and pulled her close so that her breasts pressed pleasingly into his chest. 'I wanted to spend a few minutes alone with you,' he murmured. 'You smell good – new perfume?'

'Just talc,' she replied, blushing with delight. He tipped her chin up and kissed her, one hand covering a generously proportioned breast and fondling it.

'Don't,' she protested, trying to push him away, but he backed her up until her thighs were against the desk. Deftly, he undid the buttons on her pale pink blouse to reveal a plain white nylon bra and a vast expanse of freckled cleavage. He bent his head and dropped several hard kisses on her yielding flesh, making her gasp.

With the expertise born of long practice, he undid the clasp on the back of her bra with one hand then, as it slid downwards, stared reverently at the voluptuous perfection of her ripe orbs. Large but firm, they were tipped by jutting crimson nipples which reminded him of raspberries.

He took one between his lips and flicked his tongue against it, then sucked gently while she went rigid in his grasp. He stroked her back and shoulders until he felt her relax in his arms. When he lowered her onto the desk, she tried to scramble back to her feet.

'We can't,' she moaned. 'Not here.'

'Yes, here,' he said firmly, liking the idea of fucking her over Duncan's desk.

'I didn't think you fancied me,' she said weakly.

'Of course I do – can't you tell?' He took her hand and guided it to the hard bulge in his trousers, watching her blush as she touched it gingerly.

'Unzip me,' he ordered her. She gave him a startled glance, but he held her eyes with a compelling grey stare until she fumblingly obeyed him. He drew out his member and wrapped her limp hand around the shaft, noticing that her eyes had now glazed over. He wondered how many men she'd had and wouldn't mind betting that her experience was pretty limited. Struck by an off-putting thought, he said, 'Penny – you have done this before, haven't you?'

'Yes,' she whispered, squeezing the rigid column in her hand inexpertly.

He threw her pleated navy-blue skirt over her waist and hooked his hands in the waistband of her tights and white cotton knickers. As he peeled them down her wide hips, he thought they were definitely knickers rather than briefs or panties, because they came right up to the waist and were of a voluminous cut that none of his girlfriends would have been seen dead in.

Her thighs were clamped tightly together and he eased them apart, hoping she wasn't going to be difficult to arouse. She had a luxuriant bush which he brushed aside to reveal the tightly furled leaves of her vulva.

Sensing the tension that suffused her body, he dropped to his knees and planted several kisses on the dark fronds of her fleece, then began to lick languidly at her furrow, gradually inserting his tongue deeper into it as she writhed on the desk under his ministrations.

Although there was nothing he wanted more than to plunge into her and hump her until the irritations of the day had receded into insignificance, Jasper knew better than to enter any woman until she was ready. So, even though his erection was throbbing impatiently in her limp grasp, he persevered, pleasuring her with his lips and tongue until her thighs were splayed widely apart and her breath was coming in uneven gasps.

When he felt the trickle of warm moisture flooding her saliva-slick quim, he got to his feet, positioned himself at the entrance to her inner chamber and thrust smoothly into her.

Instantly she was transformed. She wrapped her sturdy legs around his thighs and began to claw wildly at his back in the grip of a hitherto unsuspected passion. Glad he hadn't bothered to shed his jacket, Jasper drove determinedly into her, watching the magnificent heave of her bosom as she jammed her hips upwards to meet each strong movement.

Half hoping that Duncan would return unexpectedly and walk in on them, and not caring that various documents had been sent sailing in all directions, Jasper had to exert himself to keep up with her. Her eyes were closed and her hair had fallen over her face as she moved frenziedly and not very rhythmically under him.

She came suddenly with a cry so loud he hastily clapped his hand over her mouth, in case one of their colleagues heard and came to investigate.

He redoubled his efforts, impaling her relentlessly so she was almost pushed off the other side of the desk. Grasping her by the waist, he made a dozen last deep thrusts and came in a scalding flood of fluid high up inside her.

The sudden ringing of the phone right next to them made them both jump. Penny opened her eyes and stared at it like a terrified rabbit.

'What shall I do?' she asked frantically.

'Ignore it,' he advised her.

'I can't – it's probably Duncan. He said he'd call when he arrived at his meeting to get some figures I'm supposed to have ready.' Unperturbed, Jasper reached out a hand and picked it up.

'Yes?'

'What the hell are you doing answering the phone?' snapped Duncan. 'Where's Penny?'

'Responding to a call of nature,' replied Jasper smoothly. 'Here she is now.'

He passed the phone over while she rolled her eyes wildly and looked as if she thought it might bite. As he pulled out of her with a much louder squelching noise than he'd expected, he could hear Duncan barking questions at her.

'I'm . . . I'm not sure,' she faltered in reply. Duncan's roar of annoyance was clearly audible, making Jasper glad that their combined juices were now leaking out of Penny and all over the highly polished surface of the desk.

He straightened his clothing while she hung up and began to scramble hurriedly back into her tights and knickers.

'He's furious,' she said, almost overbalancing. 'I've to phone him back in a couple of minutes with the figures.'

61

'I'll leave you to it,' he said, heading for the door.

'Jasper . . .'

'Um?' He paused with his hand on the handle.

'We . . . we can do this again, can't we?'

'Sure,' he returned absently, wondering if anyone would snitch on him if he vanished to the pub for an hour or so.

As her taxi pulled up outside Latimer's, Saskia didn't need to glance at herself in the mirror of the silver compact she carried in her bag to know that her hair and make-up were immaculate.

Trying to get her relationship with Boyd on a more intimate footing was proving more difficult than she'd anticipated. She'd managed to engineer it so that they had dinner together once a week or so, but so far he'd made no attempt to take her to bed.

She considered her position. She could always make the first move herself; she was almost certain he wouldn't reject her – what man in possession of the usual hormones would? She thought of her looks as yet another weapon in an impressive armoury which included her acute intelligence and a keen head for business. But, knowing that men didn't value anything easily come by, she was too shrewd to do that – no, he had to make the running.

But she was uneasy about his feelings for Jonquil – she thought she'd detected a certain warmth in his eyes when he looked at her. She hadn't counted on finding him interested in another woman, just when she was ready to hot things up.

What was going on there? As far as she was aware, Boyd only knew Jonquil through the video project, but intuition told her there was more to it than that. Tonight she intended, if she could, to find out exactly what.

Once inside the restaurant she allowed the waiter to relieve her of her coat and then usher her into the bar where Boyd was waiting. She was wearing a cinnamon silk trouser-suit which drew attention to her slim figure and the length of her legs. The ivory silk top under it hinted discreetly at the lush curves of her breasts and, as usual, every man present looked up and watched her walk across the room, some admiringly, some hungrily.

Over drinks and dinner they discussed company business but, once coffee had been served, Saskia brought up the subject on her mind.

'Are you happy with the way the video project's shaping up?' she asked, pushing a lock of blonde hair behind her ear, her green eyes watchful.

'Pretty much. The production company has an excellent reputation and they're nice people.'

'I'm not altogether convinced – they seem disorganised.'

Boyd sat back in his seat and stirred his coffee thoughtfully. 'I can see why you'd think that, but I've been closely involved with both the budget and the production schedule and it comes across as a fairly tight operation to me.'

Saskia raised one perfectly arched eyebrow. '*Fairly* tight?'

'I know you prefer everything completely cut and dried, but we can afford to be relaxed about this and let them handle it their own way.'

Saskia leant forward across the table, knowing that the movement would make her breasts push against her silk top.

'You're busy developing the new software,' she said huskily. 'You don't really have time to oversee the promotional videos as well. Why don't I take over the project?'

Boyd grinned at her. 'Because I'm enjoying it – it's a new area for me and I'm finding it fascinating.'

Keeping her smile in position required some effort, but she managed it. 'Where do you know Jonquil from?' she asked, making it sound like a casual enquiry.

'She was at university when I was doing some part-time teaching.' There was nothing in his expression which gave anything away.

'That must be a while ago.'

'Seven years.' Was it her imagination or had he, just for a split second, looked angry?

'An old friend, then?'

'Not really, we lost touch and it was a surprise to both of us when we met again, a short while ago.'

'Were you close?' She asked the question lightly but, veiled by her thick, dark lashes, her eyes were fixed attentively on his face.

63

'I thought we were but it appeared I was wrong. More coffee?'

She shook her head and considered continuing digging, but he'd swivelled in his chair and was indicating to the waiter that he wanted the bill. Better leave it for now and wait for the next opportunity.

When he dropped her at her house, she didn't ask him in. Tonight she wanted something she didn't think was on Boyd's current agenda. She leant back inside the car to say, 'I'll let you have those projections on Monday.'

'Okay, have a good weekend.'

She let herself into the house and punched in the code of her alarm system before kicking off her shoes and padding along the thick oyster-coloured hall carpet to the kitchen.

The house was three storeys high and narrow, but it was well located and beautifully decorated and furnished. The kitchen was streamlined and functional in almond-green and white, the tiles cold beneath her stockinged feet.

She stroked Veda, her silver-grey Persian cat, which purred and wound herself around her ankles as she straightened up and went to pour herself a cognac. She took the drink upstairs, followed by the cat which leapt onto the bed and curled up. From the drawer of her bedside table she produced a card and sank onto the bed before dialling the number on it.

'Is Terry free tonight?' she asked when a male voice answered.

There was a pause before he said, 'Yeah. Where do you want him to go?'

She gave him the address then took off her trouser-suit and silk top and hung them up, before slipping on a peach satin kimono over her white lace bra and panties. A matching suspender belt held up her pale stockings.

When the doorbell rang fifteen minutes later she went down to let him in and then led the way back up to her bedroom, feeling his appreciative gaze on her swaying backside as she did so.

He was a good-looking, fleshy-featured man in his late twenties with impressively broad shoulders and curly blond hair slicked back with gel.

When he spoke it was with an Essex accent. 'How do you want it to go tonight?'

'First I want you to get undressed while I finish my drink,' she purred. She sank languidly onto the bed and made herself comfortable.

He grinned at her and, with his eyes holding hers, tugged at the knot of his tie. As he shed his clothes, taking his time about it to reveal a muscular, well-exercised body, she smiled to herself.

The discreet escort agency wasn't cheap, but it was worth every penny and it ensured that she got *exactly* what she wanted without any complications.

Once he was naked, his enormous member already erect, she slid from the bed and picked up two leather belts.

'Lie down,' she ordered him.

Obediently he stretched out on the bed and allowed her to lash his wrists to the bed head. She rested one hand on his phallus in a casual caress and then, without warning, flicked him across the chest with the other belt. He didn't flinch and, if anything, his shaft grew even harder.

That was what she liked about Terry; she could do anything she wanted with him and he got off on it all. She let her kimono slither to the carpet and proceeded to alternately slap him with the belt and stroke and kiss his supine body.

After a final stinging blow across the thighs, she removed her bra and panties and climbed astride him. He couldn't take his eyes off her honey-skinned breasts as she mounted him.

'Bend your knees,' she commanded, then leant back against them as she arched her back and began slowly and voluptuously to ride him.

Being in control – that was what it was all about.

Chapter Six

Jonquil was so absorbed in her work that, when the phone in her office rang, she jumped and knocked her cup of coffee over. She looked wildly around as it spread rapidly across her desk and just managed to snatch her handwritten notes out of the way before they were soaked.

Grabbing the box of tissues from the windowsill, she dumped half the contents onto the puddle and picked up the phone.

'Hello.'

'Jonquil, it's Boyd.' At the sound of his deep voice, her stomach lurched and she was aware of a wicked little lick of lust high up in her sex as he continued, 'Are you OK? You sound upset.'

'I'm fine – I just knocked my coffee over, that's all.'

'You didn't used to be so clumsy,' he remarked. 'Have you been drinking? It's a bit early in the day, isn't it, even for you?'

At the teasing note in his voice, she found herself laughing reluctantly, half-amused and half-exasperated, particularly since it was only nine-thirty in the morning.

'My liquid intake so far has been limited to one and a half cups of coffee,' she retorted. 'What can I do for you?'

'I wondered how the scripts were going.'

'Fine, so far. You'll be getting a copy of the latest drafts tomorrow, so you can take a look at them before the meeting on Friday.'

'I think that would be a good day to show you round the warehouse we've bought – it's currently being converted into an automated distribution facility. Filming will have to wait until it's up and running, but it might be interesting for you to see it at this stage.'

'Fine,' she said. 'What time?'

'I'll get my driver to pick you up from home first at around ten, then he can collect Hal and Natalie from Soho.'

'You don't need to do that; I can get the tube,' she protested.

'And have you turn up looking like you've been through a car wash without a car? I'm surprised you didn't come down with flu, after getting so wet yesterday.'

'I was OK once I'd had a hot bath.' She paused before adding, 'Thanks for getting your driver to take me home, by the way.'

'I like to keep my staff busy,' he told her blandly. 'See you on Friday.'

Although it was almost the end of October, Friday was one of those freak days when the sun shone brightly down and the temperature soared, so that it felt more like early September.

Nevertheless, aware of the fact that it could change very swiftly, Jonquil dressed in a black cashmere sweater, a black and white houndstooth check jacket and a black skirt.

It was only when they arrived at the warehouse that she realised that her clothing was totally inappropriate. The massive, echoing interior was in the process of being ripped out and piles of timber and rubble lay everywhere. When the car dropped them, they went in to be confronted by what was little better than a building site.

Boyd was talking to a couple of men and studying some plans laid out on a stack of planks. He was wearing a hard hat, battered leather jacket and jeans which rode low on his lean hips, his feet encased in stout boots.

He came forward to greet them, followed by one of the other men carrying three hard hats which he handed to them. Boyd regarded Jonquil's clothing doubtfully.

'I should have warned you to wear something that didn't matter. You're going to get dirty.' Hal and Natalie were both as casually dressed as usual and looked completely at home in their surroundings.

'I'll be OK,' said Jonquil, cursing the fact that whenever she was seeing Boyd, she found herself making a huge effort with her appearance, but this time she'd badly miscalculated.

He began to show them round and it was all so interesting that she forgot to watch her step and scuffed the toes of her high-heeled black suede shoes when she walked into a pile of masonry.

Swearing under her breath and envying the others their more practical footwear, she found herself at the bottom of a ladder leading up to the next level. Hal and Natalie had already climbed it and Boyd was waiting for her, holding it steady.

'Maybe you ought to wait down here,' he said. 'You're not dressed for scaling ladders.'

'I'll be fine,' she said immediately, determined not to be a liability.

She slung her neat black shoulder bag bandolier-style across her chest and put her foot on the first rung. It was only when she'd ascended halfway that she realised Boyd would be able to see right up her skirt and that in all probability her stocking-tops and suspenders would be on display, not to mention her lacy black briefs. Blushing in embarrassment, she glanced down, but he was staring straight ahead of him, holding firmly onto the sides of the ladder.

Unfortunately the disturbing thought made her lose her concentration and one shoe with its smooth leather sole slipped off the rung of the ladder, twisting her ankle painfully. She lost her footing, then gasped as she found herself scrabbling frantically for the rung, hanging desperately on with her hands and feeling like her arms were about to be torn from their sockets.

She heard Boyd yell, 'Hold on, I'm coming! Hal – steady the ladder from up there!'

A few seconds later, he was directly below her and one strong arm grasped her firmly by the waist and supported her until she'd managed to get her feet back on a rung.

'I'm OK now,' she said shakily. 'You can let go.'

'Not until you're safely back on the ground,' he growled. 'Just take it slowly and come down a step at a time. I'm right behind you.'

Feeling a complete fool and very aware of the pressure of his arm around her, Jonquil made her way back down, trying

69

not to wince every time she put any weight on her damaged ankle.

'You'd better sit down,' said Boyd, not relinquishing his hold on her. She caught her breath as a sickening pain shot through her ankle and it turned again, making her lose her balance.

He swung her off her feet and carried her over to a stack of bricks, saying urgently, 'What's the matter? Have you hurt yourself?'

'I . . . I've twisted my ankle.'

'Let's have a look.' He eased her shoe off and felt at her ankle with gentle fingers. 'Can you wiggle your toes?' She could, but it hurt. 'Better get you back to the offices; we've a nurse there who can strap it up for you.'

Natalie joined them and then Hal. 'Are you OK, Jonquil?' Natalie wanted to know.

'I'm fine.'

Taking a mobile phone out of his pocket, Boyd asked his driver to bring the car round. Before she could protest, he scooped Jonquil up in his arms again.

Feeling ridiculous, Jonquil tried to wriggle to the ground. 'I can walk,' she protested, but he merely tightened his grip as he strode towards the door, followed by the other two.

Jasper wasn't having a good day.

A letter had just arrived reminding him that he was behind with the payments on his BMW and threatening repossession if he didn't bring them up to date. Gloomily, he lit another cigarette and asked himself why he was having such a hard time of it at the moment. Without a car, there was no way he could do his job; he could hardly turn up for meetings on the bus.

He knew Duncan wasn't in today so there was no need to rush to get to work on time. Instead, he made some more coffee and contemplated his options.

He wondered whether Jonquil would be good for another loan, but she'd been pretty sticky about the last one. In retrospect, he wished he hadn't told her it was to pay off a gambling debt, but he'd been desperate. She'd be on his case now if he tried to borrow any more and probably even if he didn't.

He put in a brief appearance at work and then made his way to a drinking club he frequented and ordered a whisky. He was soon joined by a couple of acquaintances.

'How's it going?' asked Gerrard, a portly man in his fifties who still bore the scars of teenage acne. He signalled to the barman to pour Jasper a refill.

'Could be better,' said Jasper, offering them both a cigarette. 'The job's going nowhere and I've had a run of bad luck on both the horses and at the casino.'

'I had a rough time earlier this year,' Colin told him sympathetically. 'The wife was on my back, the Inland Revenue were after me for some taxes they said I hadn't paid and I bought a quarter share in a greyhound that was so slow *I* could outdistance it. Do you know what I did?'

'What?' asked Jasper.

'Changed my game. Tried my hand at poker and won every time.'

'Poker,' said Jasper thoughtfully. 'It's years since I played that.'

'Fancy a game? We're meeting a few other blokes later for a session.'

'I might just do that.'

After all, what did he have to lose except more money?

'For heaven's sake, Boyd, I can walk,' Jonquil protested, but he ignored her and scooped her off the back seat of his car and into his arms.

'Not up two flights of stairs, you can't. Have you got your keys to hand?' he asked.

She rummaged in her bag, feeling thoroughly flustered. What a disaster of a day. Not only was her ankle throbbing like mad, despite the painkillers the nurse had given her, but she'd had to suffer the indignity of being carried around the Docklands building as if she were a small child.

It hadn't helped that being held so closely against Boyd's hard chest had started her having thoughts she was better off not having and she'd had to fight a tantalising desire to

71

put her arms around his neck, pull his head down and kiss him.

He strode up the two steep flights of stairs as if she weighed no more than a couple of bags of shopping, then in through her front door once she'd unlocked it.

He deposited her on the sofa saying, 'Which is the bedroom?'

To her mortification, she felt herself blushing. 'Why do you want to know?'

'Because this is the perfect opportunity to drag you in there, throw you down on the bed and have my way with you while you're too weak to resist and can't run away,' he retorted, straight-faced.

She gazed at him mutely, trying to ignore the wayward flare of heat in her groin his words had provoked. Just the thought of him having his way with her made her feel aroused, despite the pain she was in.

'I want some pillows to put behind you,' he told her impatiently. 'I don't want to go before I've made sure you're comfortable. Is Eam . . . Damon coming round this evening?'

'Yes.'

'Will he make you something to eat?'

'I should imagine so.'

'OK, then, I'll get those pillows.'

She watched him walk into the bedroom wishing that internally she wasn't squirming with excitement. The trouble was, the longer she spent with Boyd, the more difficult it was getting not to throw self-respect to the winds, drag him onto the nearest horizonal surface and *insist* he screw her, so it was with a feeling of great relief she eventually heard the front door close behind him.

How could she have been so foolish as to try and climb a ladder in high-heeled shoes? She could at least have taken them off. Now she was immobile and in pain, not to mention having spent a good deal more time alone in Boyd's company than she'd have chosen to.

Jasper walked into the first pub he came to and ordered a double whisky. What a fool he'd been, continuing to play poker when it had been obvious he was on a losing steak. But he'd been convinced that his luck would change with just one more turn of a card.

Now he was down another three hundred pounds with no apparent way of paying off any of his debts. He downed his whisky and looked at his watch. A desire to forget his troubles, at least for a short time, made him finish the drink and retrace his steps to retrieve his car. As he headed for Streatham, he hoped fervently that Nadine was in.

She opened the door in a fluffy white towelling robe and no make-up, which made her look about sixteen. She appeared surprised, and not altogether pleased to see him.

'What are you doing here?' she demanded.

'Aren't you going to ask me in?'

Reluctantly, she moved to one side. As soon as she'd closed the door behind them, he drew her into his arms and breathed in her fragrance, his hands moving across her back over the soft towelling.

'I was thinking about you and wanted to see you,' he murmured.

'I'm not wild about people dropping round unannounced. Call first in future, please,' she said, but she made no objection when he parted the front of her robe to reveal her voluptuous figure.

He caressed her avidly, savouring the texture of her smooth-skinned breasts with their crinkled velvety areolae. He weighed them in his hands, enjoying their fullness and the way her deep pink nipples hardened under his touch.

Swiftly aroused, she sank to her knees and unzipped his trousers, drawing his already erect member from the confines of his briefs.

'You really *did* want to see me,' she murmured, pressing her lips to the glans and then teasingly circling it with her tongue. Slowly, she eased the end between her full lips and let it slide into the warm cavern of her mouth.

One thing she liked about Jasper was that he always smelt and tasted so good because he showered frequently, unlike some men she'd known. She took as much of his rod into her mouth as she could, then commenced a moist sucking, knowing that it would drive him wild.

He leant back against the wall and buried his hands in her silky dark hair, forgetting all his problems in the delicious heat of the moment. She sucked until his manhood had swollen to huge erectness and his groans of pleasure indicated that if she kept it up much longer, he'd come.

But that wasn't part of her plan just yet, and she let it slip from her mouth, then explored it with her tongue, strumming the ridge running down from the head, before licking her way to the base and kissing the heavy spheres of his testicles.

She rose to her feet and he swung her round so she was the one with her back against the wall. He covered her mound with his hand and massaged it, feeling the welcome stickiness against the palm of his hand. She opened her legs and he tickled the tiny triangle of her clit, aware of it twitching under his touch. She was already very wet but he pushed three fingers inside her and swivelled them around, feeling her internal muscles clutch at them as he explored her satiny inner chamber.

She moaned and bore down on them, prompting him to work them rhythmically in and out of her, his thumb rubbing her engorged nub. She felt the tingling heat building in her female core and her hips moved of their own volition as she rapidly scaled the heights of ecstasy.

'Oooooh!' she cried as she came in a rush of erotic sensation that left her weak and breathless.

Jasper scooped her up and strode into the bedroom, where he deposited her on the bed and then quickly shed his clothes. She got onto her hands and knees and pushed her curvaceous bottom tantalisingly towards him.

He knelt behind her, grasped her by the hips and plunged into her, then reached for her breasts while she ground her derrière against him, eager to have him as deeply inside as possible.

He shafted her with long, leisurely strokes, caressing her breasts and teasing her nipples into jewel-hard points. Absently, he admired the graceful contours of her back and hips, thinking she had a body designed for fucking. She turned her head to flash him a salacious smile.

'Quicker,' she gasped and he obligingly quickened his pace

until his thrusts were fast and furious and he lost sight of everything except the eruption building in his loins.

As if from a great distance, he could hear the sound of her generous buttocks slapping against his thighs; then his body tensed, he made several last jerky plunges and ejaculated into her with a force that felt like a volcano discharging molten lava.

'You idiot!' she said an hour later, sitting bolt-upright in bed and pulling the sheet up so her naked breasts were hidden from his appreciative gaze. 'I despair of you – when will you learn that gambling's a mug's game. Now what are you going to do?'

'I'm not sure,' he admitted. He sat up too and fumbled for his cigarettes.

'I heard Jake discussing you with the manager yesterday,' she told him. 'They're about to put the screws on. Jake asked me to have a quiet word with you and suggest that, for your own good, you settle your account as quickly as possible.'

'I can't settle it. Unless . . .' He wound a lock of glossy brown hair around his hand and kissed her softly on the lips.

'Unless what?' she prompted him.

'Unless you lend me the money.'

Nadine pulled away from him and got out of bed, belting the robe around her narrow waist before turning to face him. 'You've got a nerve. Why should I? I work hard for every penny I earn and I'm not about to hand it over to you so you can pay off your debts, or more likely blow the lot on a horse.'

She bent down, picked up his trousers and threw them on the bed. 'Get dressed. I'm going to take a shower and, when I've finished, I expect you to have gone.'

As Saskia drove along the Gloucestershire country lanes between hedgerows studded with scarlet berries, she tried to focus on how beautiful everything was.

It was another mild sunny day and the trees were looking gloriously autumnal as they turned from green to shades of gold, russet and vermilion. In the valley to her left, a faint mist

75

hung over the river which was swollen almost to overflowing from the recent rain.

She eased her foot off the accelerator and slowed to a crawl, trying to ignore the sinking feeling in her stomach which was increasing with every mile she got closer to her parents' house.

It was her father's birthday and she kept glancing at his present, bought after much deliberation and now carefully wrapped in bright green paper and tied with white ribbons.

Another car came into view in her mirror and, as the lane was too narrow for it to pass her, she reluctantly increased her speed.

All too soon, it was time to signal left and pull off the road onto the gravel driveway leading to her parents' Queen Anne house. It was a beautiful building constructed from weathered Cotswold stone, a mellow honey colour in the late afternoon sunlight, but the sight afforded her no pleasure.

A wine-coloured creeper swarmed over the upper left-hand corner, but it had been hacked back ruthlessly so it didn't encroach on any of the windows. Taking her time about switching off the ignition and unfastening her seat belt, Saskia thought, not for the first time, that it was so like Daddy to fight a constant battle to stop nature from getting out of hand.

She got slowly out of the car and smoothed the front of her elegant ash-grey dress. There was a single strand of perfectly graded pearls around her slender neck, her only other jewellery an antique silver bracelet and matching ring.

She took her bag from the passenger seat and then lifted out her father's present, staggering slightly under the weight. The front door opened and her mother stood on the threshold, beautifully dressed in an azure-blue silk dress, her permed hair sprayed into a rigid blonde helmet around her pinched face.

'Hello, Mummy,' Saskia called, shutting the car door with her backside.

'Hello, Saskia – you're late.'

'Surely by only five or ten minutes.'

'Your brother managed to get here on time.'

With a great deal of effort, Saskia kept a smile on her face. 'Well, I'm here now.'

'So I see. Why on earth are you wearing that ghastly colour?

It doesn't suit you, it makes you look washed out.'

Saskia ascended the shallow flight of steps and leant forward to kiss the air next to her mother's powdered cheek, then followed her into the immaculately clean and tidy house.

'Hi, Sask – you're getting fat,' her brother Basil greeted her from the comfort of a winged armchair drawn up in front of the small fire which flickered in the massive stone hearth.

'Hello, Basil – how are you?' As usual she found herself already itching to slap his smug, well-fed face.

'Blooming, sister dear, blooming and prosperous.'

Basil, a merchant banker, was a couple of years her junior, but good living had already taken its toll on his appearance and he looked ten years older. His face was mottled, jowly and sprinkled with broken veins, while his stomach strained at his brightly patterned waistcoat.

He was drinking a glass of sherry, the decanter on a small table just next to him. Their father, a much older and balder version of Basil, came into the room at that moment.

'Happy birthday, Daddy,' she said, and slid her carefully wrapped present towards him. He grunted and bent down to rip it open to reveal a new set of expensive golf clubs.

She'd gone to a lot of trouble to get something she thought he'd like and even consulted a golf professional, but she wondered why she'd bothered as he grumbled, 'I don't need a new set of golf clubs – I've already got some perfectly good ones. You might as well have these, Basil, since your sister seems to have money to throw away.'

'Cheers,' said Basil, prodding the end of one with the toe of a highly polished brogue.

'Basil got your father this,' her mother told her proudly, indicating a bad painting of a ship in an ugly frame, which Saskia happened to know he'd found in the attic of the house he and his wife were renting.

'What are you up to these days, Sask? Still got your little job in Docklands?' Basil asked. He made it sound as if she spent her day making coffee and answering the phone. Without waiting for a reply, he turned to his father. 'Guess who I saw yesterday? Old Roderick Hawkins. He asked after you.'

'You can come and give me a hand in the kitchen, Saskia,'

her mother told her. 'But go and wash your hands first while I find you an overall to put on over that dress. I expect it cost a pretty penny, even if it doesn't do anything for you.'

After enduring half an hour of her mother's fretful monologue in the kitchen, there was still the meal to be got through. She hated pheasant anyway, but Basil loved it – and what Basil loved, Basil got.

Saskia had never known why her parents had always doted on her brother while treating her with barely concealed dislike. Nothing she ever did met with their approval and even now, when her career was going so well, they spoke of her job slightingly.

'How's Caroline?' her mother asked when there was a pause in the conversation. Caroline was her brother's wife, but she rarely attended family gatherings.

Saskia didn't particularly like her sister-in-law, whom she considered empty-headed in the extreme, content to while away her days shopping and meeting friends for lunch, but she had a certain sympathy for her refusal to be made uncomfortable by her parents-in-law.

Although they'd never been downright hostile, for fear of being estranged from their beloved son, neither had they been welcoming. As it no doubt suited them to have Basil to themselves without the intrusive presence of his wife, a polite fiction was maintained that Caroline was too busy with charity work to see much of them.

Saskia was well aware that her sister-in-law's commitment to helping the needy was limited to attending charity balls and other functions where she could dress up and drink a lot of champagne.

Saskia glanced covertly at her watch. Only another hour or so, and then she could leave and be back home by nine-thirty, where she could fix herself a huge brandy and send for Terry to come and screw her until she didn't even remember she had a family, let alone one as unpleasant as hers.

The interminable meal dragged on while she concentrated on thinking about her beautiful, tranquil house. It was her bolt-hole, her refuge from the world, and she wanted nothing more than to be back there.

At long last she was able to take her leave, telling herself as she raced along the dark country lanes towards the motorway, that at least she could probably get away without seeing them again until Christmas.

Chapter Seven

'Fancy an evening at the theatre, darling?' asked Damon. They'd just been watching a film on TV and, at the unexpected question, she turned her head to stare at him in astonishment.

'You hate the theatre,' she said.

'I know I do, but Kevin's getting up a party and he asked if we wanted to go.'

Jonquil enjoyed seeing plays but had never been able to persuade Damon to go with her. The thought that Kevin was involved made her go off the idea a bit, but not enough to stop her asking, 'What's on?'

'*Cat on a Hot Tin Roof.*'

That clinched it; she loved Tennessee Williams. 'OK. When are we going?'

'Thursday.'

'Great, I'll look forward to it.' She didn't particularly want to spend any time in Kevin's company, but at least at the theatre the opportunities for conversation would be limited.

He cleared his throat. 'Kevin was wondering if Boyd might like to come with us.' She might have known there'd be catch. 'Well, do you think he would?' he continued after a pause.

'I haven't the slightest idea,' she returned.

'Will you ask him?'

'You ask him,' she suggested.

'Kevin thinks it would be better coming from you.'

'I'm sure he does, but I'd rather not. If the invitation's from Kevin, he should call Boyd himself.'

'He's tried to phone him, but he's just getting the run-around. He can't get past the lovely Saskia's assistant's assistant.' Damon cleared his throat again. 'You know, darling, you're really not being very helpful about this.'

'That's because I don't want any more involvement with Kevin's blatant little schemes,' she told him crossly, 'so I won't come.'

'You've got to come,' he said in dismay. 'I told Kevin you would.'

'Only if you drop the subject of Boyd and don't bring it up again between now and Thursday.'

He must have realised that she meant it because he subsided sulkily back against the cushions.

The sight of the thickset man in the dark suit sitting on the bonnet of his BMW did nothing to improve Jasper's mood, as he left work after a long day in which he'd failed to make a single sale.

'Can I help you?' he asked, the polite words tinged with sarcasm. 'Only that's my car and I was rather hoping to drive it away without the addition of a new mascot.'

Even as he spoke, he knew that the man was here to collect money. The only question was, for which particular debt?

'Correction, mate,' said the man, whose eyebrows met in the middle without a break. 'This car belongs to the leasing company, otherwise I'd have taken it off you by now and flogged it to set against the money you owe.'

Jasper took out his cigarettes and lit one. 'You'll have to give me more of a clue. I'm not sure exactly which of the lengthy line of my creditors you represent.'

He knew he was behaving recklessly in letting the man know that he had more than one debt and was therefore probably in serious financial straits.

'Like that is it? I'm Hogg; I work for one of the casino's business associates and he's sent me to make sure you pay up without any more messing us around. You can think yourself lucky that we aren't having this conversation in front of your boss and workmates.'

'OK,' said Jasper, wearied by the whole hopeless situation. 'I rent my apartment. I lease my car. I don't have a single asset to my name, unless you count a few decent clothes, and I owe money all over London. The bottom line is I can't pay you – either now or in the foreseeable future. If you want to try to kick the shit out of me, this is as good an opportunity as any.'

Hogg raised his single eyebrow, as though Jasper had committed some deplorable social solecism. 'If you want money badly enough, there's always some way to get it,' he told him. 'Find one.'

He rose from the car bonnet and took something out of his pocket which glinted in the light from a nearby street lamp. Jasper was horrified to see it was a Swiss army knife.

He took a step back, looking around to see if anyone was likely to come to his aid, but the car park was deserted. No coward, he nevertheless didn't fancy his chances against a man with the build of a pit bull armed with a lethal-looking knife.

He swallowed. 'Look,' he began, then broke off as with a businesslike gesture, Hogg plunged the knife into one of his front tyres.

'Find one,' he repeated pulling it out, then walked away, climbed into a grey Vauxhall Vectra and drove off.

Jasper slouched against his car for a minute until his legs stopped trembling, then resignedly took off his jacket and rolled up his sleeves in preparation for changing the wheel.

Boyd phoned Jonquil on Thursday in the early evening, getting her out of the bath. She stood dripping, wrapped in the hand towel she'd grabbed in mistake for a bath towel, as he asked about her ankle.

'It's much better, thanks,' she told him truthfully, glad he didn't know she was virtually naked. It felt disturbingly erotic to be talking to him with her bare breasts slick with soap suds. She was suddenly assailed by the unwelcome memory of how they used to take baths together and struggled to banish the arousing thought from her mind.

'I see I've got a theatre ticket, courtesy of your boyfriend's boss.'

'Really?' was all she could think of to say as she remembered how she used to sit between Boyd's strong thighs while he lazily lathered her back and then slid his hands in front of her to caress her soapy breasts.

'He doesn't give up, does he?' He sounded amused by the situation. Jonquil struggled to think of something to say, but there was an insidious smouldering in her female core and she felt hot and shivery at the same time. 'Are you going to be there?'

'Yes, I'm just getting ready now,' she replied.

'Is Damon picking you up?'

'No, he's going straight from work.'

'I'll give you a lift, then. Six forty-five all right?'

'No – don't do that, I've a mini cab booked,' she said hastily.

'Cancel it. I'll see you later.' He hung up without giving her the chance to protest further.

It was no good. Just talking to him on the phone had put her in a state of red-hot arousal. Getting back into the bath she lay back and closed her eyes while her hand glided over her soapy breasts, down her belly and between her thighs.

Jasper had bumped into an old acquaintance in a pub and managed to borrow fifty quid off him, which had cheered him up for a few minutes, but then he found himself wondering what good fifty quid was when he owed so much.

He was driving aimlessly around, feeling edgy and restless. He was reluctant to visit any of his usual haunts, in case he was waylaid by more of his creditors, but the idea of spending an evening alone in his apartment didn't appeal in the slightest.

He found himself driving past a private gambling club he occasionally frequented. He would have continued on his way, but there was a parking space right outside. What were the chances of that in the West End? He discovered that he'd pulled up, locked the car and strolled into the club without making any conscious decision to do so.

If it hadn't been for the gaming tables, the room could have been in a second-rate seaside hotel. There was a grubby patterned carpet which had once been gold and turquoise and which felt sticky underfoot, while tobacco-stained wallpaper depicting blowsy cabbage roses adorned the walls.

A plate rack ran around the room three feet below the ceiling, holding a selection of dusty Toby jugs, willow-patterned plates and dried flowers.

The dowdy decor in no way reflected the amounts of money which changed hands on a nightly basis and the dozen or so players, mostly male, were obviously indifferent to their surroundings and were all concentrating on their chosen games.

Jasper bought fifty pounds' worth of chips then took a seat by the roulette table, watching for a while to see if there was any sort of pattern.

One man, an Arab, seemed to be on a winning streak. Every bet he made paid off and when he placed a huge stack of chips on thirty, Jasper followed suit. After all, it was his thirtieth birthday coming up soon.

He held his breath as the little silver ball bounced slowly to a halt, paused over the adjoining number, then rolled into thirty.

Trying not to betray his elation, he gathered up the huge stack of chips the croupier pushed over and then hesitated. Should he stay and simply bet what the Arab backed, see if he could win more, or should he collect his winnings and get out now before he lost the lot and probably more besides?

The decision was made for him. The other man rose to his feet and left the table, cashed in his chips and departed. As he strode out to his car a few minutes later, Jasper was almost delirious with relief.

Over five thousand pounds. It wouldn't pay off all his debts, but it would go a long way towards placating his creditors until he could get his hands on the rest of the money.

'Congratulations – it must be your lucky night.'

The husky female voice from just behind him made him pause in the act of opening his car door. He turned and saw a skinny blonde woman he'd vaguely noticed in the club. He'd been too preoccupied to pay her any attention, but now he eyed her speculatively. Presumably she made a habit of hanging around the club, ready to latch onto winners, and was after sharing his winnings.

She looked to be in her late thirties and was attractive enough in a blowsy, over made-up way. Getting lucky had made him feel randy as hell and Nadine was working.

He flashed her his charming smile and asked, 'Were you playing tonight?'

She smiled back and tossed her blonde hair provocatively away from her face. 'Can't afford to, love. I'm a single mum with no one putting food on the table but me. Talking of which, why don't you take me for something to eat and I'll help you celebrate?' She jiggled her hips suggestively, lest he be in any doubt as to what was on offer.

He was on for that – but only that. He didn't feel like watching her eat her way through an expensive three-course meal as foreplay. Glancing around, he saw a narrow alley running down the side of the club and nodded towards it.

'If you want to help me celebrate, let's go down there.'

She looked affronted. 'I'm not a pro, you know.'

He took the wad of cash out of his pocket, peeled off a hundred pounds and proffered it to her. She bit her lip and hesitated. He was well aware that she'd much prefer that they go on somewhere together as if they were on a date, before ending up in bed after which she'd expect him to leave a discreet present.

But bugger that – she was a tart and if she didn't care for being treated like one, she could throw his money back in his face. Except she wouldn't.

After a few moments, he made to put the notes back in his pocket, but she stepped forward and twitched it out of his hand. He took her arm and steered her towards the alleyway, while she muttered, 'I don't make a habit of this, you know.'

Once out of sight of anyone passing, he stopped next to some dustbins and turned to face her, reaching for her breasts. They were small but very firm with large, prominent nipples. Once he'd freed them from the confines of her scarlet polyester top, he kneaded them roughly, teasing the jutting points into hard thimbles. He flattened them against her ribcage, while she unzipped his trousers in a businesslike way, obviously keen to get to the matter in hand.

That suited Jasper. He bundled her skirts around her waist and yanked at her slippery satin panties, glad to see she was wearing stockings. He clasped her pert buttocks in his hands and squeezed them as if testing them for ripeness.

She started to jerk at his burgeoning shaft as if trying to pump water from a well. He winced and closed one hand over hers murmuring, 'Hey – don't damage it, it's the only one I've got.'

She moderated her movements while he amused himself by

exploring her body, delving casually between her thighs and fingering the sticky folds he found there. He was hampered because she didn't open her legs widely enough to give him as much access as he wanted, so he slapped her lightly on one bare buttock, making her flinch and jerk her hips towards him as he growled, 'Open wide.'

A torn sheet of newspaper blew past them, wrapping itself briefly around Jasper's ankle. He kicked it free, getting off on the squalor of the dirty alley and the fact he was buying her services.

He thrust a couple of fingers deep inside her, inhaling her musky perfume and massaging her bottom with his other hand. He smacked her across the crown of her rump, enjoying the way it made her buttocks bounce and how the sound echoed around the alley.

He realised that she'd managed to work him fairly close to climaxing and, not wanting to settle for a hand job, he grasped her by her thin waist and sat her on a dustbin. It was the work of a moment to yank her panties all the way off and thrust her thighs wide apart.

He drove into her with such force, she would have shot off the other side of the dustbin if he hadn't grabbed her hips. He nuzzled her bare breasts, her skin cool in the chilly wind, her nipples hard and puckered.

Usually an unselfish lover, Jasper used her shamelessly for his own satisfaction and made no attempt to bring her to an orgasm – after all, he was paying for it.

He pistoned relentlessly in and out of her until he felt his climax building past the point of no return, then speeded up for the last half-dozen shallow strokes and came with the force of a dam breaching its banks.

He pulled out of her immediately and zipped himself up.

'See you,' he called over his shoulder as he strode away, leaving her sitting on the dustbin with her thighs wide apart and their mingled juices trickling slowly out of her.

When Jonquil spotted Boyd's limousine gliding to a halt outside the house, she pulled on her camel wool coat and hurried downstairs as fast as her injured ankle would allow her to and opened the door just as he reached it.

She swallowed at the sight of his familiar dark good looks, already ashamed of the fact that she'd masturbated herself to two climaxes while thinking about him.

'You shouldn't have come downstairs on your own,' he admonished her. 'I'd have helped you. Here – lean on me.' Without giving her the chance to protest, he slid his arm round her waist and pulled her close, supporting her as they made their way to the car.

His close proximity seriously tried her self-control. She wanted to push him away, but at the same time to mould her body to his, and then was exasperated with herself for feeling that way.

Once he'd helped her into the car, he opened a panel in front of them to reveal a small bar. 'I wouldn't want you go thirsty,' he teased her. 'After all, I imagine half an hour's a long time for you to go without a drink.'

'Don't you think you're overdoing that particular joke?' she asked, as he deftly uncorked half a bottle of champagne.

'What joke?' His voice was innocent, but she could hear the laughter in it. 'You mean you don't want a glass of champagne?'

'I'd love a glass of champagne.' Anything to help her get through the evening, which was obviously going to be more of an ordeal than she'd anticipated.

By the time they reached the theatre, she felt light-headed from a combination of the champagne and the sheer physical pull Boyd seemed to exert over her so effortlessly. She was unable to prevent him from helping her out of the car and inside, so that to the casual observer she was sure it must appear that they were lovers entwined in a fond embrace. But no such thought must have entered Damon's head, because his face broke into a broad grin as he stepped forward to greet them.

'Is this just coincidence, or did you come together?' he asked, pumping Boyd's free hand.

'I offered Jonquil a lift,' he said, as Kevin came up.

'Glad you could make it,' he boomed, taking Boyd's arm and trying to draw him away from Jonquil. But the arm around her waist tightened and, as Damon had just taken her free hand, the four of them must have looked as though they were taking part in some strange dance.

The bell went at that moment and Boyd moved towards the steps leading to the circle, taking Jonquil with him. The crush of other people meant that both Kevin and Damon had no choice but to relinquish their respective holds and follow the other two up the stairs.

When they reached their seats Boyd smilingly ushered Kevin and Damon into the row before they could protest, still keeping Jonquil held firmly at his side, then helped her into the seat next to his.

She could tell that Kevin, now on her other side, was fuming and she had to exert serious self-control not to laugh. The lights went down and she prepared to lose herself in Brick and Maggie's tormented relationship for the next few hours.

But she hadn't reckoned on the fact that the seats were very narrow and Boyd was so broad-shouldered that it was impossible not to make contact with him, even though she tried to take up as little room as possible.

As a consolation prize for not sitting next to Boyd, Kevin pressed his thigh against hers, just as he'd done the night at *La Maison*. By now she disliked him so much that she couldn't bear to have him touch her and, in a reflex reaction, moved her legs to the right, where they made immediate electrifying contact with Boyd's.

She heard him chuckle under his breath and, unable to stop herself, pinched him on the arm.

'What was that for?' he whispered.

'You know,' she hissed back.

'Shhh!' said someone directly behind them.

Jonquil had always found the play sexy, but tonight's production brought out every last iota of its repressed sexuality. As Maggie and Brick smouldered their way through the first scene set against a backdrop of a hot Mississippi night, Jonquil found herself becoming more and more aroused until she broke out in a fine film of perspiration.

When the lights went up at the interval Kevin immediately leaned across her, saying, 'Boyd, I wonder if we could talk about—'

'Sure. Let's head for the bar.' He rose to his feet without

waiting for a reply and pulled Jonquil to hers.

'I don't want a drink, so I'll just stay here,' she said, smiling sweetly up at him. It would serve him right to have to endure Kevin's unsubtle pitch throughout the interval, without her to hide behind.

His eyes glinted dangerously. 'Is your ankle paining you?' he asked. 'How thoughtless of me. But don't worry, you don't have to do without a drink – I'll carry you there.' The thought of being borne through the crowds in Boyd's arms made her want to faint with embarrassment.

'No!' It came out as a shriek as he bent to pick her up. Lowering her voice, she continued as calmly as she could, 'My ankle isn't hurting at all and I can manage perfectly well, thanks.'

'Isn't she brave?' he smirked to the other two. 'Come along, then.' He clamped his arm around her waist and led her towards the bar, with an exaggerated solicitousness which made her long to slap him.

She wondered what Damon was making of Boyd's proprietorial behaviour towards her but, when she glanced over her shoulder, he was deep in a whispered conversation with Kevin.

'What's everybody drinking?' Boyd asked as soon as he'd helped her into a chair in the crowded bar.

'I'll go,' Damon instantly offered, primed no doubt by his boss.

'I wouldn't hear of it,' drawled Boyd. 'Jonquil?'

'A vodka and tonic, please.'

'A double vodka and tonic for Jonquil. Kevin?'

'A single will be fine,' she snapped.

'Whisky, please,' said Kevin. 'And I'll have a double.'

'Damon?'

'I'll have a double whisky too.'

Boyd vanished into the throng, leaving Jonquil thinking that at that moment she didn't know which of the trio she disliked most. Boyd, for shamelessly manipulating the situation for his own amusement; Kevin, for being so rude and self-seeking; or Damon for getting her into this in the first place and now meekly doing everything his employer told him to.

She was still fuming when Boyd came back with their drinks.

90

She gulped hers down recklessly while Kevin began to tell him exactly what his company could do for him.

But he'd barely got into his stride when the bell went and Boyd immediately rose to his feet, saying to Jonquil, 'Drink up, we'd better get you back to your seat.'

'Damon can help her,' said Kevin. Damon leapt to his feet at once.

'Yes, come on, darling – lean on me.'

She wondered if it would have crossed his mind to offer of his own accord, if Kevin hadn't prompted him. She knocked back the rest of her drink and stood up, then staggered slightly and wished she'd left some of it.

Boyd steadied her, blocking Damon's way as if by accident, then said casually over his shoulder, 'We're fine, thanks.' Damon looked so chagrined and Kevin so thunderous that Jonquil had to choke back a giggle.

When they arrived back at their seats, Kevin gestured impatiently at her to precede him into the row. She deliberately ignored him, forcing him to say, 'I'm sure Jonquil wants to sit next to Damon, and who are we to separate two love-birds?' making her cringe with embarrassment. She glanced at Boyd, saw the satirical gleam in his eye, and had to suppress another giggle.

'I need her next to me to explain the plot whenever I lose the thread,' he explained with a straight face.

The rest of the play passed in a blur, overshadowed by the one she felt she was taking part in, which seemed even more complicated. Drinking vodka on top of a couple of glasses of champagne hadn't helped and she felt light-headed and giddy when they stood up to leave at the end.

'I hope you'll let me buy you supper,' Boyd said affably to Kevin.

'We'd be delighted,' replied Kevin, baring his yellowing teeth in a relieved smile that Boyd wasn't about to vanish into the night without another chance of hooking him in.

'I've booked a table at the Terrazza. Is that okay, or would you prefer somewhere else?'

'The Terrazza's fine,' said Kevin, rubbing his hands together at the prospect.

A car was waiting just outside and Boyd opened the door and, somewhat to Jonquil's surprise, ushered Kevin and Damon in before her. He bent down and said to Kevin, 'Everything's taken care of. My driver will take you both to the restaurant, then home afterwards and the bill will be put on my account. Thanks for the performance, I really enjoyed it.'

Jonquil wondered which performance he was referring to as Kevin spluttered, 'Aren't you coming with us?'

'No, I can see you and Damon are dying to talk business and it just bores me, so I'll take Jonquil home.' He slammed the door and the car pulled away.

'Here's our ride,' announced Boyd as another car glided to a halt next to them.

'That was absolutely *shameless*,' she rebuked him as soon as they were settled into the comfortable seats.

'It was, wasn't it?' he agreed unabashed, then they both burst out laughing. 'I only hope that he'll take the none-too-subtle hint and stop bothering me. I already have an excellent distribution deal.' There was a silence; then he turned towards her in the darkness. 'What are you doing with someone like Damon? He's a professional 'yes' man who'll obviously do anything to further his career, including using his loyal girlfriend as bait.'

'Damon has lots of good qualities,' she defended him.

'He was so preoccupied with helping the obnoxious Kevin with his scheme that he didn't seem to notice that I had my arm around you as if *we* were the couple. If you and I were together I'd make damned sure that no other man got so close to you.'

'He knew you were only doing it to help me keep the weight off my ankle,' she flashed.

In the dim light in the interior of the car she could see that his face was an enigmatic mask, but his eyes were glinting again as he said, 'Was I?'

His mouth came down on hers, catching her completely off guard. Confused and aroused, she responded instinctively, every cell in her body craving his kiss and his touch.

They sank back onto the seat, his hand smoothing over her glossy hair, while she slid her arms around his neck and parted her lips against the onslaught of his probing tongue.

She found herself pressing her breasts avidly against his hard chest, her breathing becoming ragged as he explored the warm velvet of her mouth.

He stroked the curve of her hip, then her thigh, tracing the smooth contours over her skirt while she lost track of time as the car glided silently through the dark autumn night.

She was on fire for him, so aching with lust that she moaned softly and he pulled her closer, his lips drifting over her neck, then downwards to the soft hollow at the base of her throat.

One hand slipped under her skirt, warm and arousing, as he stroked her stocking-clad thighs, sending wanton shivers of desire through her. She could feel her hidden core moistening and the delicate folds of her most intimate parts becoming swollen as he caressed the soft skin above her stocking-tops.

Unconsciously, her thighs parted so he could touch her even more intimately over the thin silk of her panties. A spasm of sheer erotic pleasure lanced through her body and she moaned again, a slave to the sexual heat that threatened to consume her.

She wanted him. She wanted him so badly that nothing else mattered. She fumbled with his zip and drew out his member, tingling waves of lust lancing through her as she saw that it was, if anything, even bigger than she remembered. Even bigger and very, very hard.

It was no good – she had to have it inside her right away. Swiftly, she dragged her panties off, hitched up her dress and climbed astride him, poised to lower herself onto the enormous shaft, already delirious with the prospect of being so satisfyingly skewered.

With a sudden deafening screech of brakes, the car skidded to a halt and the air was rent by a cacophony of blaring horns. She would have been thrown to the floor if Boyd hadn't shot out an arm and steadied them both, holding her close with the other.

'*What the—!*' he exclaimed and lifted her to one side of him before pressing the button that made the glass which separated them from the driver move smoothly downwards.

'Sorry, sir.' The chauffeur sounded shaken. 'Some idiot just shot across a red light without stopping.'

'OK, carry on, but take it easy.' The glass slid silently upwards again.

'Where were we?' Boyd muttered with a crooked smile, reaching for her. But the shock had brought Jonquil to her senses and she realised with a flush of shame that if they hadn't just had to do an emergency stop, by now she'd be rising and falling on his phallus, riding him hard towards their mutual satisfaction.

She moved away from him saying shakily, 'No, Boyd.'

'Why not? You want me as much as I want you.' He tried to draw her into his arms but she held him away.

'That has nothing to do with it,' she said shakily. 'I'm in a relationship with Damon and I want you to respect that.'

'You don't belong with him – you belong with me,' he replied, with a raw edge to his voice.

She moved along the seat to put as much distance as she could between them, afraid that if he touched her again she'd be unable to control herself. Anger at her own humiliatingly brazen actions made her speak more vehemently than she intended.

'That's what I thought, seven years ago, but I was as wrong then as you are now,' she blazed. 'Can't you get it into your head that I'm in love with Damon and nothing you can do or say will ever change that? Anything between you and me is in the past and that's the way it's going to stay. The only relationship I want with you is a professional one, so don't *ever* touch me again.'

The car turned into her road and she fumbled with the door handle, throwing the door open and scrambling out before it had come to a complete stop.

Chapter Eight

Jasper had just got in from work, after another unsuccessful day. He threw himself onto the sofa and dialled his sister's number, before tucking the phone under his chin and rifling through the mail he'd just picked up from the mat. He dropped it onto the coffee table, grimacing at the fact that there was nothing but brown envelopes.

'Hi, Jonquil, it's your favourite brother.'

'George – how are you?'

'Very funny. I'll be in your neck of the woods in an hour or so – can I just call round for a few minutes?'

'Sure. I'm working but I'll be glad of the excuse to take a break.'

'Does that mean Damon's not there?'

'No, he isn't here.' Jasper wondered vaguely why she suddenly sounded annoyed.

'OK, see you soon.'

Fervently hoping that her brother wasn't coming round to borrow more money, Jonquil got back to work.

'Well . . . thank you,' she said when he handed her the cheque, trying to conceal her surprise. 'But you were broke a couple of weeks ago – where did you get the money?'

'That, my dear sister, is none of your business.'

She looked perturbed. 'It's just that . . . Jasper – did you win this money on a horse?'

He flicked his floppy fair hair back from his face and looked down his aquiline nose at her, a quizzical expression on his face. 'That's rich. I come round to repay a debt and all you can do is give me the third degree about where I got it from.'

'Please look me in the eye and tell me you didn't win this money on a horse.'

'Didn't I promise not to bet on the gee-gees any more?' he said lazily.

'You did, and now I want you to tell me that you kept that promise.'

'I wish I'd put you a cheque in the post – I wasn't expecting an interrogation.'

Jonquil regarded the cheque in her hand suspiciously. 'You must have won it. You don't suddenly find this sort of money under your pillow.'

Jasper got up saying, 'Time for me to go and no, I didn't win it on a horse, but that's all I'm going to tell you.' He kissed her on the cheek adding, 'Lighten up – everything's fine.'

'Have you had your invitation to the Halloween Ball?' Natalie asked, having phoned Jonquil to see how the scripts were going.

'What Halloween Ball?'

'Boyd's company's. We've all been invited – it'll be a laugh.'

Casting desperately around for an excuse, Jonquil was unable to think of one. In retrospect she was really embarrassed about the scene in the car with Boyd and the last thing she wanted to do was attend some ball he was giving. Unable to think of anything that wasn't an out-and-out lie, she decided to fall back on part of the truth.

'I don't want to take Damon,' she admitted. 'You remember his boss, Kevin, who was at my party? He invited Boyd, Damon and me to the theatre so he could make another attempt at getting some of Boyd's business. The two of them spent all evening trying to sell him on the idea, but he knew exactly what they were doing and was obviously really amused.'

'You don't have to take Damon – why don't you come with us? My current squeeze would love to have a woman on either arm. He'd imagine that all the other men there would think he was knocking us both off and they'd be viridian with envy.'

'I . . . I wouldn't feel comfortable going without a partner.'

That wasn't actually true, but she had to convince Natalie that she had a valid reason for not attending.

'It might look anti-social if you don't go. We like to present a united front when we're working on a project and you're a key member of the team at the moment. Why don't you bring your handsome brother?'

The message was unmistakable – she was going, whether she liked it or not.

'OK, I'll ask Jasper,' she said reluctantly.

Boyd glanced at the clock on the wall, then at Saskia who was sitting next to him on the sofa in his office, studying a spreadsheet.

'It's almost seven,' he said. 'Do you want to knock off?'

She looked up and smiled. 'I'm getting hungry,' she admitted, 'but we could really do with finishing this tonight and it'll take at least another couple of hours.'

'Shall we go and get something to eat, then on to my place to wind it up?' he suggested. She sat back in her chair and thought about it, crossing her long stocking-clad legs. 'What I really feel like is eating slices of pizza with my fingers, sitting on the floor,' she told him.

He grinned at her. 'We could go to Mario's. I don't suppose they'll mind if we leave a big enough tip.'

She tapped him playfully on the arm. 'The other diners might think it's a bit odd. I've got a great pizza delivery service just down the road. How about coming back with me and I'll order a couple?'

'Sounds good.' He stood up and stretched, then went to look out of the window where the lights of the buildings sparkled on the inky waters a long way below. There was a rigidity to his stance that reminded her he'd seemed preoccupied recently.

'Are you OK?' she asked.

'I'm fine, thanks. Let's go.'

Once they'd arrived at her house, she showed him into the airy sitting room with its pale aqua-tinted walls and oyster-coloured carpet, opened a bottle of chilled Orvieto and then phoned for their takeaway.

'Excuse me a minute,' she murmured and headed upstairs. Once in her bedroom, she divested herself of the jacket of her elegant cyclamen-pink suit, spritzed herself with perfume and

97

pulled out the pins so her blonde hair fell loose around her shoulders.

She was wearing an ivory silk blouse through which the luscious contours of her breasts in her lace bra were clearly visible. She considered herself appraisingly in the mirror – should she change into something more provocative? No, it wouldn't do to be too obvious, even though she'd decided tonight was going to be the night.

'Have I ever told you that you're gorgeous?' said Boyd lazily when she reappeared in the sitting room.

'No, but you can if you want to.' She flashed him a seductive smile, sat on the floor next to his chair and picked up the paperwork on one of the deals they were considering. They discussed it until the cartwheel-sized pizza arrived. He joined her on the floor and they ate straight from the box.

'That was delicious,' she said with satisfaction when all that remained were a few greasy crumbs.

'I'd never have had you figured for a takeaway pizza sort of woman,' he returned. 'I thought Michelin-starred restaurants were more your thing.'

'They are – some of the time,' she purred, pushing her silken hair back from her face. 'But I don't want to be a high-powered business woman twenty-four hours a day. There are other things I enjoy as well.'

'Such as?' He stretched out his long legs in front of him and leant back against the sofa.

'Riding, particularly in the country, tennis, swimming in a turquoise sea under a tropical sun, sitting up in bed watching the late night film on TV while eating cheese on toast – lots of things.'

'You can't have much time to do any of them – I work you too hard.'

'I love my work,' she assured him, laying her hand on his thigh for a fleeting second. She saw his eyes taking in the curve of her breasts and leant forward, ostensibly to pick up a sheaf of papers, but knowing her blouse would gape open and reveal an intoxicating glimpse of her creamy cleavage.

She was taken by surprise when he rolled her suddenly onto her back and kissed her hungrily. Trying to conceal her exultation, she remained passive in his arms for a few moments before tentatively responding. It would never do to come across as too eager at this stage.

His body felt hard and virile against hers as his tongue explored her mouth and he caressed her breasts over the silk of her blouse with detached expertise. When he'd coaxed her nipples into jutting points, he deftly undid her buttons before sliding his hand inside to fondle the smooth-skinned orbs over the lace of her bra.

She stroked the taut muscles of his back and sensed the coiled strength and tension in them. She could feel the hard column of his erection against her hip and knew he was already very aroused.

One hand glided over her buttocks, tracing the contours of the firm globes, pressing her harder against his manhood. She remained passive in his arms as he kissed her neck and then slid one hand up her skirt to find the bare strip of flesh between her stocking-tops and ivory lace panties.

There was something about the way he was touching her that Saskia found unnerving – there was an almost mechanical edge to it. It reminded her of the way she used Terry, the escort, and she didn't find it a comfortable thought. She was assailed by the unwelcome suspicion that he was thinking about Jonquil and the idea was so unpalatable that she stiffened.

'What's the matter?' he muttered in her ear, one hand stroking her upper thigh.

'You're moving too fast for me,' she gasped as his fingers brushed over her lace-covered mound.

'Relax,' he murmured, intensifying the pressure on her sensitive flesh. A tingling surge of sheer erotic sensation zapped through her, making her shiver with reluctant desire. He eased his hand between her thighs and commenced an insidious massage of her vulva over the narrow strip of fabric concealing it.

His touch was so assured that she was aware of her sex moistening and softening. The tiny triangle of her clitoris blossomed into a blunt nub and hectic messages of arousal surged around her slender body.

But despite all that, she was tempted to call a halt to the

proceedings. The thought that he'd rather it was Jonquil he was holding, but was making do with her because she was there, was galling for a woman who put a high price on herself.

But then he slid his fingers under the crotch of her panties and deep inside her and she knew she was lost – there was no way she could call a halt to the proceedings until she'd achieved her satisfaction. OK, she'd go with it, but she'd make damn sure that he didn't stop until she was completely satisfied.

He explored her internally with a delicate, tickling touch that had her squirming voluptuously on the carpet, deliciously impaled. Her skirt rode up around her waist and her thighs fell wantonly apart as he bent over her, intent on his task.

The heat was building swiftly as he rubbed her throbbing clit with his thumb, making her moan and writhe, wanting more than he was giving her.

He withdrew his hand and peeled her panties down her thighs. His breath felt warm against her quim as he parted her outer labia and began a lengthy exploration with his tongue. He licked his way over every inch of her moisture-slickened vulva, swirling it into each crease and crevice, teasing her by flicking it across her aching bud until she thought she'd explode.

He plunged it into her hidden channel, drinking her female juices thirstily, then strumming her clit like the strings of a guitar. She felt her climax building fast until she trembled on the brink, then she cried out as she came in a lengthy series of convulsions which rippled endlessly through her.

He was stripping off his trousers as she rose to her feet and, ignoring him, left the room with a come-hither sway to her hips.

When she reached the top of the stairs she glanced over her shoulder and saw him, magnificently naked, coming out of the sitting room. Once in her bedroom she removed her skirt, blouse and bra before stretching out on the bed and waiting in just her suspender belt, stockings and high heels.

He came into the room, his erection rearing up massively between his thighs and advanced upon her. She wound her arms around his neck as he positioned himself at the whorled entrance to her sheath, before plunging into her and burying his member up to the hilt.

100

She locked her long legs around his thighs and let him sweep her along with him on a hectic roller-coaster ride. She couldn't fault his performance; he was tireless, but there was a coldness about it which she found off-putting.

He worked her to another climax, varying his strokes in a way that drove her wild, before eventually pausing for a brief moment, then driving into her with half a dozen swift, shallow thrusts and erupting in a powerful surge of release.

When Jonquil reluctantly asked Jasper if he'd like to accompany her to the Halloween Ball, she was surprised that he seemed keen on the idea, telling her that parties were good places for both picking up women and making contacts.

It was fancy dress on a Halloween theme with evening attire as an option for those who didn't want to go to the expense or trouble or either hiring or making a costume.

Jonquil couldn't see herself dressed as a witch or a ghoul, so she opted for a saffron silk gown with a scooped neckline which she'd bought in New York for her employer's Christmas party last year.

When Jasper came to pick her up she was struck by how attractive he looked. She'd never seen him in a dinner jacket before and thought how much it suited him.

'If you ever find yourself unemployed, you can hire yourself out as an escort to women who want a personable man to attend functions with,' she teased him.

'As you're my sister, it's a discounted rate tonight,' he said. 'I'm only going to charge you a hundred pounds and the cost of a gourmet dinner. Being at a woman's beck and call is hungry work.'

'How would you know? Anyway, there's a buffet,' she informed him, 'so you'd better take the opportunity to fill your pockets with sausage rolls – that should keep you going for a few days. Of course, the company you hired the tuxedo from might take it amiss when you return it with the pockets full of crumbs.'

Jasper looked pained. 'You don't think I've hired this, do you? I had it made for me – can't you tell by the impeccable fit? You look beautiful, by the way. You really suit that colour.'

101

He held out her coat for her and helped her into it. As they went downstairs, he asked casually, 'Just out of interest, why isn't Damon taking you?'

'Because on this particular occasion he'd be an embarrassment.'

On the drive there Jonquil told him about Damon's determination to get some work out of Boyd. When she mentioned the name of Boyd's company, Jasper's head jerked towards her.

'Is that who you're working for at the moment? Why on earth didn't you tell me?' he demanded.

'Probably because you never show any interest in my work,' she retorted. 'I love you dearly, Jasper, but I find your total self-obsession a bit much at times. Whenever we get together we always talk about you – or hadn't you noticed?'

'We don't, do we?' He sounded genuinely bewildered.

'We certainly do.'

'I'm beginning to wish I'd turned down your invitation, if you're going to spend the evening pointing out my shortcomings,' he complained.

'Anyway – why are you so interested in the fact that I'm working for Boyd?' she asked curiously as he manoeuvred the BMW expertly through the heavy traffic.

'Because I'm looking for a better position and he's in a position to give me one.'

'Don't you *dare* ask him for a job,' she blazed. 'I could do without him thinking that I only know people who want something out of him. I mean it, Jasper, either promise me that you won't even hint you're looking for a new opening, or you can drop me on the next corner and I'll go on my own. It was bad enough Damon behaving in a way that made me ready to faint with embarrassment, without my brother humiliating me even further.'

'OK, OK, I'll just be my amusingly charming self and restrict my activities to trying to get off with the best-looking woman there,' he placated her, wondering why she sounded so agitated.

'Don't you have a girlfriend at the moment?' she asked after a pause.

'Sort of, but like you she thinks I'm a totally worthless

102

individual. I'm sure she only continues to see me because I'm dynamite in bed.'

'Not to mention unbelievably modest. Honestly, Jasper, I don't know how you manage to attract women – your ego is visible from across the street.'

Boyd had hired a ballroom in a hotel for the occasion and it was already crowded by the time they arrived. They went to the bar and Jasper bought drinks while Jonquil scanned the crowd for someone she knew. She spotted Saskia across the room, looking coldly beautiful in an ash-blue satin gown which accentuated every slender curve.

'You made it, then?' Jonquil turned to see Natalie, almost unrecognisable in a witch's costume complete with pointed hat and false hooked nose. If she hadn't still been wearing her horn-rimmed glasses, Jonquil would have had trouble identifying her. Natalie's partner was wearing a scarlet jumpsuit with a matching hood embellished with two rubber horns.

'Hi, Natalie. Yes, I came with my brother, as you suggested. You two look terrific – I took the easy option.'

Jasper returned carrying their drinks and they chatted for a while until Natalie's partner bore her off to dance. Jasper, who was idly surveying the crowd, suddenly let out a low whistle.

'Who's that *stunning* blonde?' he asked, putting his arm around Jonquil's shoulders and turning her slightly so she was looking in the right direction.

'That's Saskia, Boyd's business manager.'

'Introduce me,' he urged her.

'I wouldn't have thought she was your type. I believe she's known as the ice queen.'

'I'm imagining what she'll be like once I've thawed her out.'

'You and most of the men present.'

'Hello, Jonquil, I'm glad you could make it.' The sound of Boyd's deep voice behind her made her jump. She'd been looking out for him, but hadn't spotted his tall, broad-shouldered frame. She turned round and saw that, like Jasper, he was in a dinner jacket and, like Jasper, he looked devastatingly attractive in it.

'Hello,' she said, to her annoyance feeling her heart pounding agitatedly in her chest. His face was set in taut lines and he

103

looked angry about something. The way she'd called a halt to their passionate embrace in the back of his limousine must still be rankling.

He turned to glare at Jasper, whose arm was draped negligently over her shoulders and subjected him to a hostile survey, which Jasper was obviously oblivious to as he was gazing at Saskia, his grey eyes narrowed with carnal intent.

'Am I to take it that, despite your declaration of undying love for him, Damon's history?' Boyd asked, his voice harsh.

'No, he just couldn't make it.'

'I see you had no difficulty finding a stand-in at short notice.'

Jonquil's eyes widened at the barely concealed fury in his words, wondering what on earth was the matter with him. She nudged Jasper in the ribs with her elbow, saying, 'Let me introduce you – this is my brother. Jasper, this is Boyd, whose company I'm currently working for.'

Boyd's face cleared and he held out his hand, suddenly smiling. 'It's a pleasure to meet you.'

'It's good to meet you, too. Jonquil tells me she's writing some scripts for you and that you're working her hard.'

'I certainly am, but she's doing an excellent job. What's your line?'

'Medical equipment sales, at the moment.' He caught Jonquil's eye and grinned at her, but to her relief didn't follow up by angling for a job.

'Are you enjoying the party?' Boyd asked affably.

'I certainly am, but I'd enjoy it even more if someone would introduce me to that gorgeous creature in the blue satin dress.'

'I think I can manage that. Let's go on over.' He led the way, chatting affably to Jasper, and touched Saskia on the shoulder. She smiled up at him, nodded coolly at Jonquil, then her eyes lighted on Jasper. Her lips parted slightly and her gooseberry-green eyes darkened.

'Saskia, this is Jonquil's brother, Jasper.' His eyes holding hers, Jasper raised one hand to his lips and kissed it.

'You are without a doubt the most beautiful woman I've ever laid eyes on,' he breathed. 'Will you dance with me?'

'Only if you promise not to deliver any more ridiculous lines like that.' She spoke tartly, but she was aware of a searing heat in her loins and an almost overwhelming desire to drag him off to the nearest hotel bedroom and find out if he really was as sexy as he looked. She'd always preferred fair-haired men.

'Would you like to dance?' Boyd asked Jonquil when the other two had joined the throng on the dance floor.

'Thank you, but my ankle isn't up to it.'

She flashed him a distant smile and walked away.

Chapter Nine

Saskia applied another coat of mascara to her long lashes, asking herself if she was making a terrible mistake. It was one thing finding Jasper the most attractive man she'd met in years, it was altogether another doing something about it.

She'd made the decision a while ago that Boyd was the man for her. Between them they could build a business empire that would dominate the computer world. But Jasper was so unbelievably sexually charismatic, that she'd barely been able to think about anything else since she'd met him. So when he'd asked her out for dinner, she'd found herself accepting, even though it was against her better judgement.

He was due to pick her up in half an hour but, even at this stage, she was wondering if she should tell him that she'd changed her mind – she'd formulated her plan regarding Boyd and she should stick to it. But even though she'd achieved her aim and he'd taken her to bed, it didn't seem to have changed anything between them and she was almost certain he still hankered after Jonquil.

She opened her lingerie drawer, wondering which of the flimsy wisps of silk and lace she should pick. She was aware that if she opted for anything overtly sexy, it would be a tacit admission to herself that she was considering going to bed with Jasper and she *never* did that until she'd got to know somebody well.

Except Terry, the escort, but that didn't count.

All her underwear was expensive and figure-flattering, but there was a subtle difference between the beige lace bra and briefs set and the black silk teddy with the high-cut legs and plunging front.

Thinking 'what the hell', Saskia slipped out of her robe and pulled the teddy over her head, enjoying the sensual caress of the fine fabric against her smooth skin. She drew a pair of cobweb-fine black stockings up her long legs and fastened her suspenders into place, then regarded herself dispassionately in the mirror. Did she look good or would she be better in the ivory camisole and French knickers? And what did it matter, since he wasn't going to see her anyway?

Her black silk suit with the cropped jacket and round neck was a triumph of understated elegance she'd bought in Milan. It had been expensive but it had been worth every penny. Once she was dressed, she checked her appearance in the mirror and, satisfied that she was immaculately groomed, picked up her bag and made her way downstairs, trailed as usual by Veda, her cat.

When she opened the door a few minutes later, Jasper was leaning casually against the wall of the porch, his fair hair blowing in the wind. There was a slight smile curving his mouth and he carried a bunch of fragrant white roses.

The sight of him made her knees go weak and she was aware of a gathering heat high up in her sex. A vision of him making love to her, his lean body moving over hers, flashed across her mind and the idea made desire course through her body like an inexorably rising tide.

'I didn't think you could possibly be as beautiful as I remembered you,' he told her, 'but you are.' He handed her the flowers and stepped inside.

'I didn't think you could possibly be as corny as I remembered you,' she countered, 'but the roses are lovely and at least you've avoided the cliché of red ones.' She indicated the sitting room. 'Go in while I just put these in water.' Veda came out to see if she was missing anything and Jasper bent to rub the cat under the chin, making her purr ecstatically.

'What a gorgeous cat,' he commented. He looked around him. 'And what a gorgeous house – you all go together perfectly.'

He strolled into the sitting room and, when she rejoined him a couple of minutes later, he was sitting on her sofa, Veda sprawled across him, pawing absently at his knees while he stroked her.

'Would you like a drink?' she asked coolly, determined not

to let it show that a volcano of carnal desire was threatening to erupt in her loins.

'A vodka martini, please.'

Saskia busied herself mixing them in the nineteen-thirties' silver shaker she'd found in an antique shop, before going back to the kitchen to get the ice and the triangular glasses which she kept in the freezer.

'You're the first woman I've ever met who can mix a perfect vodka martini,' he said, after taking an appreciative sip. 'What else are you good at?'

She flashed him a smile that dazzled him. 'My job.'

She sat opposite him and crossed her stocking-clad legs, an alluring sight he had difficulty tearing his eyes from. He had even more difficulty in not striding across, taking her in his arms and kissing her thoroughly.

The cat decided it was time for a change and leapt off Jasper's knee before padding across to drape herself over the back of Saskia's chair.

They chatted for a few minutes, then she picked up the cocktail shaker and brought it over to refill his glass, bending over him with a curtain of silken ice-blonde hair veiling her face.

Jasper's senses were assailed by a delicate wave of Joy and, without thinking about it, he caught her around her slender waist and drew her down next to him on the sofa.

Their lips met and a charge of sheer unadulterated lust shot through her, turning her into a quivering mass of yielding female flesh. His clean masculine scent, the persuasive movement of his lips on hers and the feeling of his arms around her, made her hotter for him than she remembered ever having been for a man.

A shiver of eroticism passed over her and she pressed her breasts against his chest, arching her spine and parting her lips invitingly.

His hands glided lazily down her back, stroking her over the fine silk of her jacket, arousing her more swiftly than she'd have believed possible. He trailed a series of feather-light kisses down her throat and into the hollow of her collarbone.

Her head fell back and she didn't protest when he undid

109

the top button of her jacket to reveal the smooth flesh of her décolletage. He took his time about kissing every inch of it, before unfastening the second button which exposed the enticing valley of her deep cleavage and the lacy edges of her teddy.

He lifted his head to murmur, 'Lovely,' before dropping endless searing kisses between her breasts. Deftly, he undid the rest of the buttons and slipped the jacket down her arms, groaning as he took in the full effect of the black silk of the teddy against her honey-coloured skin.

He stroked her shoulders and her bare arms, while deep dark pleasure uncoiled within her and she caressed his neck and ran her fingers over his floppy fair hair.

Jasper allowed his fingertips to brush over the outer swelling of one breast before circling it and then drifting over the taut peak of her nipple in a lazy caress. He continued to stroke her breasts as if they were made of the most delicate porcelain, until her nipples had hardened to demanding points and her eyelids had fluttered closed over her green eyes.

Slowly, he slid her shoulder straps down her arms so she was naked from the waist up, then wondered if he'd be able to control himself, she was so exquisite.

He kissed the soft crinkled tissues of her areolae, teasing her rose-coloured nipples with wicked flicks of his tongue until she moaned and reached to undo his tie.

He shrugged out of his jacket and helped her with the knot, then lifted her so she was half-lying on the sofa. He unzipped her skirt and drew it down her hips, a faint groan escaping him when he saw the full length of her legs in her dark stockings, emphasised by the high cut of the teddy.

He stroked her belly and hips, then the pale bands of flesh above her stocking-tops, his eyes fixed hungrily on the two tiny black pearl buttons holding the teddy closed over the delicate swelling of her mound.

But he wasn't about to lose control and continued to work her slowly and skilfully up the spiral of arousal. When she was moaning with need, he paused and let his fingers rest on the buttons, his palm making gratifying contact with a damp patch on the strip of silk concealing her most intimate places.

She parted her thighs in mute invitation.

'Are you sure?' he murmured, his own raging excitement tempered with an unexpected feeling of protectiveness. She nodded without opening her eyes and he undid the buttons, exhaling sharply as he feasted his eyes on the damp tendrils of her pale fleece.

He stripped off his clothes and knelt between her thighs, using his lips and tongue to give her further pleasure until, with a sudden cry, her back arched and her slim frame was convulsed by a series of spasms which left her panting weakly, her mouth forming a soft oval of surprise.

He positioned himself above her and entered her in one smooth movement, while she pushed her pelvis upwards, soon adjusting to the rhythm of his controlled thrusts.

No stranger to sexual encounters, Jasper was aware of an unfamiliar sense of awe that this beautiful creature was allowing him to make love to her.

She was so perfect, so yielding and fragrant that he wanted it to go on forever. But his considerable self-control was almost exhausted and at last he was overtaken by his own ecstatic release, then rolled to one side of her, gathering her possessively in his arms. They lay in sated silence for a while, until she pushed her hair back from her face and sat up.

'I know just what we need now,' he said, sitting up, too.

'What's that?' she asked.

'Another flask of vodka martinis. I'll make them.'

'Go ahead,' she invited him, swinging her legs to the floor and rising to her feet. Jasper padded across the carpet, unselfconscious in his nakedness, while she slipped silently from the room and upstairs for her robe.

When she came back, he was nowhere in sight and for a heart-stopping moment she thought he'd gone, although the silver flask and two clean frosted glasses were on a tray on the coffee table. Then she heard splashing from the downstairs cloakroom and he emerged and grinned at her.

'That's not fair,' he said indicating her robe. 'I've got a choice of sitting here in all my glorious nudity as if I'm posing for figure drawing in an art class, or going to the trouble of dressing again.'

111

'I like your glorious nudity,' she told him, 'but do whatever makes you feel more comfortable.'

'In that case . . .' He reached for his jacket and took out his cigarettes.

'I'm afraid I don't allow smoking in here,' she told him, her voice suddenly crisp.

He put them regretfully away, then suddenly glanced at his watch. 'I've just realised that we're nearly two hours late for the table I booked. Do you want me to call, apologise profusely, and see if we can have it in half an hour or so?'

She reached for her vodka martini and took a sip. 'We could send out for something or I could see what I have in,' she suggested.

'That,' he said, taking her hand and kissing it, 'sounds like a wonderful idea.'

Damon reached for another poppadom and spooned a lavish helping of mango chutney onto it, followed by a large portion of raw onion saying, '. . . so once I'd finished my report, Kevin said I'd saved the company at least ten grand and we could . . .'

Jonquil bit lethargically into her own poppadom and wished Damon wouldn't eat so much raw onion. It meant that if he stayed the night he'd reek of it and it was a smell she hated.

They were in her local Indian restaurant on Friday evening but she wasn't having a particularly good time. Usually, she enjoyed eating out, but she hadn't felt like curry tonight. Damon, however, had, and had immediately quashed her suggestion that they should go for a pizza instead, on the grounds that he'd been looking forward to a curry all day.

She realised that he was looking at her expectantly.

'Sorry – what?' she said vaguely.

'Weren't you listening? I was telling you about my report.'

'Sorry, I've got a lot on my mind.'

'Are you OK? You haven't seemed yourself recently.' He bit another large chunk off his poppadom and chewed it, his hazel eyes resentful.

'This project isn't going as well as it might.'

'In what way?' he asked, signalling the waiter to bring them two more Kingfisher beers. Jonquil rearranged her cutlery on the tablecloth.

'The scripts are proving problematic.'

For scripts, read 'Boyd', she thought to herself. The Halloween Ball had been nothing but an endurance test. Her face had ached with the effort of smiling and trying to look as though she was having a good time. She'd wanted to leave early, but had difficulty in dragging Jasper away from Saskia.

'It's early days yet, isn't it? You can sort it out as you go along,' said Damon, dragging her back to the present. 'Why don't you discuss it with Boyd?'

'He's part of the problem,' she muttered, half to herself.

'Then you need to spend more time with him,' he suggested. His face lit up. 'I know, why don't we all go out to dinner together? Then you can talk about it in relaxed surroundings.'

Jonquil looked at him suspiciously and pushed her red-gold fringe back off her forehead. 'When you say "all", who exactly do you mean?'

Damon shifted on his seat. 'Well . . . you, me, Boyd, Kevin . . .'

'What on earth has Kevin got to do with my scripts?' she demanded.

Damon's cheeks became tinged with colour as he ploughed on. 'You'd be surprised what a lot Kevin knows. He'd be able to ask the right questions, get information out of Boyd you might not think of – it's worth a try.'

'For goodness' sake, Damon!' she exploded. 'I gave the party you asked me to for him *and* went to the theatre with you both. I suffered considerable embarrassment on both occasions and I've done all I'm prepared to do to help your obnoxious boss get his greedy hands on some of Boyd's business. It's not my fault Kevin screwed it up, and if I never set eyes on him again it will suit me just fine. Why does everything always come back to you and *your* career?'

She regretted the words as soon as they were out of her mouth, but it was too late to take them back. She'd half-expected Damon to blame her for the fact that he and Kevin had been banished to dinner on their own after seeing the play, but he'd said very little on the subject. Now she realised

113

why – he'd been gearing up for yet another attempt and she was annoyed about it.

As well as that, since Boyd had reappeared so disturbingly in her life, she'd been finding Damon less attractive and it worried her. They'd been getting along fine until then, but now, whenever they made love, she found herself unable to enjoy it.

'I was only trying to help,' he said huffily.

At that moment the waiter trundled a trolley up to the table and began to unload the dishes they'd ordered, saying the name of each as though it were an incantation.

'Chicken pasanda, mixed vegetable, saag paneer, dhal, brinjal, pilau rice, nan,' he chanted placing them all on the table. By the time he'd finished and wheeled his trolley away, Jonquil had herself under control.

'What I mean is,' she said, trying to placate him, 'I'm not on the sort of terms with Boyd that I can keep inviting him to things. He's going to start thinking I'm after him.'

Damon dug sullenly into the chicken pasanda without replying. Although the food was good, she found herself picking at it and the silence at the table became oppressive.

The door opened at that moment and Hal came in with one of the cameramen from the production company, bringing a flurry of cold air with them. They were just being shown to their table when Hal spotted her and came over, unwinding a frayed wool scarf from around his neck.

'Hi,' he greeted them. 'How are you? Is the food any good here? I haven't been before.'

He surveyed their array of dishes appraisingly as Damon nodded and said through a mouthful of curry, 'Pretty good.'

'Terrific ball the other night, wasn't it?' continued Hal.

Jonquil's heart sank as Damon's jaws ceased their movements and he looked from Hal to her and back again. She hadn't mentioned it to Damon because she didn't particularly want to get into the reasons she hadn't invited him.

'What ball?' he demanded.

Hal's large, pleasant face became a study in consternation and he looked helplessly at Jonquil.

'A Halloween Ball,' she told Damon reluctantly.

'Enjoy your meal,' said Hal and hurried off, obviously glad to be going.

Damon looked puzzled. 'You didn't mention you'd been to a Halloween Ball.'

'It was a work thing. Shall we order another nan?'

'Whose work thing?'

'Boyd's,' she admitted.

'Why didn't you ask me if I wanted to go?' He looked so hurt that she felt guilty.

'Because I knew that you'd use it as an opportunity to badger Boyd and I couldn't bear being so embarrassed again.'

'You're so naive, Jonquil,' he told her patronisingly. 'That's the way we do business on the fast track – grabbing every opportunity that presents itself. Boyd knows the way the game's played and expects it. All I want is just one more crack and I'm sure I can convince him that he needs us.'

'Damon, Boyd knew exactly what you were doing that night at the theatre and he was playing with you.'

She spoke slowly and clearly, tired of the whole situation and wanting it to end. She could see that Damon was never going to let it drop and would continue to pester her about it well into the following year, if she didn't put a stop to it now.

He flushed. 'It was just a breakdown in communications, that's all. He obviously really likes you – any fool can see that. Won't you invite him to dinner at your apartment and work on him for me? Wear that low-backed frock you've got and give it the soft lights and sweet music treatment. If you're really nice to him and ask it as a personal favour, I can't believe he'd turn you down.'

Jonquil sat back in her seat and pushed her plate away.

'Exactly how nice would you like me to be? she asked with deceptive calm.

'As nice as you have to be to get me the work,' he blurted out.

'Go to bed with him, you mean?'

He wouldn't meet her eyes. 'I didn't say that.'

'Damon, listen to me. Boyd has absolutely no intention of giving you any work. He told me so.'

His mouth fell open. 'When?'

'In the car on the way home.'

'Why didn't you tell me?'

'I mistakenly thought that you'd have got the message.' She threw her napkin down and got to her feet. 'I think we should call it a day and not see each other any more. Goodbye.'

She grabbed her coat and stalked out of the restaurant.

Chapter Ten

Boyd tapped on the door of Saskia's office and pushed it open.

'What can I do for you?' she asked coolly. Their sexual encounter hadn't been mentioned by either of them afterwards and, even though both of them had enjoyed it on a physical level at the time, neither of them particularly wanted to repeat the experience. Saskia burnt for Jasper with a carnal heat she'd never experienced in her life, but no one who knew her would ever have guessed – including Jasper.

Boyd had been relieved when he'd discovered she'd been seeing Jonquil's brother. It had been a mistake to take one of his employees to bed, however beautiful and sexy. But she'd been cool with him ever since and he was keen to get their relationship back on its previous footing. She was important to his business and he didn't want her so pissed off with him that she left.

He sat down opposite her and pushed a fax across her desk. 'This just came through. What do you think?'

She studied it for a few minutes, before saying, 'It's an interesting proposition, but we'll need to know a lot more about this company before taking it any further. I'll get someone onto it.'

'I'll leave it with you. Good weekend?' he enquired

A sensual smile played briefly about her lips, then she hastily banished it and rearranged the papers on her desk. 'Not bad. How about you?'

'I went down to my house in Kent and did some work on the new software.'

Saskia looked up in concern. 'I wish I could persuade you only to work on that here, where we've got tight security. Someone could break into your apartment or house and steal the development work.'

'Relax. I've excellent security at both the apartment and the house,' he told her. He rose to his feet and indicated the fax he'd brought to show her. 'Let me know when you get the results of the investigation.'

He went back to his own office and sat with his feet up on the desk, thinking about Jonquil. Then, on impulse, he picked up the phone and punched in her number.

'Hi, it's Boyd.'

'Yes?' She didn't sound at all pleased to hear from him, but he persevered.

'Can we meet for lunch? There's something I want to talk to you about.'

'I've a Friday deadline for the current script and it's tight as it is,' she prevaricated.

'The deadline's now Monday. Are there any quiet restaurants near you?'

'There's a pizzeria just down the road in the row of shops next to the lights. Will that do?' She knew she sounded ungracious, but she didn't care.

'That'll be fine,' he assured her. 'Twelve-thirty?'

'OK, see you then.'

The pizzeria was done out entirely in black and white and Jonquil always felt as though she ought to dress in the same monochrome theme, so as not to strike a jarring note.

But, as it was a chilly day she opted for a v-necked angora sweater in deep violet, worn with a pair of charcoal-grey trousers and flat black leather boots.

She arrived early and, as the waiter was throwing the napkin over her knee, Boyd came in. She noticed crossly that two attractive women at the table by the window both gave him an appreciative once-over as he crossed the restaurant.

'Have you ordered anything to drink?' he enquired, taking the chair opposite her.

'Not yet.'

'Can we have the wine list, please?' he asked the waiter, who dashed off to get it.

'I don't want any wine, thanks. Just mineral water for me,'

she said. At his raised eyebrow, she continued, 'Don't even bother to make your usual joke about my drinking – it wasn't funny the first time. What was it you wanted to see me about?'

'I've just been so totally belittled I think I've lost the power of speech,' he complained. He looked so rueful that, despite her annoyance with him, she felt the laughter bubbling up and had to work hard at keeping her face straight. The waiter returned with the wine list, but Boyd waved it away, saying, 'Just a mineral water and a glass of house red, please.'

He picked up the menu and studied it briefly, then when the waiter had taken their order he turned back to her.

'We need to discuss the visit to the Spanish factory.'

'When are we going?'

She'd known it was coming up and had been looking forward to it – she hated winter and the thought of some sun was very appealing, particularly as it would just be Hal, Natalie and herself going. Boyd had told Natalie that his presence was unnecessary as the manager of the factory spoke excellent English and would be able to tell them much more about it than he could.

Since splitting up with Damon, Jonquil had been brooding about him. He'd phoned her a couple of times and tried to get her to change her mind about finishing with him, but she'd made it clear he was wasting his time. Even so, the fact that they'd broken up had left quite a gap in her life. A trip abroad would help take her mind off it.

She'd decided not to let Boyd know that she was no longer seeing Damon, in case he took it as an indication that she'd changed her mind and wanted to resume a relationship with him. She just hoped that keeping the fiction alive wouldn't become complicated.

She became aware that Boyd had just replied to her earlier question.

'Sorry, what did you say?' she asked.

'I said I'd like to go next week, if possible. I thought we might fly out on Thursday and come back on Friday.'

Taken by surprise, she heard herself say accusingly, 'Natalie said you weren't going.'

'I wasn't planning to, but I've business there.'

Damn. She hadn't bargained for Boyd's presence. Now she wouldn't be able to relax for a moment.

'Next week's fine, as far as I'm concerned.' She knew she wasn't hiding the fact that she was put out, but what did he expect?

'Have you come up with anything for the script yet?' he asked.

'No. I thought it was pointless until I'd seen the operation.' It came out sounding surly so she took a gulp of her mineral water and struggled to get a grip, reminding herself for the thousandth time that Boyd was the client. 'Is anyone else going besides Natalie, Hal and the two of us?' she asked, struggling to keep her tone civil.

Boyd busied himself unwrapping a bread stick before replying, 'Natalie and Hal aren't going at the same time. They're flying out the following week.'

'I don't want to go to Spain alone with you!' she blurted out. 'Why can't we all go together?'

'Because they can't make it next week and I can't make it the week after,' he snapped, his face hard. 'If you're worried that I'm going to use it as an opportunity to get you into bed, you needn't be – you made your feelings very plain, the other night.'

He took a deep breath before continuing. 'If you're in love with Damon and are sure he's the right man for you, I promise I won't try to come between you again. I'd really like us to be friends and I give you my word that it will be strictly business, from now on.'

'Do you mean it?' She was suspicious and she felt she had every right to be.

'Yes. I promise that I won't touch you again.' There was a gleam in his eyes as he added, 'Unless, of course, you get overcome by lust, drag me into bed and beg me to screw you.'

As that was partly what she was afraid of every time they were alone, she dropped her eyes in confusion. Luckily, at that moment, the waiter brought their pizzas and she was able to avoid any reply.

When the man had gone and they'd both started eating,

Boyd said, 'I believe Saskia and your brother are currently an item.'

'So he said.'

'I hope it works out for them. I know that Saskia can come across as a bit cold, but she's got a warmer side, once you get to know her.'

'Really?'

He shot her a searching glance across the table. 'You don't like her, do you?'

'I hardly know her.'

'Maybe I can help rectify that. Why don't you and Damon come for dinner on Saturday and I'll invite Saskia and Jasper as well? Look how I'm selflessly laying myself wide open to Damon's salesmanship again, just to help everyone get along.'

'He won't be around on Saturday,' she told him hastily.

'No? Come on your own – I know you'll be missing him and it'll help take your mind off it.'

Jonquil struggled to cut through the crust of her asparagus and mushroom pizza, trying desperately to think of a reason not to go. But she'd already missed the opportunity to say she was doing something else.

'Jasper may have other plans,' was the best she could come up with.

'I'll get Saskia to ask him and then give you a call. How's your pizza?'

Jonquil was dreading the dinner party. She knew that Boyd's wife, Julie, was bound to be there – all married couples spent Saturday nights together. She wasn't looking forward to seeing her again, but supposed that it had always been inevitable that their paths would cross at some stage.

Boyd's apartment was in a thirties' mansion block in Hampstead with some of the original Art Deco features still intact. He'd insisted on sending his driver for her and, after a brief argument, she'd accepted. Getting a mini cab on Saturday night could be difficult.

She spent almost two hours on her appearance, determined to look as presentable as possible if she was going to be spending the evening with two of the most stunning women she'd ever met. Did Julie and Saskia get on? It would be interesting to see them together.

When he opened the door, a girl wearing an apron over a mauve t-shirt and matching flower-print skirt was hovering just behind him.

'This is Christine,' he said. 'She's giving me a hand this evening, so I don't have to keep vanishing into the kitchen.'

He was casually dressed in a black cashmere sweater worn with a pair of stone-coloured cotton trousers and, even though Jonquil had arrived determined to coast through the evening in neutral, unfazed by anything, her mouth still went dry at the sight of his strong body lounging near to her, his hands in his pockets.

She handed her coat to Christine and followed him into the sitting room, mentally gearing herself up to confront the woman who'd caused her so much misery, then stopped dead – the only people in the room were Jasper and Saskia.

'What can I get you to drink?' Boyd enquired.

'Dry white wine, please.'

Where was Julie? Still getting ready? Jasper and Saskia were sitting very close together on the sofa and Jonquil suddenly got the distinct impression that Boyd was glad someone else had arrived, because they looked as though they could barely keep their hands off one another.

She had to admit that they looked stunning together. Saskia was wearing a simple striped silk jersey dress in black, cream and indigo, which left her arms bare and stopped several inches above the knee to reveal a discreet amount of shapely thigh. Her pale blonde hair was loose and her make-up understated, except for a deep pink lipstick which emphasised the luscious curves of her lips.

Jasper's silver-grey linen and silk-mix suit had a hint of blue in the weave and his tie was a conservative burgundy stripe worn with a white shirt.

Boyd handed her a glass of wine and she murmured her thanks before taking a sip. 'This is a lovely apartment,' she said, since neither Jasper nor Saskia appeared to be about to initiate a conversation.

'It could do with redecorating and refurnishing. I thought

about asking Saskia to advise me, since she's made such a beautiful job of her house but, as I already shamelessly overwork her, it didn't seem fair.'

Ask Saskia? Why not Julie?

'Thanks for the compliment,' said Saskia. 'But my taste wouldn't be yours. Why don't you just call in a team of interior designers?'

'That would be too impersonal,' he replied. 'I'll get round to doing something about it, one day.'

Christine appeared in the doorway and caught Boyd's eye. 'The first course is ready,' she announced.

They went through to the dining room where Jonquil immediately noticed that the candlelit dining table was only set for four. A great wave of relief assailed her, but she wasn't sure exactly what Julie's absence signified. What was going on? Was the other woman no longer part of Boyd's life?

Christine appeared carrying a tray holding four small white pots of mushrooms baked with garlic and Camembert. While she deposited one in front of each of them, Boyd poured them all glasses of crisp white wine.

The cheese was still bubbling and obviously molten, so Jonquil dug her spoon in cautiously and waited a few moments before transferring the contents to her mouth. Her head was spinning and she felt totally confused, not sure what to think.

'Delicious,' Saskia commented. 'Did you make this, or did Christine?'

'I'm tempted to say I did and bask in your admiration,' Boyd joked. 'But the truth is, I had it sent round from a nearby restaurant. Christine's the proprietor's daughter and she's putting things in the oven and taking them out at the right times for me.'

'It tastes great,' agreed Jasper, before continuing, 'Saskia tells me that you're branching into some interesting new areas of software. Do you do much development work yourself?'

'I do, as it happens. That's where my real interest lies and, since I have Saskia to handle most of the actual running of the business, I can concentrate on new projects. I think you said you were in medical equipment sales?'

Jonquil shot Jasper a warning glance, worried that he was

about to make a pitch for a job, but he merely nodded and they went on to discuss the latest emerging technology.

It occurred to Jonquil that she needn't worry about Jasper approaching Boyd – if he was after a job he'd ask Saskia and, if he did, that would be between them and nothing to do with her.

She looked across the table at Boyd as he talked about his latest project, thinking that his enthusiasm for his work had never waned. The flickering light from the candles cast softening shadows on his hard-boned face, making him look younger.

It wasn't difficult to imagine them seven years ago, enjoying an evening together, knowing that later, when the others had left, she and Boyd would retire to the bedroom and make love into the early hours.

Or perhaps he'd take her on the sofa, their clothes strewn on the carpet in an untidy heap, his hands on her breasts, his manhood pistoning in and out of her as they . . .

She jerked her mind away from its arousing train of thought with a great effort, hoping nothing had shown on her face. She pressed her thighs together under the cover of the tablecloth in an attempt to subdue the wayward tingling sensation her libidinous thoughts had aroused.

The main course was a deliciously fragrant chicken dish served with marble-sized roast potatoes and a platter of green vegetables. Jonquil was surprised to find herself ravenously hungry and ate heartily, telling herself wryly that it was the only sensual pleasure she was going to enjoy that evening.

As they left the table, Boyd said to Jasper, 'Do you want to take a look at the new software? It's not ready to launch yet and there are a still a couple of problems to be ironed out – but it's not far off.'

'That would be great,' Jasper said enthusiastically. 'When do you plan to put it on the market?'

'Probably next spring.'

Boyd led the way into his office, a pleasantly untidy room dominated by his computer equipment. He lifted a painting from the wall to reveal the steel door of a wall safe and tapped four numbers into a miniature key pad next to it.

He took out a disc and loaded it into the computer, then

punched in a password which Jasper saw with surprise was JONQUIL.

They all gathered round the screen and watched as Boyd demonstrated the software. Even to Jonquil, who wasn't particularly computer-literate, it looked impressive. It was over half an hour later when they returned to the sitting room, after Boyd had carefully replaced the disc in the safe.

Jonquil asked to use the bathroom and, if she'd harboured any doubts that Julie might live there some of the time, they vanished when she saw the exclusively masculine toiletries on the shelf under the mirror and on the ledge around the bath.

Even if Julie did live in the country and only came up for the occasional night, she'd have left at least a few of her things lying around, but there wasn't as much as a bottle of perfume or a jar of hand-cream.

Jonquil picked up the silver-topped bottle of Boyd's favourite cologne, opened it and inhaled deeply, then put it back and stroked his black towelling dressing gown which was hanging behind the door, feeling faintly ashamed of herself for giving way to her feelings.

Soon after she'd returned to the sitting room and they'd had coffee and brandy, Jasper and Saskia exchanged glances, then got up.

'Time we were going,' said Jasper. 'It's been a terrific evening.'

'Yes, thanks, Boyd.' Saskia stood on tiptoe and kissed his cheek.

'Do you want a lift home?' enquired Jasper, looking at his sister.

'It's out of your way – my driver will take her,' returned Boyd, not giving Jonquil a chance to reply.

'Night, then.' Jasper took Saskia's hand and they headed for the door. As soon as they'd left the apartment, he pulled her around the corner out of sight of Boyd's front door and enfolded her in his arms.

'I could barely eat for thinking about taking you to bed,' he muttered into her hair, making sure she could feel the rigid length of his erection against her hip. 'That dress is just *so* sexy, I don't think I can wait until I get home.'

'We don't have to.' Saskia drew him along the corridor to the door next to the lift and pushed it open to reveal a small storeroom.

He hustled her inside and flicked the light on, pushing the door to behind them. With a cat-like smile playing around her lips, Saskia bent over a wide shelf which was stacked with a selection of cleaning materials.

She drew her skirt up around her waist to expose her shantung French knickers which clung lovingly to the curves of her bottom. Jasper swallowed and stepped forward to caress the firm globes, sliding his fingers into the silk-covered cleft between her buttocks.

Slowly, he drew the French knickers down her hips, his eyes devouring each inch of honey-coloured flesh as it was exposed to his burning gaze. When the undergarment fell around her ankles in a whisper of silk, he groaned at the sight of the perfectly formed derrière turned so provocatively towards him.

'I'm waiting,' she told him huskily, parting her thighs so he could see the deep pink folds of her vulva, already glistening with her juices, and framed by her softly curling blonde fleece.

He stroked the overlapping folds, provoking a renewed flood of moisture which drenched his exploring fingers. He caressed the swollen crest of her clit until she moaned and pushed her bottom demandingly back against him.

He unzipped his trousers and took out his throbbing shaft, using it to stimulate her until he couldn't wait a moment longer and penetrated her with infinite care, an inch at a time. When she tried to hurry the proceedings by butting her rump back at him, he grasped her hips and held her still.

When he was piercing her to her very core, he withdrew with agonising slowness and then pushed stealthily back in again.

'Are you trying to drive me out of my mind?' she wailed softly. 'Screw me properly.'

Holding her trapped, bent over the shelf and with his member huge but motionless inside her, he lifted her hair and pressed hot kisses on the back of her neck, his hands finding her breasts and caressing them so arousingly that she moaned again.

Unable to hold back a moment longer he commenced a leisurely thrusting with long, deep strokes which had her gasping as she moved with him, her arousal mounting fast.

He slipped a hand inside her dress where it closed over one perfectly formed orb, toying with a jewel-hard nipple and working her to boiling point. His other hand delved between her thighs from the front to stimulate the throbbing point of her clit.

'Aaaaaah!' she cried as she came, and a series of carnal spasms trembled through her slender frame. Panting weakly, she held onto the shelf as Jasper increased his pace, making each firm stroke shallower as he felt himself approaching the point of no return.

Her pleasure was so intense that her knees trembled and she could hardly stay on her feet. Bracing herself against the shelf, she met every staccato thrust with an answering jerk of her hips, her internal muscles clutching at his organ, feeling herself quickly scaling the dizzying heights of arousal again. She cried out and bit her lip to stop herself – anyone might be passing and hear them.

Another climax gathered and broke, then while the erotic convulsions were still passing over her, she felt Jasper explode inside her in a copious discharge which filled her completely.

They sank to the floor together and lay for a while surrounded by mops and brushes before Saskia pushed her hair away from her face.

'Let's go back to my place and do it again,' she invited him.

When he'd seen the couple out, Boyd picked up the phone and spoke to his driver, then turned to Jonquil.

'Dave's on his way back from picking something up from the airport for me and he's got a flat tyre. He says he can be here in half an hour, or I could call a cab for you, if you'd prefer it.'

Knowing that she might have a long wait for a cab at that time on a Saturday evening, Jonquil forced herself to smile and say, 'Half an hour's fine.'

'More coffee?' he asked.

'Please.' He picked up the empty pot and went into the

kitchen, leaving her alone with her thoughts.

It crossed her mind that the flat tyre could be a ruse on Boyd's part to keep her there. In a few minutes, he might join her on the sofa, take her in his arms and kiss her.

The idea made her pulses race and an anticipatory heat began to build in her belly. As she was now convinced that Julie was no longer in his life and she herself had split up with Damon, there was nothing to keep them apart – was there?

Except her pride and a determination *never* to give Boyd the opportunity to treat her so badly again.

But the knowledge that they were alone in his apartment and an overwhelming desire to feel his hard body against hers, his hands caressing her, made Jonquil lick her lips nervously. A sudden wayward thought occurred to her, a thought that had her stomach churning with excitement and her female core throbbing urgently.

What if she allowed Boyd to make love to her and experienced one more time the heights of ecstasy that only he had ever been able to take her to?

Then, afterwards, she could tell him that it had meant nothing to her and walk away, a belated revenge for his treatment of her years ago. The idea was so arousing that she could barely breathe. She craved his lovemaking and, right at that moment, it was all she could think about.

He came back into the room at the moment and she hoped fervently that he couldn't tell which way her thoughts had turned.

She accepted a cup of coffee and waited for him to make his move, breathless with anticipation and burning up with desire. But instead, he began to talk about the Spanish factory and how it fitted into the rest of the organisation.

She shifted restlessly on the sofa, her body craving his touch, sure he must be able to tell how she was feeling, but he seemed annoyingly oblivious. Her sex felt swollen and the crotch of her panties had worked its way between her sex-lips, where it was now uncomfortably wedged. Surely she wasn't going to have to make the first move?

The phone went.

'Hello? Hi, Dave – did you get it fixed?'

There was a pause then he said, 'We'll be right down.' He turned to Jonquil. 'Dave's outside – I'll get your coat.'

He insisted on seeing her safely into the car, then, with a cheerful wave, strode back into the building, leaving her seething with frustration.

As she sank back onto the comfortable leather seat, Jonquil wondered why, on this one night when her physical desire had overcome her prudence, Boyd had exhibited a hitherto unprecedented restraint.

Damn him. Damn him to hell.

Chapter Eleven

Saskia's doorbell rang in the early evening, just after she and Jasper had arrived back at her house after work. When she went to answer it, Jasper heard her exclaim, 'Basil – what on earth are you doing here?'

Whoever Basil was, she didn't sound at all pleased to see him, making Jasper think it was probably an ex-lover.

'Hi, Sask. I'm meeting the old folks here in fifteen minutes or so.'

'I'm afraid that now isn't very con—'

Jasper didn't hear her finish her sentence or invite the mysterious Basil in but, a few seconds later, a corpulent man with a high colour put his head round the sitting-room door, making Jasper suspect he'd just pushed his way past her. Prepared to evict the intruder, Jasper waited to see if that was what she wanted.

Basil walked in and took up a position in front of the fireplace, his hands in his pockets, without acknowledging Jasper's presence. The sight of his loudly patterned waistcoat and too-tight suit made Jasper wince.

'What do you mean, you're meeting the old folks here?' demanded Saskia from the doorway.

'They're coming with me to take a look at a house I'm thinking of buying,' Basil said, as if that was all the explanation necessary.

'Why aren't you meeting them at your own house?'

Basil shrugged and jingled his keys in his pocket. 'Caro's having a few friends round and told me she didn't want the elderly parents cluttering up the place, so I told them I'd see them here.'

Not an ex-lover then, thought Jasper – this must be Saskia's brother. When he'd asked her about her family, she'd been unforthcoming, but had said her parents lived in the Cotswolds and her brother in London. She'd changed the subject very quickly and it hadn't come up again.

'Why didn't you ring and ask if that would be convenient?' she asked, glaring at Basil.

'Stop being such a pain in the backside, Sask. It's not as if you'd be likely to be doing anything better.'

Basil appeared to notice Jasper, who was sprawled gracefully on the sofa, his long legs stretched out in front of him, for the first time.

'Or have I interrupted something?' he said, with such a meaningful smirk that the instant dislike Jasper had felt hardened into something stronger.

'Sorry, Jasper,' said Saskia, flashing him a smile. 'This is my brother, Basil, and I'm afraid that his unexpected arrival has made me forget my manners. Basil – Jasper.'

Jasper nodded, his attention diverted by the sight of Basil's socks. He tipped his head back and stared down his nose at them – they appeared to be red, yellow and purple tartan. Was the man colour-blind, or what?

'What do I have to do to get a drink around here?' Basil's bloodshot eyes lighted on the drinks tray and he crossed to pour himself a generous measure of whisky, slopping some onto the highly polished surface of the table.

He knocked half of it back in one go, then stood rocking backwards and forwards in front of the fireplace, surveying the elegant, airy room dismissively. 'This place is a bit poky, isn't it? How much did you pay for it?'

Saskia sank onto the arm of the sofa next to Jasper, her arms folded in front of her, and didn't reply.

'The place I'm thinking of buying is three times the size,' Basil continued. 'No wonder you've never invited us here – it'd be difficult fitting us all in the same room at once.' He guffawed loudly at his own wit, then glanced at his watch. 'I can't think where the aged parents are – probably got lost trying to find this back street.'

'Why are they coming to look at a house *you're* thinking of buying?' she asked. 'You don't usually welcome their opinion on anything unless you want them to . . . oh, I see, you're hoping for a loan from them.'

Basil's high colour went even ruddier. 'Not a loan, exactly,' he said. 'After all I am the son and heir. More an advance of the inheritance. What do you do, old chap?' He addressed Jasper for the first time, obviously not keen on the direction the conversation had taken.

Jasper's distaste for Basil's rudeness to Saskia, not to mention his clothes, manifested themselves in a cold stare. There was a pause while Basil looked at him properly for the first time, took in his beautifully cut suit and hand-made shoes and obviously decided he was worth taking notice of after all.

'I'm in merchant banking, myself,' Basil said, taking out a cigar and putting it between his lips.

'I don't allow smoking in here,' Saskia told him.

'Don't be such a bossy bitch, Sask. Is she always ordering you around, old chap?'

He fumbled in his pockets for a lighter, while Jasper rose slowly to his feet. If *he* didn't get to smoke in Saskia's house, he damn well wasn't going to let her pig of a brother light up against her wishes.

'I'm allergic to cigar smoke,' he lied pleasantly. 'Last time someone smoked in the same room, I had to spend three days on a ventilator, so I'm very much afraid that if you attempt to light that, you go straight out of the door.'

Basil's mouth fell open, emphasising his sagging jowls and he shot Jasper a shifty, appraising look. Jasper had been at school with men like Basil and he'd got his measure – he was a bully who wouldn't be likely to risk a physical encounter with a man in much better shape.

Reluctantly, Basil put the cigar away, while Jasper continued, 'Actually, Saskia and I are just about to go out, so I'm afraid you'll have to wait for your parents in your car.'

'Eh? Oh, that's OK – you two toddle off. I'll just make myself at home here. I'm sure the ancients will want to take a look round, anyway.' He settled his bulk comfortably into an armchair. Jasper glanced at Saskia and saw that she was looking horrified.

'I'm afraid that's not possible,' he told him firmly. 'Saskia's alarm is the new fingerprint-activated type so she's the only person who can put it on, and crime's so high around here she couldn't risk leaving the house unprotected. Talking of which – is that Volvo estate outside yours? Because it looks as though some kids might be vandalising it.'

'What?' With speed surprising in a man of his bulk, Basil lumbered out of the house yelling, 'Hey you little buggers – get away from there!'

The two small girls who lived next door were standing hand in hand next to his car, each clutching a pair of miniature pink ballet shoes, obviously waiting for their mother to take them to their ballet class.

'Come on – grab your bag and let's get out of here,' Jasper urged Saskia.

They hastily left the house where, to Jasper's glee, the children's mother raced down the path to confront the man yelling at her children. The smaller of the two girls burst into tears and the woman swept her into a comforting embrace before rounding on Basil.

'How *dare* you shout at my daughters! Get away from them this minute!'

'They were vandalising my car,' protested Basil, bending down to see if he could spot the damage.

'Vandalising your car at five and seven years old? Don't be ridiculous!'

Just at that moment, another car drew up and Saskia caught a glimpse of her mother's pinched face staring disapprovingly out of the window.

'Oh no, here are Mummy and Daddy – that's all we need,' she whispered, torn between laughter and dismay. The elderly couple got out and her father rushed to his son's defence, while her mother rounded on her.

'What's going on here? What trouble have you dragged Basil into now?'

'Hello, Mummy. How are you?'

'Never mind how we are – explain yourself at once.'

As the children's father had now come down the path to join the fray and everyone was shouting at once, Jasper, who disliked scenes, decided it was time to go.

He took Saskia's hand and said to her mother, 'Lovely to have met you – goodbye,' and headed for his BMW. He drove swiftly off, then, half a mile down the road, was alarmed to notice that her shoulders were shaking. He pulled over immediately saying, 'Don't cry. I'm sorry if I upset you. Do you want me to go back and smooth things over?'

She turned brimming eyes towards him and burst out laughing. 'That was the funniest thing I've ever seen in my life. How *could* you tell Basil that those two sweet little girls were vandalising his car?'

'They might have been,' he protested. 'Children turn to crime young these days and they *were* standing right next to it.'

She dabbed at her eyes with a tissue and then kissed him passionately. When at last she drew away she said, 'Drive to the nearest decent restaurant – I'm going to buy you a lavish dinner. I don't think I've ever seen Basil made to look such an idiot in my life.'

The restaurant he chose was the type with banquettes around the wall and they sat side by side rather than opposite each other. While they studied the menu, he stroked Saskia's thigh under the cover of the tablecloth.

'If you keep that up, I won't be able to decide what I want,' she murmured as he gradually edged her skirt higher and higher until his hand made contact with the bare flesh above her stocking-tops.

'I'll order for you,' he told her, allowing his fingers to slide under the lace of her panties where they sent an electrical charge of lust zapping through her. She inhaled sharply, aware that if he continued touching her, she wouldn't be able to think straight. Jamming her thighs together, she tried to read the menu but he began to massage her mound over her briefs.

It was hard to keep her legs closed when he was provoking such exquisite sensations and an incandescent heat was growing within her, setting her loins on fire.

'Jasper – stop that!' she hissed, as the waiter approached them and stood with his pen poised over his pad.

'To start, the lady will have . . .' began Jasper, probing her female valley caressingly. She didn't even hear what he said, she was so busy fighting the urge to let her thighs loll wantonly apart.

Her eyes glazed, she reached for her drink and took a gulp, shivering as he increased the pressure so that the heat in her groin spread slowly through her body and made her feel icy-cold and red-hot at the same time.

She must have relaxed without realising it, because she became aware that he'd managed to slide a couple of fingers into the delta at the top of her thighs and began to stroke the tiny bump of her clitoris with his forefinger.

She gulped audibly and the waiter turned expectantly towards her, obviously thinking she was about to say something. Jasper rubbed her nub with a deft rhythmic movement which sent a fiery fizzing sensation through her body. Her lips parted but nothing came out and if she'd been able to pull herself together sufficiently, she'd have elbowed him painfully in the ribs.

'Madam?'

'And a green salad,' she gasped.

Jasper finished giving the rest of their order while she sat next to him, barely able to breathe as she realised that she was fast approaching a climax.

'Please stop,' she whispered.

'That isn't what you usually say,' he returned, but Saskia was too far gone to protest further and gripped the edge of her seat, willing herself not to cry out.

Her wrists went numb and she was dimly aware of a pulsing sensation in every nerve-ending; then an intense wave of pleasure crashed over her and, in full view of a couple of dozen diners, she climaxed, her eyes fluttering closed and her head falling back on her shoulders.

As the erotic tide gradually ebbed and she came slowly back to reality, she hardly dared open her eyes, afraid that everyone in the room would be staring at her. But when she risked a brief glance through her long eyelashes, she didn't seem to be the focus of attention.

She took a gulp of her wine before saying feelingly, 'You bastard.'

Jasper looked hurt. 'Women are always complaining that

men don't give them enough orgasms.'

'They don't mean in public places.'

'Don't worry – no one suspected anything. It's too dimly lit and they're all intent on filling their faces.'

Still in an erotic daze, she ate her starter, washing it down with copious amounts of wine. When her main course arrived accompanied by a large dish of sautéed potatoes, she was moved to expostulate. 'You know I don't eat fried food.'

She stared at them as if hypnotised. They were beautifully golden and crisp and smelt divine. Just looking at them made her mouth water.

'Everyone should indulge themselves every once in a while,' Jasper informed her, spooning a large portion onto her plate. Slowly she picked up her knife and fork and raised one to her lips. It tasted like the most delicious thing she'd ever eaten and, suddenly ravenously hungry, she made short work of her meal.

'Shall we be really sinful and have a pudding?' Jasper asked.

'Nothing else is going to pass my lips except black coffee,' she vowed. 'I'll have to exist on a couple of lettuce leaves and a glass of mineral water for the rest of the week, to do penance for this.'

As the waiter poured their coffee, she decided it was time to exact revenge. Reaching under the table, she laid her hand on Jasper's groin and was gratified to feel his member harden instantly.

She unzipped his trousers, delved into them and drew out his shaft, fumbling to free it from his briefs.

'Let's see how you like it,' she murmured.

It was a cold, crisp morning, but at least the sun was shining as Jonquil hurried into the production company to see Natalie so they could go through the latest drafts of the scripts together. Shooting had started in earnest now and the pressure was on to keep one jump ahead.

'You'll never guess where we ended up last week,' said Natalie, pouring them both coffee before they settled down at the conference table.

'Where?' Jonquil asked.

'Boyd's country mansion in Kent. It's not far from where we were filming and when it came on to rain we drove over there to wait it out.'

Every cell in Jonquil's body leapt to attention. This was where she might get final proof that Julie really *was* out of Boyd's life.

Steeling herself for the fact that there was a slim possibility she might not like the reply, and trying to sound casual, Jonquil forced herself to ask, 'Did you meet his wife?'

Natalie looked startled. 'I didn't think he was married.'

'I'd . . . I'd heard he was and that he kept her stashed away in the country.'

Natalie pushed her horn-rimmed glasses back up her nose. 'I don't think he can be – there was certainly no sign of any female in residence. He gave us a tour and I didn't spot as much as a pair of women's shoes or a lipstick.'

Jonquil's heart began to jump around her chest so frantically that she had difficulty catching her breath. Boyd *wasn't* married – he was free. There might be a future for them, after all.

Hal walked in at that moment, his arms overflowing with videos and files. 'Hal, have you ever heard that Boyd's married?' said Natalie. 'Jonquil seems to think that he is.'

'No, he's not,' replied Hal. 'He mentioned a couple of months ago that he was unattached when we were talking about something.'

Jonquil barely heard what else was said. Maybe it was fate that had brought Boyd back into her life – maybe they *were* meant to take up where they'd left off. But a still, small voice of common sense told her that Boyd had still behaved abysmally when he'd dumped her for Julie, even if the marriage hadn't worked out.

She remembered the day it had happened as if it were yesterday. Julie had been the girl next door to Boyd when he was growing up. Her mother had been an alcoholic and her father a philanderer, prompting Boyd to take her under his wing. When Jonquil had met her, she'd been disturbed by the casually possessive way in which the other woman treated him. Even worse, Julie was absolutely gorgeous.

It seemed that every time she called, he went running, telling Jonquil that she had man trouble and needed him. Things came to a climax during Jonquil's last week at university, when, instead of taking her to the summer ball, he went hurrying up to London to see Julie. Two days later, one of Jonquil's friends showed her the announcement of his engagement to Julie in the paper.

Not waiting for his return, she packed her bags and left, then got on the next flight to New York, where she'd stayed for seven years.

But perhaps Julie had put some sort of pressure on him. He'd made it clear he cared for her and she might in some way have manipulated him into proposing.

Maybe it was time to forgive and forget.

For the first time in as long as he could remember, thanks to Saskia, Jasper didn't wake up every morning feeling dissatisfied with his lot.

There were still problems. His job, for one thing, and the fact that, although he'd managed to settle all his other debts, he currently owed the casino almost fifteen hundred pounds.

Determined that nothing was going to mar his life with her, and having a shrewd idea that she wouldn't like it if she found out that he gambled, he decided to tackle the second problem first.

He hadn't placed a single bet since having the win in the gambling club, but fate must be smiling on him to have cast Saskia in his path, so surely fate would be kind enough to let him win enough to clear his debts completely. After that, he'd never so much as buy a lottery ticket.

He knew what he had to do, but he waited until all the indications seemed positive. On the day that he found thirty pounds in the pocket of a suit he hadn't worn for a while, then drew the lucky ticket in the monthly office raffle and won a bottle of whisky, he wondered whether it was the right time to make his move.

His conviction that today was his lucky day was borne out when he discovered that Duncan, his boss, was going to be out for the rest of the afternoon. Leaving the office after the exchange of some good-natured banter with the besotted Penny, Jasper headed the direction of the casino.

When he arrived it was fairly quiet, but that suited him – the fewer distractions the better. Nadine was at the blackjack table and, when he sauntered over to say hello, she didn't look exactly delighted to see him. Luckily, there was no one at her table, so they were able to exchange a few words.

'Hi, Nadine – how are you today?'

'Not any better for seeing you in here,' she retorted.

'What's the matter?' he asked, taken aback by the hostility of her greeting.

She placed her hands on her hips and looked him up and down. 'In the first place, I'd hoped you'd learnt your lesson that gambling takes much deeper pockets than you've got and that you wouldn't show your face here again. In the second, you haven't been in touch for ages, so don't come over to me and expect me to throw down the welcome mat.'

'Sorry,' he said vaguely, deciding to ignore the first complaint. 'I didn't think you were bothered whether you saw me or not.'

'The occasional phone call would have been nice. A short while ago, I was seeing you at least twice a week and then suddenly – silence.'

'Sorry,' he repeated.

'Anyway, what *are* you doing here? Is it to pay off the rest of your account, to see me, or – and I suspect this is the most likely – have you come to throw more of your money down the drain?'

'I thought I'd just try my luck at the roulette table.'

Nadine glanced around the room and then lowered her voice. 'Jasper, don't be a fool. I know you've paid off half your debt – don't risk sending it sky high again.'

He grinned at her. 'I'm feeling lucky today and, once I've won enough to pay it off, I'm cutting up my membership card and you won't ever see me in here after that.'

'I wish I had a tenner for every mug I've heard saying they felt lucky – I'd be able to retire.'

He leant across and kissed her on the mouth. 'Don't worry about me. Everything's going my way.'

Saskia had been unsettled by Basil's unexpected arrival on her doorstep. It was so typical of him to have turned up without warning, not caring if it was convenient or not. What a pity she hadn't been out.

But then she'd have missed Jasper's masterly handling of the situation. She'd never had anyone stand up for her before and it had felt great. The fact that Jasper hadn't been fazed and had refused to allow her to be bullied, had raised him even higher in her estimation.

Even though he currently dominated her thoughts and she wanted to be with him all the time, she was realistic enough to be been aware that he was something of a lightweight and not the sort of man she'd had in mind for herself at all. Boyd had fitted the picture much better, but she'd never felt a tenth for Boyd what she felt for Jasper, despite the fact that her boss was infinitely more successful.

But Jasper probably just hadn't found his niche yet. She knew he was unhappy in his current job and she was waiting for the right opportunity to help him draw up a new career strategy. Any man who could deal with a bully like Basil with such ease, could go far given the right encouragement and incentives.

At the thought of Basil accusing the two small, well-behaved girls next door of vandalising his car, Saskia felt laughter bubbling up. It was such an unaccustomed feeling that she surprised herself. She'd never been out with a man who made her laugh the way Jasper did and it felt strange.

Strange but good.

As Jasper was leaving the casino, his face set and white, Jake, the assistant manager hurried after him and caught him up.

'That was a big loss you just took,' he said, trying and failing to look sympathetic. He paused before continuing, 'We're worried about your ability to pay it off.'

Jasper managed to resist the temptation to push past the man and hurry out of the building somewhere he could be alone.

'I paid off the last one, didn't I?'

'Not all of it – there was still half of it outstanding when you came in here today, and now it's nearly ten times that.' Jake

141

coughed and looked at his shoes. 'Actually, a decision was recently taken to withdraw your credit, but unfortunately for some reason it didn't reach the floor. I'm afraid we're going to have to insist that you repay the full amount within a week.'

'That's impossible,' Jasper protested. 'You'll have to give me more time than that.'

'A week,' repeated Jake and walked off.

Jasper had left his BMW in the car park at work and he was still in a state of shock when he went back to collect it. The thought that kept running through his head in an endless refrain was that this was going to cost him Saskia.

He knew he hadn't a hope of paying the money off and inevitably, however hard he tried to conceal it, she was going to find out and then she'd ditch him for being such a loser.

He was just getting into his car when Duncan came hurrying out of the building shouting, 'Wait a minute – I want a word with you!'

Jasper sat staring straight ahead of him with the driver's door still open, waiting for Duncan to waddle his way across the car park.

'Where the hell have you been all afternoon?' his boss demanded.

'Trying to put my life right,' he muttered.

'What's that supposed to mean?' yelled Duncan, infuriated by the blank way Jasper was gazing through the windscreen. When he didn't reply immediately, Duncan ranted, 'You've been skiving off, that's where you've been, just like you always do when my back's turned. Well, I've had it with you!'

'Sod off, Duncan,' snarled Jasper.

He slammed the door, put the car into gear and screeched off as Duncan screamed, 'You're fired!' after him.

Chapter Twelve

Jasper didn't dare tell Saskia that he'd been fired. She was away on business for a while and he hoped to have found a new job by the time she returned. He applied for virtually anything in sales and, a few days later, managed to get an interview.

His gambling debt continued to hang over him like a rock about to crash down from a great height, particularly as he knew that another visit from Hogg was inevitable and this time the damage would probably be to his person rather than his car.

The only thing he could come up with was to ask Jonquil. He knew she didn't have anything like the amount of money he owed, but perhaps she could be persuaded to take out a loan on his behalf. With no job and no security, he knew he hadn't a hope in hell of getting one himself.

Thinking he'd strike while the iron was hot, he phoned her, intending to rush into an explanation of his problem, hoping to get something moving as soon as possible.

But when he got her answering machine he paused, deciding it was a subject best approached with caution, and instead left a message inviting her round for a meal the following evening. He'd have to be diplomatic about it, work round to it by degrees and make sure she knew that he realised how dumb he'd been.

She'd be furious of course, and probably give him a good bollocking, but if she *could* get a loan, and he managed to get a new job, he could pay off his debt and at last be free.

As Jonquil sat in a mini cab on her way to Jasper's, the following evening, she kept brooding about Boyd. Why hadn't he tried to get her into bed on Saturday? On virtually every other occasion they'd been alone, he'd wasted no time before trying to make love to her.

At last he seemed to accept that it was over between them, ironically just as she was burning up with lust for him. How could she let him know that she'd changed her mind? She hadn't been able to sleep last night, for wanting him there in her bed, his arms around her, his body moving over hers.

As a result, today she felt bad-tempered and edgy. She'd told Jasper she didn't feel like going out, but he'd said there was something they *had* to discuss, which filled her with foreboding.

'A huge drink for my favourite sister,' he greeted her, kissing her and handing her a large glass of claret, before she'd even taken her coat off.

'You don't look too good – what's up?' she asked.

'I've just lost my job,' he admitted. 'But don't worry – there's another in the pipeline.'

'Oh, Jasper, I'm sorry,' she said in dismay.

'Don't be. If I had to spend another day looking at Duncan kitted out in his idea of sartarial elegance, I'd have cut off one of his polyester ties and set fire to it. Anyway, are you hungry? I'll see how the spuds are doing.'

Jasper had pulled out all the culinary stops and bought two large lamb steaks, some ready-scrubbed baking potatoes which were already in the oven, and a bag of mixed frozen vegetables. They discussed his job prospects while waiting for the meal.

'How should I cook the steaks?' he said, when at last the potatoes were almost ready.

'You could either grill them or fry them,' she suggested, determined not to end up doing it herself. Jasper had invited her for a meal, so *he* could damn well prepare it. He unearthed a frying pan and dropped a dollop of butter into it.

'Haven't you any olive oil?' she asked, backing away from the clouds of black smoke which began to rise from the pan.

'Nope. Don't worry – butter's great for cooking things in.' He tossed in the steaks which sizzled so viciously that she hastily closed the kitchen door on him and retreated to the sitting room. He shot out briefly in a cloud of smoke to get the bottle of claret and eventually emerged coughing and

144

triumphantly carrying two heaped plates.

The steaks were swimming in warm claret with which he'd tried unsuccessfully to make a sauce and were burnt to a frazzle on the outside and raw in the middle. He'd cooked the frozen vegetables by the simple expedient of throwing them into the fat with the steaks, so they were blackened on the outside and still frozen in the centre. Luckily her jacket potato was edible, so Jonquil concentrated on that and the claret, which was excellent.

They'd only just finished when the doorbell went. Instantly, she was aware of the tension emanating from him as he went to the window and furtively drew the curtain a couple of inches to one side, then his face cleared.

'It's Nadine,' he muttered half to himself, going to let her in. Jonquil wondered who she was and whether Saskia had anything to worry about. Her first thought on seeing Jasper's visitor was that Saskia *definitely* had something to worry about.

Even a long burgundy wool coat couldn't conceal Nadine's voluptuous figure. Jonquil took in her lovely face, glossy brown hair and sloe-dark eyes and marvelled at her brother's ability to attract the most stunning women. She noticed his expression and wondered why he looked so wary. Had he ditched her and she was unhappy about it?

The other woman stopped short when she caught sight of Jonquil. 'I'm sorry – I didn't realise you had someone here,' she said to Jasper. 'I should have phoned first.'

'This is my sister, Jonquil,' he introduced her. 'Sit down – would you like a glass of wine?'

'This isn't a social call. Jake sent me – I need to talk to you about your—'

'Let's go into the other room,' Jasper interrupted her hurriedly. He rose to his feet but Nadine stayed where she was.

'I think your sister had better hear this – maybe she can talk some sense into you. If you don't pay off your account at the casino by the weekend, there's going to be trouble. They're determined to get the money – whatever it takes.'

Horrified, Jonquil looked from one to the other, as Nadine continued, 'Trust me when I say you can't afford to stick your head in the sand and hope the problem will go away. You have to raise the money somehow and do it quickly.'

'How much do you owe?' Jonquil wanted to know, her voice faint with anxiety.

'Almost fifteen thousand pounds,' he confessed, unable to meet her eyes.

'You *idiot!* Where the hell are you going to find that sort of money?' she wailed.

Nadine stood up. 'I'd better go.' She turned to Jonquil. 'He *has* to find it, or things will get unpleasant. I warned him to stay away from the tables, but he didn't listen.'

As soon as the door closed behind her Jonquil said, 'You promised me when you borrowed that money from me that you'd never gamble again.'

'I promised never to bet on horses again, and I haven't,' he pointed out, his face white.

'That's why you invited me here tonight, isn't it? To ask for another loan. You surely can't imagine that I have that sort of money.'

He looked at her beseechingly. 'I . . . I thought you might be able to borrow it.'

'How? I've just taken out a mortgage on the apartment and I borrowed to my limit to buy that.'

'I know, but if you put the apartment up for security, surely they'll let you have another fifteen thousand? I promise faithfully that I'll pay it off every month and it won't cost you a penny.'

'You've just lost your job,' she pointed out bluntly. 'So don't you think that might prove difficult? Wouldn't Saskia lend you the money?'

'I wouldn't ask her and she must never know about this — because she'd dump me. What am I going to do?'

'I'll go and see both my bank and building society tomorrow and see what I can raise, but I don't hold out much hope. If that fails, I'll rack my brains and try and come up with something else.'

The following day, she saw the assistant manager of her bank who was dry and dismissive and told her that he doubted her ability to pay off a hefty loan in addition to her mortgage. She had no more luck when she tried her building society. When she returned home, she rang round several more and then in desperation tried a loan company, but even they wouldn't lend her the sum she wanted.

Reluctantly, she had to phone Jasper and admit defeat, but told him she'd see if she could come up with any more ideas while she was away in Spain.

He sounded despondent, making her wonder if she ought to stay and make sure he was okay, but she reminded herself that this was a business trip she was going on and, even if she wanted to, she couldn't cancel it. Besides, she didn't want to.

It was with a sense of pleasurable anticipation that she did her packing. Until she'd become convinced that Boyd really was unattached, she'd been dreading it. But now it seemed like the ideal opportunity to let him know she'd had a change of heart.

The idea of resuming their relationship was so exciting that she felt the blood fizzing through her veins and hot little tingles of lust kept shooting through her groin; then she felt guilty for feeling like that when her brother was in so much trouble.

Jasper hoped to be able to tell Saskia on her return to London that he'd been offered a new job. He'd always been good at interviews, but he was uncomfortably aware that his track record wouldn't stand close scrutiny. There was also the problem of a reference from his last employer, because he was certain Duncan wouldn't give him one.

As he announced his arrival at the software company, he found himself praying for a female interviewer. But he wasn't surprised to find that it was a man in his early fifties, who introduced himself as Mr Simpson without mentioning a first name.

The interview lasted less than an hour and, as the man was escorting him back to reception after they'd finished, Jasper thought cautiously that it hadn't gone *too* badly, although he'd had to be evasive when asked tricky questions like why he'd left his last job.

'Jasper, you old bastard, haven't seen you in ages,' said a voice from behind him, just after he'd shaken Mr Simpson's damp hand and assured him how much he'd like to work for the company.

'Gavin!' said Jasper with genuine delight. He and Gavin had worked for the same firm a few years ago and had always got on well. 'Do you work here? I've just had an interview.'

'I've been here two years.' Gavin glanced at his watch. 'Got to run – I'm late for a meeting. How about getting together later for a drink?'

'Sure. Where do you suggest?'

'How about that pub we used to drink in in Islington?'

'Okay. See you there, say at six-thirty?'

'Six-thirty.' He slapped Jasper on the back and hurried off.

Jonquil stood on the balcony of her hotel room overlooking the Mediterranean and sighed contentedly. The sea glittered under the midday sun, the surface unbroken except for the wake of a graceful white yacht heading unhurriedly towards the horizon. She couldn't believe how hot it was – it must be almost eighty degrees, even though it was November. A knock on her door had her reluctantly leaving the balcony to find Boyd waiting for her.

'Are you ready for lunch?'

'I'm starving.'

It was a long time since breakfast, a bowl of cereal taken on the run as she'd dressed in what felt like the middle of the night, even though it had been approaching five.

'Okay, lunch on the terrace then it's a half-hour drive inland to the factory,' he said as she locked her door. 'Paulo's expecting us around two.'

They took a table under a red-and-white striped parasol with a stunning view over the lush, landscaped gardens and beyond that the sea.

'I wish we had time for a swim,' she said, looking longingly at the two gleaming turquoise swimming pools connected by a waterfall, over which was a small wooden bridge. The spray thrown up formed a mist through which arced a rainbow, created by the sunlight on the tiny drops of water.

'We should be back by late afternoon,' he told her. 'We can have one then.'

He was sitting opposite her, casually dressed in a white t-shirt and a pair of stone-coloured cotton trousers. The sight of the dark hair on his arms and at his throat made her mouth go dry and she felt the usual stirring of desire that just looking at him seemed to evoke.

She swallowed and took a gulp of her mineral water, aware that the heat was having an effect on her libido. Tantalising images of Boyd shafting her in various lewd positions danced in front of her eyes and made her want to suggest that they forget about visiting the factory.

It would be much more enjoyable to go to her room, and spend the afternoon in bed with a warm breeze stirring the curtains and the ceiling fan revolving slowly above their heads, Boyd's naked body moving with hers as he—

'Omelette for the lady,' the waiter announced, breaking into her wanton daydreams and placing her meal in front of her. 'Swordfish steak for the gentleman.' He dashed off again to return with an enormous dish of mixed salad and a pepper grinder.

Jonquil came back to earth and blushed at her own thoughts, hoping that the fact she was wearing dark glasses had concealed the nature of them from Boyd and that nothing had shown on her face.

'This looks delicious,' she said, picking up her knife and fork and cutting into her omelette.

'Today I'll give you a tour of the factory, with Paulo there to answer any questions I can't, and tomorrow I'll go back on my own to take care of my other business. You can sunbathe or explore if you like – you may as well make the most of it, and the flight back isn't until six.'

'That will be great,' she murmured, wishing he'd be with her. They could lie on the beach side by side and he'd take a tube of suntan cream and rub it slowly into her sun-warmed skin, while she—

'. . . about the Northern European operation?' he asked.

The heat in her belly had very little to do with the temperature and she shifted uneasily on her chair as she said, 'Sorry, what were you saying?'

He repeated the question while she wondered how she was

going to get through the afternoon and evening until the time when somehow – she wasn't sure exactly how – they'd end up in each other's arms and sink slowly, limbs entwined, onto the cool cotton sheets of the bed.

She became aware that he was waiting for a reply and tried desperately to remember what he'd just asked, eventually having to say, 'I'm sorry, but a combination of the early start and the heat seems to have scrambled my brain.'

'Don't worry about it,' he returned pleasantly. 'It is a bit of a shock to the system; it was just below freezing when we boarded the plane only a few hours ago and it must be approaching eighty here. Relax and eat your lunch.'

The tour of the factory was interesting and Jonquil made several pages of notes, but she was glad when they got into the hire car and headed back to the coast in the late afternoon. The sun was just beginning its leisurely descent towards the horizon by the time they pulled up outside the hotel and she hurried up to her room to change into her favourite hot pink bikini.

Boyd had said he had a call to make, so she went down to the pool on her own. She stretched out on her stomach on the sun-lounger, undid the back of her bikini top and sighed happily as the sun's rays fell on her pale freckled skin. All the other guests had vanished, presumably to shower and change before dinner, and she had the poolside to herself, except for a muscular young attendant who was busy stacking chairs. She noticed the admiring glance he gave her and wished that Boyd would look at her like that.

She was tired after the long day and the faint rustling of the breeze in the palm trees and the gentle splashing of the waterfall made her feel sleepy. She must have dozed off because, the next thing she knew, she felt a warm hand on her back and then heard Boyd growl, 'Why the hell aren't you wearing any sun cream?'

'What?' she asked groggily, half sitting up and then hastily lying back down again as her bikini top fell off. She heard his sharp intake of breath and knew he'd caught a glimpse of her naked breasts.

'You know how easily you burn,' he admonished her, his

voice hoarse. 'Where's your cream?'

'There,' she muttered, reaching behind her and trying to fasten her bikini so she could sit up. He picked up the sun block and unscrewed the cap, before brushing her hands out of the way and squeezing a large dollop between her shoulder-blades. It was so unnervingly like her feverish fantasies that she felt as if her self-control wouldn't stand it.

'I don't need any,' she protested. 'I'm just about to swim.'

She caught a glimpse of his strong, muscular legs and felt faint with longing at the sight of them.

'The sun will still catch your shoulders, and they're already pink,' he retorted. She subsided back onto the lounger and had to bite her lip to suppress a moan of sensual delight as he began to massage the cream into her overheated skin.

It was agony and it was ecstasy as he worked his way up to her neck, his strong hands moving gently but arousingly. She felt her nipples hardening into taut peaks and struggled not to squirm with pleasure. He rubbed the lotion into her shoulders and along her arms, then squeezed another glob onto the small of her back.

As his long fingers skimmed the edge of her bikini bottoms, she felt a slow smouldering in her female core, a smouldering that threatened to break into a sizzling blaze of sheer, unadulterated lust.

She pressed her pelvis into the lounger, digging her nails into the palms of her hands and trying not to give way to the temptation to sit up and pull him down next to her, their bodies melting into one another in a passionate embrace.

The way he was massaging the small of her back with a lazy circular movement almost made her lose the last tenuous threads of her self-control and the heat in her loins was so great she thought she was about to spontaneously combust.

Just when she thought she couldn't stand it another moment, he stood up and moved away. He peeled his t-shirt off in one smooth, graceful movement to reveal his powerful shoulders, flat stomach and narrow hips.

A moment later, he'd dived cleanly into the pool, making barely a splash as he entered the water, then set out for the far end, employing an athletic crawl. Jonquil moaned softly and wondered if she were about to pass out from wanting him so badly. She was on fire for him, practically incandescent with arousal.

She fumbled to fasten her bikini and stumbled to her feet. She had to cool off and get a grip of herself before she did something stupid. She dived into the pool, the cool water closing blissfully around her overheated body.

She swam up and down a dozen times until sanity returned and the smouldering in her loins subsided to a demanding throbbing, then turned on her back and floated, looking up into the sky to see that the approaching dusk had turned it to amethyst above the horizon.

Boyd made his way over to her and, if she'd had the strength, she'd have swum in the opposite direction because, with the water running down the firm planes of his chest, she was tempted to throw herself into his arms, her body moulding itself to the contours of his.

She turned hastily onto her stomach and held onto the side of the pool, so he wouldn't notice the marble-hard points of her nipples thrusting shamelessly against the thin cotton of her bikini.

'I'm going in now,' he told her.

'OK, I'll just have a bit longer in the water,' she managed to say.

'I'll meet you in the bar. Will seven-thirty be OK?'

'That's fine.'

She closed her eyes so she didn't have to torture herself watching him climb out of the pool and then towel himself dry. When eventually she was sure he'd gone, she got out and went over to one of the changing cubicles. If she didn't bring herself to a climax immediately she'd explode. She couldn't even wait until she got back to her room.

The wooden cubicle still held the heat from the day as she sank onto the bench and dragged her bikini briefs off. With her thighs wide apart and her eyes closed, she began to feverishly stroke her aching bud, conjuring up lascivious images of Boyd screwing her on a sun-lounger.

She was already so aroused that, within a couple of minutes, she was almost there. Her hand was moving faster and faster between her slim thighs, when a sudden sound made her eyes fly open.

To her horror, the pool attendant was standing in the doorway, his burning gaze fixed on her exposed vulva, the massive bulge in his skin-tight jeans paying silent testament to his arousal.

Poised on the brink of a desperately needed orgasm, Jonquil couldn't stop herself and her hand continued with its lascivious task. As her body was convulsed by a shameless wave of pleasure, she had a mental image of what she must look like, her thighs splayed in whorish abandon, her sex glistening and swollen.

She heard him gulp and, over the faded denim of his jeans, saw him clutch what was undoubtedly a huge erection. He was only young, around nineteen or twenty, his body fit and strong.

Their eyes locked and there was a question in his as slowly, he unzipped his jeans. Her mouth dry, Jonquil licked her lips and watched as he took out a large, heavily knobbed phallus. Without making a conscious decision, she found herself kneeling on the bench with her back to him, her thighs invitingly parted.

He came silently up behind her and removed her bikini top with one swift tug, then clasped her breasts with his large hands, his rod hard and hot against the cleft between her buttocks. He kissed her neck, muttering compliments in broken English, then with one jerky thrust his member was inside her.

It was a coupling completely lacking in finesse. Roughly fondling her breasts, he drove strongly in and out of her, his muscular body taut and straining.

Jonquil found herself suddenly excited by the sheer animal quality of their encounter – there was a freedom and anonymity to it that she found strangely liberating. Arching her back, she ground her bottom into his groin, inciting him to even greater efforts.

The silence was broken only by his grunts and her gasps, as she felt herself driven back up the spiral of arousal. With a loud moan, she came again, just before he erupted powerfully into her, crying out in Spanish.

As she sagged weakly on the bench, brushing her damp hair out of her eyes, Jonquil had a fleeting vision of Boyd walking in and discovering them. The idea made a final little shudder of sheer erotic pleasure ripple over her, milking the last drops of fluid from her unknown lover.

He eased himself free and zipped up his jeans, his expression both triumphant and dazed, while she fumbled for her discarded bikini. He passed it to her with a big grin, then slipped silently from the cubicle.

The pub in Islington was now a wine bar and, over a bottle of Fitou, Gavin filled Jasper in about the company.

'It's not like the old days of doing business over four-course lunches,' he said regretfully. 'It's all noses to the grindstone, shoulders to the wheel and so on. The money's not bad if you make enough sales, but the base salary's pretty low. Old Simpson's a bit of a shit. As the senior sales manager, he sets the targets and they're pretty impossible ones – I'd like to see him try to meet them himself.'

Jasper immediately felt depressed. A low salary plus commission wasn't much use to him; he needed a high salary *and* a generous commission on top of that. And Simpson sounded as much of a pain in the backside as that bastard Duncan had been.

'I've got several interviews lined up,' he said easily, 'and I'm in no hurry, so it's just a case of waiting until someone makes me an offer I'm happy with.'

'Our stuff's getting more and more difficult to shift,' admitted Gavin. 'There are new products hitting the market every day and our software's starting to look obsolete in comparison.' He laughed and topped up their glasses. 'Let's face it – ours *is* obsolete, but there's sod-all money spent on research and development.'

'I saw some interesting new software recently,' Jasper told him. 'It's a real breakthrough – state of the art and all that – but it's not on the market yet.' He went on to describe Boyd's latest development, which he'd found really impressive. 'When it eventually hits the retail outlets, it'll just walk off the shelves,' was his final comment. He glanced at his watch. 'Fancy something to eat? There's an Italian round the corner.'

'Do you want to eat in the hotel or drive down the coast to the port?' Boyd asked when they were sitting over drinks on the terrace.

Jonquil had taken a long cool shower, wondering how she could have behaved so out of character as to let the pool attendant screw her in that casual way. Wanting Boyd must really be getting to her – she'd better make sure that tonight was the night, before she did anything else foolish.

After her shower, she'd dressed in a sleeveless emerald-green silk top with a low v-neck, worn with a short white linen skirt and high-heeled cream sandals.

At Boyd's question she took a sip of her chilled fino and then slowly uncrossed her legs and crossed them again before replying, willing him to look down and notice, but he seemed oblivious and was gazing out to sea.

Before he'd promised never to try to get her into bed again, whenever they were together she'd always been aware of the way in which his deep blue eyes lingered on the curves of her body or her legs. But since then, he never seemed to look at her and she was finding it agonisingly frustrating.

'I don't mind. Which would you prefer?' she said in reply to his question.

'Let's go down to the port, then we'll have a choice of restaurants to eat in.'

They drove along the busy coastal highway with an ozone-laden breeze wafting in through the open windows of the car, making Jonquil think that cold, damp London seemed like a million miles away. Fleetingly, her thoughts returned to Jasper and his problems, but she told herself to put him from her mind. There was nothing she could do until she got back to England, so there was no point in worrying about it.

The port was bustling with noise and life, the open-fronted restaurants busy, and all with enticing savoury aromas floating out. Most of them overlooked the marina where immaculately painted yachts were moored on the dark water.

Throughout the meal, she found she couldn't stop looking at Boyd, her eyes lingering on his cheekbones, the curve of his mouth and the way his long fingers toyed with his wine glass.

Conversation between them was desultory, Jonquil was preoccupied by her overwhelming physical needs and he seemed distracted by something. She allowed herself to wonder what it would be like between them later – it had been seven years since they'd last had sex. Would it still be as good?

At around half past ten he glanced at his watch and yawned. 'I'm beat,' he said. 'Shall we go back to the hotel?'

As they walked towards the car she allowed her hand to brush against his, hoping he'd take hers, or put his arm around her, the way he had that night in the theatre. But he didn't and she suddenly felt too inhibited to take the initiative.

They drove back in silence, collected their keys from reception and took the lift up to their floor. At her door, she turned towards him, a faint tinge of colour gathering in her cheeks at the irrevocable step she was about to take.

'Would you like to come in for a nightcap?' She tried to imbue the words with as much sensual promise as possible.

'I'm shattered and I think I'd better get to bed,' he returned cheerfully, 'but thanks for the invitation.'

With dawning dismay, she watched him walk away.

'Boyd,' she called after him. He turned round as she leant back against her door in a provocative pose, certain her raw need for him must be evident in both her body and her expression. 'Are . . . are you sure?'

'Yes, thanks.'

Unbelievably, he unlocked his door, grinned at her and went in, leaving her with a teeming mass of conflicting emotions. She wasn't sure whether she wanted to hit him or march into his room and *demand* that he take her to bed.

It was a few moments before she managed to pull herself together enough to let herself into her room, where she spent a restless night disturbed by dark erotic dreams.

Chapter Thirteen

When Jasper had a phone call from Gavin, suggesting they meet for lunch the following day, he took it as a hopeful sign that he might be offered the job.

They arranged to meet in a pub just off Oxford Street. Gavin was already there when Jasper arrived, a pint of bitter in his hand. They took their drinks over to a corner table and Gavin began to talk about football. Jasper couldn't help but notice that he seemed agitated and kept drumming nervously on the table top.

'Are you OK?' he asked when the other man suddenly went silent in the middle of saying something and began to tear up a beer mat with trembling hands.

'Yes, fine thanks. That is . . . well . . . there's something we've got to talk about.'

'Go ahead,' Jasper invited him, wondering what this was all about.

'It's the job,' blurted out Gavin. 'It's yours if you want it.'

'Really?' Jasper was careful to look only mildly interested. He didn't want Gavin to think he was desperate – it would hamper the small amount of bargaining power he had.

'There's . . . there's a condition.' Gavin clawed at his tie and loosened it, then took a deep draught of his beer.

'What condition?'

'That . . . that you bring the new software you were telling me about with you.'

Taken completely aback, Jasper could only stare at him for a few moments, wondering if Gavin had been drinking before they'd met last night and had been so far gone he'd completely misunderstood the situation.

'It isn't mine to bring,' he explained. 'You've got hold of the

157

wrong end of the stick. Boyd was just showing it to me because I was interested – it's his development and his company are going to market it next spring.'

'I told Simpson about it and he wants it for our company,' babbled Gavin, mopping his brow with a handkerchief. 'If you can deliver it, you get the job, a good salary and a generous starting bonus.'

Thinking the other man must have been working too hard and was losing it, Jasper tried again. 'I can't deliver it – it doesn't belong to me.'

'You could get hold of the disc and copy it, though, couldn't you? We could get it out by December and clean up over the Christmas period.'

Jasper's brows drew together. 'You want me to steal it?'

Gavin reached for his drink and sent an ashtray crashing off the table, obviously uncomfortable in his role of messenger.

'It'll be well worth your while. It's just a bit of industrial espionage – it happens all the time.'

'Yes, sure and people get sent to prison all the time. Forget it, Gavin, I'm not turning into a thief to get some poxy job I don't really want anyway.' Jasper drained his glass and stood up. 'You can tell Simpson to stuff it, if those are the terms.'

Gavin clutched his sleeve. 'He told me to offer you ten thousand to start with and then go up to twenty if I had to. Think about it – it's a lot of money.'

'I've already thought about it and the answer's no.' Jasper pulled away and headed for the door, his face set in angry lines.

When Jonquil eventually woke up at around ten after a largely sleepless night, it was to find a note from Boyd pushed under her door telling her that he'd pick her up from reception at three-thirty to drive to the airport.

She regarded the note sourly for a few moments, then crumpled it into a ball and threw it in the wastepaper basket. As she stepped under the shower, she asked herself what on earth had gone wrong last night. Hadn't she made the situation plain? She thought that she'd been sending out a fairly obvious message, but maybe he'd not picked up on the signals. Whatever the reason, she'd just blown the best chance she was going to get in the foreseeable future to resume her relationship with him.

She didn't feel in the mood for sightseeing, so she decided to take a walk along the beach and then stretch out by the pool with a book. Normally, she'd have been delighted to spend a November day in the sun, but she was unable to stop herself brooding about the previous night.

She had to admit she felt at a loss. If dining under the stars together in hot, romantic Andalucia and then inviting him into her room for a nightcap hadn't done the trick, what hope would she have in chilly, autumnal London?

Boyd picked her up promptly at three-thirty, looking so infuriatingly gorgeous that she had difficulty in not grinding her teeth together in frustration.

'How was your day?' he asked cheerfully as they drove along the coastal highway.

'Fine, thanks,' she returned shortly. 'What about yours?'

He talked for a while about his meeting then they lapsed into silence. To their surprise, as they approached the airport it was to find it in chaos, with hundreds of cars and taxis gridlocked and the police trying to get the traffic moving again with a lot of furious gesticulating. People on foot were swarming around carrying luggage and looking angry.

'What do you think's going on?' asked Jonquil, bewildered by the situation, as Boyd hastily reversed and turned the car around, before they became irrevocably caught in the snarl-up. He found a parking space on the outskirts of the airport and undid his seat belt.

'It could be anything – a bomb scare maybe, or a strike. I'll go and find out.'

He came back ten minutes later and said, 'There's a twenty-four hour strike by the air traffic controllers, so it appears we aren't going anywhere tonight. The problem's going to be finding somewhere to stay. A lot of the hotels are closed off-season, and the ones that are open are going to be inundated by people wanting rooms. There's a queue a mile long at the telephones, so I think we'd better drive straight into Malaga and start looking.'

Jonquil's heart started to thud so strongly in her chest that she was sure it must be echoing around the car. *She was going to get another chance to get him into bed.*

She was so excited by the thought that, for a while, she was unable to speak and merely nodded and sat staring unseeingly out of the window as they headed into Malaga.

But the strike had started that morning and all the hotels were already overflowing with disgruntled travellers. After trying half a dozen with no success, Boyd pulled up at a phone.

'I'm going to call Paulo. Maybe he knows somewhere in the area that's a bit off the beaten track and not likely to be full.'

When he came back he looked happier. 'Paulo's sister has a small hotel in the hills above here and he said that it's unlikely that anyone has driven that far in search of a room. He's given me directions and he's going to phone and tell her we're on our way.'

That suited Jonquil fine. Settling back in her seat, she vowed that tonight she was going to abandon her passive role and not wait for him to make the first move.

She was going to make him screw her – whatever she had to do.

Several hours later, Jasper could still barely believe Gavin's proposition. The two of them had worked for the same company for over a year and had regularly spent evenings in the pub together, without him ever having suspected that the other man was a few cards short of a deck.

To be fair, Simpson had obviously put him up to making the proposal, and he hadn't looked very comfortable with his role. But even so, to suggest that Jasper should commit burglary was going a bit far.

Not that he couldn't use twenty grand – that would be all his problems solved in one go – but to calmly suggest that he *steal* new software development took some believing.

As he heated up some baked beans for his evening meal, he found himself wondering how difficult it would be.

Getting into Boyd's flat wouldn't be a problem. Saskia had a set of keys in her house and Jasper had the key to that. Opening the safe wouldn't be too difficult, either. He'd noticed what code Boyd had keyed in and remembered it, because by coincidence it was the figures of the year he was born.

And as he knew that the password to get into the computer was JONQUIL, copying the disc would only take a few minutes. Easy, really.

Paulo's sister's hotel was nestled in a fold in the hills high above the coast and was reached by a steep winding road overhung with cypress trees.

It had a red-tiled roof, green shutters and small black wrought-iron balconies full of terracotta pots crammed with geraniums, hibiscus and bougainvillaea.

'What do you think?' asked Boyd, taking off his dark glasses.

'It looks fine,' she replied, thinking that, as a background for her planned seduction, it would do very well indeed.

They left the car and went inside to find a deserted reception area, but a ring on the old-fashioned bell-push on the counter summoned a woman who came hurrying in from a door at the back, bringing an appetising aroma of cooking with her. Boyd introduced himself and she nodded and smiled.

'Si, Paulo, he telephone and say you come. Please to sign in and give me passports.' After they'd registered, she handed over a massive brass key saying, 'Room sixteen. Is a very nice room, up stairs then to end.'

'I think there must be some mistake,' said Boyd. 'We need two rooms, not one.'

'Paulo, he say only one room. All others taken.'

Glancing outside at where their solitary car was parked, Boyd tried again. 'You must have another, surely? They can't all be taken at this time of year.'

She nodded vigorously. '*Si*, old peeples.'

'Old peeples?' Perplexed, he looked at Jonquil.

'I think she must mean there's a Saga tour or something booked in here,' she suggested, keeping her voice calm with an effort. The thought of having to share with Boyd had made her mouth go dry and a whole troupe of butterflies had commenced an erotic cavorting in her groin.

'We'll have to find somewhere else.' He turned to the woman. 'Are there any other hotels near here you could phone for us?'

She shook her head. 'Could you try some further down the coast?'

She began leafing through a telephone directory and then dialled several numbers, but it was obvious from her end of the conversation that everywhere was full and eventually she replaced the phone.

'No planes tonight, so rooms all full,' she told them.

Boyd appeared to be struggling with himself. He pushed his dark hair back from his brow and glanced from her to Paulo's sister and then back again. Jonquil leaned casually against the counter, thinking she hadn't often seen him at a loss and feeling a bit aggrieved that he wasn't jumping at the chance to spend the night in the same room.

'It doesn't look like we have much choice,' he eventually muttered. 'We'd better take it.'

Jonquil nodded, keeping her face expressionless with an effort. He went out to the car to get their luggage, while she picked up the key and went on ahead, praying that it would be a double room and not a twin.

When she unlocked the door and saw the large old-fashioned double bed with a snowy counterpane and carved dark wood headboard, she smiled gleefully to herself and looked hastily around to see if there was anywhere else he might sleep.

But the room boasted only the bed, a massive dark wardrobe, two bedside tables, a couple of hard upright chairs and a chest of drawers. A brief look into the immaculate bathroom showed that the bath was barely long enough for a man of Boyd's height to sit in, let alone stretch out in. When he arrived, a moment later, she'd opened the double doors leading to the tiny balcony and was gazing serenely out.

'What a lovely view,' she greeted him. 'And the air smells wonderful, all scented and herby.'

A long way below them and beyond the red-tiled roofs of the villas and apartments hugging the coast road, the Mediterranean shimmered a dark smoky indigo as the sun sank below a bank of amber cloud just above the horizon.

'I said we'd want dinner,' said Boyd, depositing their cases at the bottom of the bed without looking at her. 'Is that OK?'

'Fine,' she returned sweetly.

'I'm sorry about this.'

'Not to worry, ' she assured him, opening her case. 'Would you like first bath?'

'No, you go first. I think I'll go out for some air.' He grabbed his jacket and left the room as if it were on fire.

Humming to herself, Jonquil ran a deep steamy bath while she unpacked her case. She'd have to wear the white linen skirt again but she'd also brought a fuchsia-pink silk top as well as the one she'd worn last night, because she hadn't been able to make up her mind between them.

It had been too warm last night to bother about stockings, but it was cooler up here in the hills so she laid a pair out on the bed along with her ivory silk suspender belt, matching bra and French knickers.

She undressed and took the skirt into the bathroom with her in the hope that some of the creases in it would drop out in the steam. She spent a long time in the bath and then applied her make-up. Only when she heard him return to the room did she wrap herself in a towel and, with her damp hair waving around her bare shoulders, went out into the bedroom.

She made a shameless pretence of not expecting to find him there, gathering the towel more closely around her as he took in her state of undress and hastily averted his eyes.

'The bathroom's free,' she told him, standing in front of the mirror and drawing her comb through her hair, then deliberately letting the towel slip to the floor. She heard him gulp audibly as she bent down, picked it up and wound it back around herself, just as the bathroom door slammed behind him.

Jonquil dried her hair, then dressed in her ivory underwear and the silk top, waiting for him to finish in the bathroom so she could retrieve her skirt. When he eventually emerged in a black towelling robe, she was curled up on the bed flicking through a magazine.

She saw his eyes go to her long legs and the band of pale flesh above her stocking-tops. She stretched languorously and swung her feet to the floor before undulating across the room, conscious of his burning gaze on her silk-clad bottom.

She reappeared a minute later with her skirt, which she

163

proceeded to slip into, zip up and then smooth over her hips and belly before lifting a foot up onto the bed and adjusting one of her suspenders.

'I'll go and wait for you downstairs,' she said with a dazzling smile. Picking up her bag, she left the room.

The small bar was full of elderly people all chatting animatedly and several of them smiled at her as she ordered a dry sherry and took a seat at a table by the window. She could see her reflection in the darkened glass and decided to undo another button on her top to reveal the upper curves of her breasts, tinged with faint colour after her day in the sun.

The other guests began to drift into the dining room and she was alone by the time Boyd appeared, his hair still damp and his face set and rigid.

'Do you want another drink?' he asked abruptly.

'Why not? Another fino, please.'

She waited until he'd been served and then began to tell him about her day, talking gaily and apparently unperturbed by the way he was gazing blankly out of the window into the darkness beyond, not saying anything in reply.

Jonquil couldn't remember the last time she'd enjoyed herself so much. She hoped he was really suffering; it would pay him back for the number of times she'd tossed and turned through the night after he'd roused *her* to unfulfilled, red-hot passion.

When they moved through into the dining room, the waiter showed them to a table in the corner and immediately brought them a dish of mixed salad with spears of cold blanched asparagus arranged across it.

'Oh, good – I'm starving,' cried Jonquil, picking up a spear with one hand and the menu with the other so Boyd couldn't hide behind it. She sucked the tip of the asparagus between her full lips and proceeded to nibble daintily at it with little moans of delight that soon had him shifting uneasily on his chair.

Eventually taking pity on him, she passed him the menu, remarking, 'It's a bit limited, but it all sounds delicious.'

It *was* delicious and Jonquil relished every mouthful of her pistou, a kind of thick vegetable soup, followed by a chicken dish served with spicy potatoes.

Boyd, however, seemed to have lost his appetite and left half of his. There was a haunted look on his face and she noticed that he was drinking steadily and much faster than he usually did. She kept her own alcohol intake low, determined to keep a clear head.

After dinner, they lapsed into silence until he rose abruptly to his feet. 'I'm just going out for a walk,' he croaked.

'What a good idea – I'll come with you.'

She had to practically run to keep up with him as he strode swiftly from the hotel. Outside, a cool wind fanned her warm skin and they walked along the road below the hotel in silence for a while. She was conscious of the tension emanating from him and smiled to herself in the darkness.

Once back indoors she yawned and said, 'I'm exhausted; I think I'll go up.'

'Good idea,' he said immediately. 'I'm not tired – I'll be up later.'

'Goodnight.'

Once in the room she cleaned her teeth, sprayed herself with perfume and undid another button on her top before going back down to the bar. He was hunched over a drink and jumped when she appeared in front of him.

'There's something in the room – I heard it rustling under the bed. Please come and get rid of it,' she beseeched him. 'I think it might be a rat.'

'Unlikely,' he said, but he rose to his feet with an expression of resignation on his face and followed her upstairs. He got on his hands and knees and looked under the bed, then searched the rest of the room. 'There's nothing here,' he reassured her at last. 'You must have imagined it.'

He moved towards the door but she stepped in front of it. 'Please don't go,' she implored him. 'I know it'll come back as soon as I get undressed and then what will I do?'

'There's nothing here,' he repeated but, at the pleading look on her face, he thrust his hands in his pockets and sank onto one of the chairs. 'OK, I'll stay.'

Jonquil vanished into the bathroom with her nightdress. The nightdress was of peach silk, totally diaphanous and revealed more of her figure than it concealed. As she pulled it over her head in front of the mirror, she fervently hoped it would be enough to push Boyd over the edge.

It had thin shoestring straps and was cut low enough to expose a lot of her breasts. Her nipples were clearly visible through the fine material and a thigh-length split at one side showed off her left leg almost to the hip whenever she took a step.

She fluffed out her hair, pulled the front of the nightgown a little lower, then took a deep breath and opened the door.

He was still sitting where she'd left him and was obviously deep in thought – not happy ones, if the tormented expression on his face was anything to go by – but, as she crossed the room trying to look casual and unselfconscious, he automatically glanced up.

His strangled groan sounded as if it had been wrenched from deep inside him and his face was set in tortured lines as he asked hoarsely, 'Are you doing this on purpose?'

'Doing what?' she asked innocently, picking up her magazine and sliding between the sheets with a deliberate flash of creamy thigh.

He turned on his heel, strode away from her, then vanished into the bathroom and, a few moments later, she heard the shower going. She'd have put money on it that it was a cold one.

Hoping it wouldn't dampen his ardour too much, she discarded her magazine, switched off the bedside lamp and lay waiting for him with her eyes closed, her body suffused with languorous anticipation.

It was a long time before he came out, then she heard him moving around before eventually he got into bed and stretched out as far away from her as possible.

She waited a few moments, then slid across the expanse of smooth cotton sheet which lay between them and reached for him, feeling him go tense as she ran her fingers caressingly over the hard planes of his chest.

His hand closed over hers and the only sound was of his harsh breathing before he demanded from between gritted teeth, 'Are you trying to drive me out of my mind?' Every word sounded as though it had been wrenched out of him by force.

166

Her only reply was to nuzzle his neck, dropping teasing kisses down it, then nibbling gently at his shoulder. He swore vehemently, rolled her onto her back and then, when she attempted to wind her arms around his neck, grabbed her wrists and held them pinioned by her sides.

'Just what the *hell* are you playing at?' he growled. 'You told me in no uncertain terms never to touch you again and now you're coming onto me like a cat on heat. Are you intending to back off again as soon as I'm worked up? Is this to punish me for seven years ago?'

She could feel the hard length of his manhood against her thigh, branding her through the flimsy material of her nightdress as she murmured, 'Make love to me.'

In the darkness she could just make out the glitter of his eyes in his shadowy face as he glared down at her.

'What did you say?'

'Make love to me,' she repeated, ablaze with desire. She arched her back and pressed herself against him, in an agony of lust, the silence broken only by the sound of their ragged breathing.

'If you're leading me on only to call a halt in a few minutes, I won't make any attempt to control myself,' he warned her savagely. 'If you don't mean it, you'd better say so now, or it will be too late.'

In reply she freed her wrists, drew his head down and kissed him. The smouldering in her core burst into an inferno as his lean body covered hers; he brushed aside the fine fabric veiling her breasts and stroked them avidly.

Her nipples hardened into jutting peaks as he toyed with them, his lips hard and demanding on hers, his tongue claiming the velvet softness of her mouth with absolute possession.

His other hand glided down the curve of her hip to find the split in her nightgown and smooth over the satiny skin of her thigh, then moved slowly upwards to commence a more intimate caress which made her moan and open herself to him in mute invitation.

He found the swollen bud which was the centre of her pleasure and stroked it deftly, sending her spiralling swiftly upwards towards the peak of raw arousal. The blood surged hotly through her veins and she moaned again as his mouth left hers and kissed a moist path down to her breast.

He took her nipple between his lips and flicked his tongue backwards and forwards over it in a wickedly sensual movement. Jonquil was dimly aware of a tingling sensation in her fingertips and a demanding throbbing in her core, then an urgent heat swept over her and she cried out as she came in an unexpected explosion of pleasure.

It seemed that was all Boyd was waiting for, because before the hot waves of sheer erotic sensation had even begun to die down, he pushed her nightgown roughly upwards and positioned himself above her.

She cried out again as he entered her in one smooth thrust and commenced a fierce, undulating rhythm, carrying her along with him at a pace that left her dazed and breathless.

She clung to his shoulders, the blood coursing feverishly through her veins like molten lava, feeling herself being pushed inexorably towards further satisfaction, almost out of her mind with wanton pleasure.

There was a raw savagery about his lovemaking which took her beyond the limits of endurance in a way no other lover ever had.

When at last he groaned and his movements quickened, they came together in ferociously racking spasms which seemed to go on for an eternity and left them lying drained and sated in a tangle of entwined limbs.

Chapter Fourteen

When Jonquil woke up, her entire body felt languid and relaxed and there was a hot lingering pleasure between her thighs which was such an unaccustomed sensation that she was vaguely puzzled by it. It took her a few moments to come round and she was only dimly aware that she was lying within the circle of someone's arms.

Then it came back to her – it was Boyd holding her, Boyd who'd made love to her last night. The first time with desperate, urgent need and the second with an intensity which soon became an endless amorous exploration of each other's bodies which had gone on well into the early hours.

Her eyes fluttered open to see the dim light of dawn filtering through the curtains and she closed them sleepily again as she remembered how he'd kissed every inch of her skin.

His hands had moved over her soft yielding curves, caressing her intimately and sending her higher and higher up the steep slope of arousal until she'd begged him to take her again and give her the satisfaction she craved with every fibre of her body.

The memory made her wriggle voluptuously against him, her bottom nestling into his groin, with the result that his member hardened against her and one hand slid sleepily upwards to cover her breast, his lips nuzzling her neck.

She arched back against him, conscious of a faint ache in her muscles as he caressed her breasts and then her belly, until a moan escaped from between her parted lips.

'I can't get enough of you,' he muttered as his hand slid lower to cup her mound. He stroked her fleece until she was quivering with renewed lust, her female juices already gathering and trickling slowly from her to damp the fronds of hair which curled around her vulva.

169

She parted her thighs, bending one leg at the knee and pushing her bottom back against the granite-hard column of his erection. Two fingers slipped into her slick furrow, then continued inexorably upwards until they were moving arousingly inside her velvet-lined sheath, tracing the undulations of her internal muscles and making her squirm with delight.

Although it was cool in the room, she found herself bathed by carnal heat which spread through her body, dewing her cleavage and inner thighs with a fine film of perspiration. Boyd withdrew his fingers and spread the petals of her labia with both hands so she was completely open to him.

'Beautiful,' he breathed, before finding the swollen nub of her clit and squeezing it with a gently rhythmic pressure which sent ripple after ripple of hectic, tingling response through her.

She could hear a laboured gasping sound and it took her a few moments to realise that she was making it. Her total concentration was on the swirling vortex of sensation which had taken her over, the throbbing in her clit almost painful in its intensity.

Then, like a massive wave gathering and hanging apparently suspended in both time and motion, she knew her climax was only seconds away, but such endless seconds that it seemed an eternity before it crested and crashed over her in a dazzlingly explosion that shook her to her very core.

By the time the last eddies had surged, swirled and eventually retreated, she was weak and trembling and only dimly aware of Boyd's manhood – hot and hard – poised at the dripping entrance to her quim. Then he was inside her and he began to shaft her with long, slow strokes.

At first she was too drained to do more than lie quietly in his grasp but, as a renewed spark ignited in her loins, she began to move with him, slowly at first and then more vigorously.

A desire to take control of their lovemaking overcame her and, without speaking, she drew away from him, ignoring his grunt of protest. He lay on his back and she straddled him, positioning herself above his hugely erect phallus.

He placed his hands on her hips to steady her while she teased him by lowering herself an inch at a time, determined

170

to pay him back for the frustration she'd suffered in recent weeks.

When at last she was fully impaled on his rod, she rotated her pelvis slowly, feeling him throbbing inside her and sensing his eagerness to have her work him to his own release.

But Jonquil continued to use him for her own ends, riding him with voluptuous slowness, knowing that all the while his eyes were riveted to the bobbing swell of her creamy breasts with their coral nipples and that he was inflamed by the sight.

He tried to speed her up by thrusting his hips strongly upwards, but she was determined to take her time. She knew he was tempted to roll her onto her back and plunge frenziedly in and out of her, but pride prevented him.

The first fingers of lemon sunlight began to filter into the room, illuminating the chiselled planes of his face, now set in harsh lines as he struggled to control himself.

Smiling challengingly down at him, she began to caress her own breasts, her fingers drifting over the pale spheres and then teasing the terracotta thimbles to even harder points.

He groaned and rammed his pelvis up to meet a lazy downward push of hers, obviously driven wild by her teasing. She stopped her movements entirely and slid her finger between their bodies to find her tumescent bud and stroke it, sending ecstatic shivers feathering down her spine.

But doing that increased her own urgency and, even though she'd have liked to have kept him dangling for longer, her body seemed to have a will of its own and she found herself riding him hard, her red-gold hair tumbling around her shoulders in damp disarray.

She felt pierced to her core as she rose and fell on the bone-hard column filling her so satisfyingly. Her fast-approaching climax was like a swiftly gathering storm as she moved faster and faster, grinding herself against him to extract the last iota of sensation.

She heard him groan loudly, then his body went rigid, before he erupted powerfully into her in a boiling surge of release. There was a thundering in her ears and a dazzling flash of light behind her closed eyelids as she convulsed into the most powerful climax of her life, which spasmed through her until she thought she would lose consciousness from the sheer, mindless pleasure of it.

Later, they took a shower together and then went down to breakfast to find that all the other guests had already eaten and left for the day. They sat alone in the dining room, not saying much, while Jonquil nibbled on a sugary croissant and Boyd attacked a plate of scrambled eggs, mushrooms and fried potatoes with a ravenous appetite.

'Do you think we'll be able to fly out today?' she asked as they lingered over coffee.

'Who cares?' he returned. His eyes held hers with such intensity that she felt as though she was drowning in their dark blue depths as he continued, 'Seven years ago, I made the most stupid mistake of my life, but believe me when I say that I've paid for it, because there hasn't been a day since then that I haven't thought about you and wanted you. Can you ever forgive me?'

'Of course I can,' she murmured, then they both became aware that the waiter was hovering nearby, obviously hoping to clear the table.

'I think we'd better leave,' he said. 'I'll bet our fellow guests finished breakfast hours ago and he's cursing us for putting in such a late appearance.'

Once back in their room Jonquil was about to start packing, but Boyd cleared his throat, started to speak and then stopped.

'Is anything the matter?' she asked in concern, her heart suddenly plummeting as she wondered what he was about to say. What if he were about to tell her that last night had been great, but it hadn't meant he wanted to take up their relationship where they'd left off? Or if she'd completely misread the situation and Julie *was* still in the picture somewhere?

If it turned out he'd remained married to the other woman and was now hoping for a clandestine affair which wouldn't jeopardise his marriage, she didn't think she'd be able to stop herself from punching him.

'You know what the matter is,' he said at last.

'No, I don't,' she contradicted him.

His face hardened. 'What about Damon? Where does he fit into the picture now?'

'D . . . Damon,' she echoed, giddy with relief.

'Yes, you remember Damon – the man you're in love with. If this was just a fling to you and that as far as you're concerned things will be just the same as they were once we get back to London, you'd better tell me now.'

'Damon and I are finished,' she reassured him. 'I . . . I was never really in love with him – I just told you that because I was confused about my feelings and wanted to keep you at a distance.'

'Do you mean it?' he demanded.

'I haven't seen him for weeks,' she said truthfully. 'It's definitely over.'

He pulled her into his arms and kissed her, a long soul-searing kiss that set her ablaze for him again. They sank slowly onto the bed and Jonquil was just tugging his t-shirt free from his jeans when there was a knock on the door.

Boyd swore under his breath and they both sat hastily up and adjusted their clothing before he called, 'Come in.'

Paulo's sister stood on the threshold, holding a change of sheets and towels.

'You stay another night?' she asked, taking in their dishevelled appearance.

'Tempted though I am . . .' he murmured to Jonquil before raising his voice and addressing the Spanish woman. 'No, thank you. We'll be leaving soon.' She nodded and retreated, leaving the door wide open behind her. 'I think we'd better take that as a hint,' said Boyd reluctantly, 'and finish packing.'

Boyd's driver was waiting for them at Gatwick. It was early evening and the weather had turned bitterly cold. The heat and light of Spain already felt like a distant dream and Jonquil found it hard to believe it was only a few hours since they'd left it.

'I can't wait to make love to you again,' Boyd told her as they headed into London. 'Will you come and spend the night with me?'

'Yes,' she breathed, almost overcome by the intoxicating prospect of another night in his arms. 'But I'll need to go back to my place and get some clothes,' she added.

'That's okay – I have to go into work. I wish I didn't, but Saskia's away and there are a couple of things I need to check on. I'll get Dave to drop you off first, then he'll come back and pick you up later.'

After kissing each other lengthily, she scrambled out of the car and hastily let herself into the house, feeling the vicious wind cutting straight through her wool jacket.

She saw her answering machine was blinking and pressed the playback button as she flicked through her mail, none of which was of any interest.

'It's Jasper. I thought you'd be home by now, but your flight's probably been delayed. Call me as soon as you get in.' The message was followed by three more of increasing urgency. She was assailed by guilt as she realised that she'd been so caught up in her own affairs that she hadn't thought to phone and let him know she'd be away another night.

How could she have been so selfish? She felt even worse as she realised that she'd barely given his problems a thought until now and yet he was obviously hoping she'd still be able to come up with some way of getting him out of his predicament.

Picking up the phone she swiftly dialled his number.

'Where the hell have you been?' he demanded. 'I've phoned you several times – didn't you get my messages?'

'Yes, but only a minute ago. I'm sorry, but there was an air-traffic-controllers' strike and we were stranded in Spain for another twenty-four hours. I've only just walked in.'

'I've got to see you – can you come round?'

'Do you mean now?' she asked in dismay, the prospect of an intimate supper with Boyd and then hours spent in abandoned lovemaking receding.

'Of *course* I mean now.'

'Couldn't you come over here? I'll need to get a cab.'

'I'm well over the breathalyser limit, so I can't drive and I think someone's watching the apartment, so I daren't leave it.'

'All right. Give me an hour, I need to shower and change,' she sighed, thinking that he was really letting this get to him. She hung up, wishing the air-traffic strike had gone on much longer.

Just before she left, she phoned Boyd to tell him where she was going and to ask if Dave could pick her up from Jasper's.

'I was just about to call you.' The sound of his deep voice made her wish he was with her right at that moment. 'There's a problem at work and it looks as if I'm going to be here all night, sorting it out.'

Struggling not to be too disappointed, she managed to say, 'I'm sorry – I was looking forward to spending the night together.'

'Not as much as I was. I had plans for us,' he said regretfully, the tone of his voice leaving her in no doubt what sort of plans they were. 'Take care of yourself and I'll call you tomorrow.'

Jasper was in a bad way. Jonquil couldn't remember the last time she'd seen him unshaven. He was also fairly drunk and, by the haunted look in his eyes, planning to get drunker.

'You took your time,' he greeted her irritably, sloshing some more whisky into a smeary glass.

'Thanks a lot,' she flared. 'I've been hanging around Malaga airport most of the day, I'm cold and tired and the last thing I felt like doing was having to come all the way over here on such a freezing night, so the least you could do is say, "Hi, Jonquil, good to see you, how was your trip?"'

Jasper had the grace to look faintly ashamed. 'Sorry,' he said. 'How was your trip and can I get you a drink?'

'A glass of wine, if you have any.'

He produced a bottle of Côtes du Rhone and opened it with less than his usual expertise. Watching him struggle with the cork, Jonquil said, 'I'd lay off the whisky, if I were you – I think you've had enough.'

'I didn't ask you round so you could lecture me!' he snapped.

Jonquil picked up the coat which she'd just taken off and thrust her arms into the sleeves, not prepared to put up with his foul mood. She might as well go home and get an early night now she wasn't seeing Boyd.

'Sorry,' said Jasper. 'Don't take any notice of me. Someone's been following me around all day and I think they're parked across the road, watching the apartment.'

'Why would anyone do that?' she asked, puzzled.

'How should I know? To make sure I don't do a runner, I suppose. If it wasn't for Saskia, I'd be very tempted.'

Jonquil crossed to the window and drew back a corner of the curtain. It was true that there was a car parked on the other side of the road, but it was in the shadow of an over-hanging tree and it was impossible to see if anyone was in it.

'Are you sure you're not being paranoid?' she enquired.

'Of course I'm not being bloody paranoid. I've had three threatening phone calls since I last saw you and when I went out this morning someone had scratched, "Pay up or else" on the side of my car. Go and take a look if you don't believe me.'

'I believe you,' she said soothingly. He handed her an over-filled glass of red wine and she hastily took a gulp before she spilt it.

'Have you thought of any way of getting me out of this mess?' he demanded.

She shook her head. 'I'm sorry, I haven't come up with anything, yet.'

'If I don't get them off my back, Saskia's going to find out and then she'll leave me – I know she will.' He sounded so wretched that Jonquil went and put her arm around him.

'Why don't you tell her?' she suggested. 'She might be prepared to lend you the money.'

'I can't. She'd think I was a loser and tell me it was over.' He picked up his glass and drained it, then went to fill it with wine. 'I know,' he said, his face suddenly hopeful. 'You could ask Boyd to lend it you. It's obvious he really likes you and you could arrange to pay it back in monthly instalments – which I'd give you, of course.'

'No, I couldn't,' she retorted immediately, going cold at the idea.

What on earth would it look like if she asked Boyd for such a large sum, so soon after going to bed with him? It would come across as if she'd planned it and that the sex had just been to soften him up.

'Why not?' Jasper was obviously warming to the idea as he went on, 'He's loaded – it would just be small change to him. You can call him tonight and put it to him. I'll bet he could get it for you by—'

176

'Jasper – forget it,' she said more sharply than she'd intended, wondering whether to tell her brother that she and Boyd were an item. But then he'd probably think she'd have even more chance of borrowing the money and he was obviously too drunk to be able to focus on anything other than what seemed an easy solution to his problem.

She yawned, suddenly feeling exhausted. 'I'm shattered and I'm going to have to go,' she told him. 'I'll phone you tomorrow and we'll talk about it then. But, Jasper, please drop any idea of me borrowing it from Boyd – it's not a possibility, OK?'

She rang for a cab and, when it arrived, he went down with her to see her into it. As they walked past his BMW parked in the driveway, Jonquil noticed the threatening words scratched into the side of the otherwise immaculate paintwork, and shivered.

What if some harm came to him? Then she'd wish she'd put aside her own feelings and asked Boyd help. But surely these people wouldn't actually hurt her brother just because he owed them money?

After all, he knew who they were and if anything happened to him they must know he'd go to the police. Telling herself he'd just unnecessarily worked himself up into a state over the situation, she got into her taxi.

But as it drove off, she couldn't help but notice that the car which had been parked opposite Jasper's apartment was pulling away from the kerb.

Throughout the journey she kept turning round and was unnerved to see it stayed directly behind them. Was it coincidence or was someone actually following her and if so, why?

When the taxi stopped outside her apartment, the car drove past and she sighed with relief, but as she paid the driver she saw to her horror that it had pulled up again fifty yards down the road.

'Could you wait until I'm safely inside the house?' she asked the driver.

'OK, love,' he said obligingly. She hurried to the door and let herself quickly in, then raced upstairs and into her own apartment, double locking it and putting the chain on. She stood leaning against the door, breathing hard and wondering whether to call Boyd.

But she knew he was going to be busy all night and it didn't seem fair to burden him with her problems as well, particularly as it would mean telling him about Jasper's debt. Their new relationship was too fragile and precious to risk ruining it by acting rashly and without thinking things through and considering the consequences.

She went over to the sitting-room window and looked out, but couldn't see whether the car was still there. She got ready for bed, but sleep was a long time in coming.

Chapter Fifteen

The following day Jonquil went to look out of her window, but there was no sign of anyone watching the house and, with the winter sun streaming in and dispelling her fears, she wondered if she'd imagined that she'd been followed home from Jasper's.

She went out to buy some groceries, feeling ridiculously happy that she and Boyd were back together and then guilty because Jasper's life was in a mess and she didn't know how she could help him.

Maybe she should explain the situation to Boyd and then ask if he'd lend her the money. But she'd be taking a big risk that he'd think she'd planned the whole thing – particularly as *she'd* seduced *him* rather than the other way round.

What if she told him what had happened and then waited to see if he made the offer? But there was no reason why he should, particularly as it was Jasper's own fecklessness that had got him into debt.

The phone started ringing a few minutes after she got back from the shops and her knees went weak when she heard Boyd's deep voice on the other end.

'Did you get the problem sorted out?' she asked him.

'Yes, but I was there until five this morning. You'll never know how tempted I was to come straight round to your place instead of going back to my apartment and my lonely bed.'

'I wish you had,' she said truthfully.

'But then I wouldn't have got any sleep because there would have been better things to do. As it was, I had trouble going off because of the lascivious thoughts I was having.'

'Why don't you come round now?' she invited him, the blood surging through her veins at the thought of spending the afternoon between the sheets with the central heating turned up. Not that she'd even need it on, if they were making love; her temperature would be sky-high just from Boyd's close proximity.

'Don't tempt me, or I might just forget that I've got to find out exactly who was responsible for the problem I had to sort out last night. I prefer to leave that sort of thing to Saskia, but she's away, so I'm going to have to deal with it myself.'

'When will I see you?'

'This evening? I'm not sure what time I'll be through, but I'll ring you again, later.'

'Great,' she said happily.

'Shall I take you for a meal?'

'Why don't I make us something? It won't be anything special, but it would mean we didn't have to go out.'

'That sounds good to me. I don't think I'm going to be able to stop myself ravishing you the moment I walk through the door, so don't be wearing too many clothes.'

'How about a set of black lace lingerie?' she teased him.

'Not another word or I'll forget about work and break the speed limit on my way over.'

'With sheer black stockings and high heels,' she continued remorselessly. She heard his heartfelt groan and her breathing quickened at the erotic images that presented themselves of him making love to her while she was dressed so provocatively.

'Now there isn't a chance I'll be able to concentrate on business,' he told her ruefully. 'All I'll be able to think about will be you dressed like that with your endless legs and beautiful red hair tumbling around your shoulders.'

'It should give you the incentive to get here as soon as you can,' she said sweetly.

'I don't need any incentive,' he assured her. 'I've got to go – I'll call you later.'

In the early evening, she took out her delicate black lace underwear and put it on, then fastened her stockings and slipped her feet into a pair of high-heeled shoes before going to look at herself in the mirror.

The flimsy bra pushed her breasts upwards and together to give her a deep, creamy cleavage while the tiny panties barely covered her mound. The suspender belt around her narrow waist was indisputably sexy and the sheer stockings made the most of her long legs.

Remembering what he'd said about not wearing too many clothes, she slipped into a silk robe and belted it tightly around her waist, then opened it again to dab her cleavage and inner thighs with perfume.

She found that she was nervous about seeing him again and opened the wine so she could have a glass to calm herself down. At that moment the buzzer went and she hurried over to the intercom.

'It's me.' Just the sound of his voice was enough to make her feel overheated and she could feel herself becoming moist at the thought that within less than a minute she'd be in his arms.

She opened the front door and, as soon as he appeared at the top of the stairs, his dark hair ruffled by the wind, she leant back against the door frame and undid the belt of her robe so he could see what she was wearing underneath.

He closed the gap between them in three long strides, swung her into the apartment and slammed the door closed behind them before pushing her against the wall. His mouth swooped down on hers in a hard, demanding kiss while his hands explored her curves over the delicate black fabric of her lingerie.

Her robe fluttered to the floor and he scooped her breasts from their lacy cradle before bending his dark head and taking one coral nipple between his lips then commencing an erotic sucking that had her moaning with pleasure.

His other hand glided down her belly and over the triangle veiling her mound to delve between her thighs, which parted of their own volition.

He slipped his fingers inside her briefs and stroked the damp curls of her fleece, inhaling sharply as he felt how wet she already was. Deftly, he stroked her swollen bud, sending a tingling wash of heat over her and making her gasp.

Unable to wait another moment, Jonquil fumbled with his zip and drew out his hugely erect member. She sank to her knees and pressed a kiss on the glans, then flicked her tongue delicately over the ridge running down from it.

His manhood was hot and smooth against her lips as she trailed kisses down to the base, cupping his balls in her hand. She kissed her way back up the underside, then parted her lips to let the head slip between them to penetrate the moist cavern of her mouth.

She swirled her tongue around it, then commenced an erotic sucking while he buried his hands in her hair. She took it as far into her mouth as she could, keeping up the pressure with her lips, aware that his arousal was mounting fast.

Her own was like a tightly wound coil of heat high up in her sex, which was now slowly uncoiling to send tremors of sexual heat spiralling through her slender frame.

Reluctantly, she let his phallus slip from her mouth and rose sinuously to her feet to sashay provocatively into the sitting room.

Once there, she turned her back and drew her panties slowly down her hips. She heard his sharp intake of breath as the alabaster swell of her bottom came into view, then she allowed the flimsy garment to flutter to the carpet.

She hooked one leg over the sofa and lay along the back, gripping it between her knees, her derrière thrust alluringly upwards. His eyes devouring her, Boyd swiftly stripped off his clothes and mounted the sofa behind her.

He ran his hands along the curve of her spine, then bent to trail searing kisses across her buttocks. She felt the smooth throbbing glans of his penis butting against her slick labia, then, with one controlled plunge, he was inside her.

It was a hot and hectic coupling, both of them too excited to want to make it last. The lewd position added an erotic edge as he drove tirelessly in and out of her. Jonquil felt an urgent fluttering in her pelvic muscles then spasmed into a climax, crying out her pleasure. Boyd revved up for a few last rapid thrusts and then came too, his arm around her holding her tightly.

Jasper heard a noise and sat bolt upright in bed, straining to hear what it was that had woken him. For a few seconds he heard nothing, then the faint sound of someone moving around in his sitting room made him lever himself up and shake his head in an attempt to clear the alcohol fumes which were clouding his brain.

He got stealthily out of bed, shrugged quickly into his dressing gown and picked up the empty wine bottle from the chest of drawers.

For a brief moment his heart leapt as he wondered if it was Saskia back early and about to surprise him, but he dismissed the idea at once. Although he'd given her a key, he was sure she'd have phoned first.

The adrenalin pumping through his veins like quicksilver, he opened his bedroom door as silently as he could and stepped into the hall. Through the open door of the sitting room he saw the shadowy figure of a man, then the light snapped on, dazzling him.

'Hello, Jasper,' the man said. 'We need to have a talk.'

Jasper recognised the voice at once. It was Hogg, the man who'd slashed his tyre in the car park and there, held almost casually in his hand, was the same Swiss army knife.

'How the hell did you get in?' he demanded, considering his chances of being able to knock the knife out of the other man's hand with the wine bottle, before it made contact with his flesh.

'Easy,' grunted Hogg. 'Your locks are ancient and you didn't even have a chain on – not that that would have stopped me.'

'What do you want?'

Hogg moved closer but, instead of closing in on him, the man put the knife away and picked up a photo of Jonquil.

'Who's this?' he asked.

'What the bloody hell does that have to do with anything?' Jasper shook his head again, feeling the beginning of what promised to be a splitting headache and wishing he hadn't drunk so much.

'She was here yesterday,' commented the man. 'Nice-looking lady – is she your girlfriend?'

'My sister. Have you come to exchange pleasantries or to put the frighteners on me? You're wasting your time breaking into my apartment – I don't have the money, so I can't give it you.'

'You won't mind if I look around then?'

'Be my guest,' replied Jasper after a pause. His initial reaction had been to tell him to fuck off, but it occurred to him that if the other man searched the place, he'd see for himself there was nothing of value. He sank onto the sofa while Hogg went through his cupboards and drawers swiftly and methodically.

'Nice threads,' Hogg called from the bedroom. 'Pity there's not much of a market for second-hand clothes.' He reappeared after a couple of minutes and stood opposite Jasper. 'You don't *look* stupid,' he said, 'but you're behaving that way. What do you think's going to happen? That my boss is going to forget you owe him fifteen grand? You've got until seven tomorrow evening to come up with the dosh, and after that we're going to stop acting reasonable.'

'I don't know how often I have to say this,' returned Jasper wearily. 'I don't have the slightest hope of coming up with the money.'

Hogg raised his eyebrows and again Jasper noticed the way they met in the middle, as if he just had one long one running below his forehead.

'You'd better think of something and fast, even if it's only walking into a petrol station with a stocking over your face.' Hogg rose to his feet. 'Seven this evening, or you won't like what happens. I'll let myself out.'

Jasper put the phone down and ran his hand through his hair. That was it, then. He'd phoned every single friend and business acquaintance he'd ever had and asked for a loan, offering to pay it back at a much higher interest rate than financial institutions usually charged.

But, not surprisingly, he'd drawn a blank. Not that he'd been particularly optimistic when he'd embarked on the calls, but he was a desperate man and he felt he had to try every possible avenue.

There was nothing else for it; whether she wanted to or not, Jonquil was going to have to ask Boyd for the money. Picking up the phone, he dialled her number.

'It's Jasper,' he greeted her, then hurried on without giving her time to say anything. 'I had a visitor in the middle of the night. He broke into my apartment and made it very plain that

184

either I paid up, or he'd demonstrate a dozen different uses for a Swiss army knife.'

'Are you hurt?' she gasped in horror.

'No, but I will be the next time he drops by. My time's run out – either you borrow the money from Boyd or resign yourself to getting a call from the hospital to tell you I'm either in intensive care or the morgue.'

Jonquil's entire body went cold and she began to tremble. 'OK,' she whispered. 'He's coming round this evening – I'll ask him then.'

'That's not soon enough,' he told her, 'I need it by seven tonight.'

She rang Boyd's mobile number, but it was switched off, so she tried his secretary who told her he was away that morning but would be back in the early afternoon, if she wanted to phone again then.

Thinking that what she had to say would be better in person, Jonquil decided to go down to Docklands and wait for him there. But what she hadn't anticipated was not being able to gain access to the building as she didn't have an appointment. It was too cold in the chilly wind to stand still for long so she wandered off, keeping her eyes open for him.

She walked further than she'd intended and had just turned round and was retracing her steps when she saw his limo approaching the building from the opposite direction. She quickened her pace, but she was still quite a distance away when she saw Boyd helping a child out and then a woman.

It couldn't be. But it was. There, unmistakably, was her erstwhile rival Julie and a little boy of around three or four who *had* to be their son. Julie looked much as Jonquil remembered her, a little plumper perhaps, but still absolutely gorgeous.

Jonquil stopped dead and stared at them, the blood turning to ice in her veins. As she watched, the two adults each took one of the little boy's hands and swung him up every step in turn, making him shout with laughter.

When they reached the doors leading into the building, Julie let go of her son's hand and took Boyd's free arm, then stood on tiptoe and said something into his ear.

It was her turn to be swung off her feet, then Boyd hugged and kissed her enthusiastically. Jonquil didn't think she'd ever witnessed a scenario which screamed 'happy family!' as much as this one did.

Seething with fury, she turned and walked rapidly away.

'I'm sorry, Jasper; I can't get the money for you and that's final.'

It was early evening and Jonquil had at last got round to calling her brother after an afternoon boiling with rage at Boyd's perfidy. How could she have been so stupid as to make the same mistake twice? Hadn't the past taught her anything?

'You've got to,' Jasper urged her. 'Boyd's my only hope.'

'You don't understand. Something's happened and now he's the last man on earth I'd ask a favour of.'

'What's happened?' he demanded.

'I don't want to talk about it.'

'You can't do this to me,' he said desperately.

'*I'm* not doing anything to you. This is something you've done to yourself,' she pointed out sharply and then felt ashamed of herself. Telling Jasper it was his own fault he was in this stupid mess wasn't going to help the situation. 'You're going to have to ask Saskia. I'm sure she'd be able to get her hands on the money.'

'I can't.'

'Well, I'm not going to ask Boyd. I'm sorry, but that's just the way it is. I've got to go – I'll call you tomorrow.'

By the time Boyd rang her buzzer that evening, Jonquil had got herself under control. Pale but composed, she said, 'Come on up,' and waited in the hall for him to arrive.

'Dave will deliver dinner in about half an hour,' he greeted her cheerfully. 'I hope you can wait that long, but there's this to be going on with.' He deposited a bottle of champagne on the hall table. When he tried to kiss her, she backed away and went into the sitting room. 'What's the matter?' he asked, looking concerned.

'Nothing much, unless you count the fact that I've just

discovered the man I'm involved with has a whole other life he hasn't thought to mention to me,' she spat.

'What do you mean?' There was a puzzled frown on his face.

'I mean that I saw you at lunchtime with Julie and a little boy I can only imagine is your son.'

'And that's it – you saw me outside the building with Julie and Felix and have now decided I've a secret life.'

'You've never once mentioned her to me, so I drew the obvious conclusion she was out of the picture,' she pointed out acidly.

'If you want to know why I've never mentioned her to you, I thought that she might still be a sensitive subject – I was obviously right.'

'Sensitive subject!' hissed Jonquil. 'You bet she's a sensitive subject! I'm sure there are plenty of women out there who wouldn't mind playing second fiddle to a wife, but I'm not one of them. I have to hand it to you. You've got her well tucked away somewhere – she barely impinges on your life in London at all. I could tell just by looking at her that you're keeping her happy and that she doesn't have the least idea about your illicit liaisons – because I'd put money on it that I'm not your only bit on the side. You must cover your tracks damn well.'

A muscle began to go next to his mouth and his face looked as though it had been carved from ivory. He started to speak, stopped and then ground out from between clenched teeth, 'Seven years and nothing's changed, has it? I really thought that we were back together for good, but I see that you're just the same as you were then, consumed by irrational jealousy. I made a mistake all those years ago, I've admitted it and tried to apologise, but you just can't let go of the past, can you?'

'I'd hardly call objecting to you being a married man being unable to let go of the past!' she flung at him. 'You'd better leave – we're through!'

She turned her back and stormed towards the door.

'You didn't trust me then and you still don't,' he said in a low, harsh voice which chilled her to the core. 'That's no basis for a relationship.'

Jonquil whirled round to face him. 'It's the fact that you're

187

a cheating, conniving, two-faced son-of-a-bitch that means there's no basis for a relationship. Get out of my apartment!'

Almost incandescent with rage, she stalked into the hall and wrenched open the front door. He strode past her without looking at her, leaving her to slam the door behind him as hard as she could.

Chapter Sixteen

Emotionally drained by the events of the day, Jonquil fell into a deep sleep and didn't wake up until midmorning, conscious of a feeling of shattering betrayal.

Shortly after lunch she gave up the struggle of trying to work and decided to go out for a brisk walk. On her way back she gradually became aware of a feeling of unease and glanced behind her, wondering if anyone was following her. But the pavement was empty except for an elderly couple.

As she fitted her key in the lock she felt the same uneasy prickle feathering down her spine and glanced over her shoulder, but there was no one in sight.

She made herself a cup of coffee and then phoned Jasper, having decided to try to persuade him that the wisest course of action was for him to tell Saskia about the whole mess and hope she'd understand and lend him the money. But he wasn't in so she left a long message on his answerphone, urging him to make a clean breast of it.

She knew only too well what damage secrets could do to a relationship.

When her buzzer went later that afternoon, Jonquil's heart leapt. Was it Boyd come to tell her it had all been a mistake and he wasn't really still married to Julie?

'Hello – who is it?' she asked.

'It's Nadine,' said an unfamiliar female voice. 'We met at Jasper's, last week.'

Nadine. The voluptuous brunette who worked at the casino. What on earth was she doing here?

'Come up,' Jonquil invited her, suddenly sick with anxiety. 'What's the matter? Is Jasper all right?' she demanded before

Nadine had even reached the top of the stairs.

'Something's happened,' the other woman told her. 'He sent me to get you.'

'Is he hurt? Where is he?' Jonquil gabbled, shrugging frantically into her coat.

'We'd better hurry – I'll take you to him.'

Jonquil followed Nadine down the stairs and found a dark grey car pulled up in the driveway, a man behind the wheel. Jonquil scrambled into the back and struggled to fasten her seat belt saying, 'What happened?'

'You'll see for yourself when we get there,' Nadine replied.

'He . . . he's not dead is he?'

'Of course not – it's nothing like as serious as that,' the dark-haired woman reassured her.

Jonquil knew she'd never forgive herself if anything had happened to him. Better that she should have crawled to Boyd on her hands and knees than that Jasper should have been hurt in any way.

But somehow, at the back of her mind had always been the thought that he was getting things out of proportion and that in the end the casino would have to give him time to pay. Now, it looked as if she'd been naive to think that way.

The journey seemed endless, but eventually they drove down a ramp into an underground car park belonging to a block of luxury apartments in a converted warehouse on the banks of the Thames.

She climbed hastily out and followed Nadine and the man to the lift where she got her first proper look at him and felt a twinge of unease at his unprepossessing appearance. His eyebrows met so thickly in the middle that it looked as though he only had one and he was almost as wide as he was tall.

On the top floor, Nadine led the way across a high-ceilinged foyer then rang the bell on a beamed wooden door.

'You managed to get her here, then,' said the man who opened it. 'Bring her in.'

Once inside Jonquil looked frantically around. 'Where's Jasper?' she asked.

He looked her coolly up and down, his eyes lingering briefly on her breasts before saying, 'I haven't a clue, sweetheart.'

'W . . . what do you mean?' Jonquil asked in bewilderment, thinking she must have misunderstood.

'Come on through and I'll explain,' the man said.

'Explain now!' she flared, but he ignored her and vanished through an archway to her right. To her annoyance, the man with the thick eyebrows took her arm and propelled her into an airy penthouse with floor-to-ceiling windows.

'What on earth do you think you're doing?' she demanded, trying to shake free. 'Let go of me!'

'Let her go.' At the other man's words Eyebrows released her, while Nadine draped her coat onto a chair and sashayed over to a coffee percolator on an antique oak side table. Jonquil noticed that both men's eyes were riveted to her swaying backside.

'Coffee?' Nadine enquired, looking at Jonquil.

'No, I don't want coffee!' she retorted. 'I want to know where Jasper is.'

'Let me introduce myself,' said the man who wasn't Eyebrows. 'You can call me Mr B – that way, it's safer for everyone.'

He looked to be in his mid-forties and had a thick thatch of curly salt-and-pepper hair, small eyes and a nose that had obviously been broken at some stage because it was badly crooked.

He was wearing a grey suit in some sort of shiny fabric, while gold jewellery glinted at his throat, wrists and on his fingers. His appearance didn't inspire any confidence in Jonquil and, if it hadn't been for Nadine's presence, she'd have been very frightened.

'Nadine tells me that you know about your brother's gambling debt,' Mr B went on. 'I'm a business associate of the organisation that owns the casino and I'm responsible for collecting it.'

Nadine placed a cup of coffee on a small table next to where Jonquil was standing. 'There you go,' she murmured, adding a bizarre air of domesticity to the unreal scenario.

'If I had the money or could borrow it, I'd already have done it,' Jonquil told him desperately, 'but I haven't been able to. Jasper's tried to as well, but neither of us have the type of

191

security necessary to raise that sort of loan. If you'll just give him time, he'll pay you back in instalments.'

Mr B accepted a cup of coffee from Nadine and took a noisy gulp before looking at Jonquil.

'Anyone who wants to badly enough can get their hands on money – it's just a question of using sufficient imagination. Your brother needs an incentive and you're going to provide it.'

Jonquil was alarmed to see Nadine leave the room and even more alarmed to see Eyebrows taking an evil-looking knife from his pocket. Fear lanced through her like long shards of glass. Surely they weren't planning to kill her because Jasper owed them some money?

She stepped back, looking wildly around for some means of escape. Moving fast for such a bulky man, Eyebrows grabbed her shoulder, then got his arm around her neck from behind, holding her powerlessly captive.

With his other hand he pressed the cold steel of the razor-sharp blade painfully against her throat, making her moan with fear and claw frantically at the ham-like arm around her neck.

She could scarcely believe it when Mr B produced a camera and stood for a moment framing up a photo of them as if they were a couple at a birthday celebration.

'I'm using flash,' he told Jonquil, 'so try not to jump or Hogg might cut your pretty white neck, and we wouldn't want that would we, sweetheart? Hogg – loosen your grip, you don't want to choke the lady.'

'Sorry, boss,' grunted Hogg, relaxing the iron band pinioning her helplessly against him. Mr B took a shot and waited for it to develop, humming tunelessly to himself, then examined it critically.

'What do you think?' he asked, showing it to the other man.

'She doesn't look scared enough,' was Hogg's opinion.

'Try and look as though he's just about to cut your throat,' Mr B advised her in a matter-of-fact tone, as if the possibility might not have crossed her mind of its own volition.

Almost faint with terror, she was barely aware of him taking another snap. 'This'll do nicely,' he said as soon as the image was visible. 'Let her go.'

She slumped into a chair, her hand at her throat, while Hogg put his knife away and sat down to finish his coffee. Nadine reappeared at that moment carrying a plate of biscuits, which she offered to Jonquil first.

Jonquil automatically shook her head, feeling as though she must be going mad, while Mr B inspected the selection before taking a chocolate wafer and patting Nadine absently on the bottom. Hogg plumped for a lemon puff and they crunched in unison for a couple of minutes.

'Are you all right?' Nadine asked her. 'You've gone a bit pale.'

'Oh I'm fine thanks,' she managed to say in a trembling voice. 'I spent the journey here terrified my brother had been badly injured, then I was half-choked to death and just to add the finishing touch, I had a knife held to my throat. I've rarely felt better.'

Nadine rounded on Hogg. 'You big oaf,' she snapped, her sloe-dark eyes flashing. 'You don't know your own strength.' To Jonquil's amazement he looked cowed.

'Sorry,' he mumbled. He turned to Jonquil. 'I didn't mean to hurt you.'

'You'd better get going,' Mr B advised him. He looked across at Jonquil. 'Any idea where your brother is, this afternoon?'

'No, and I wouldn't tell you if I had,' she retorted.

'It would be in his best interests if you did, sweetheart,' he pointed out. 'Hogg just wants to show him the photo to motivate him into coming up with the dosh.'

'How?' she demanded.

'What he does to get his hands on it is nothing to do with me,' he told her, selecting a jammy dodger from the plate and taking a bite. 'In fact, it's better if I don't know.' Hogg gulped the last of his coffee and left.

'How long are you planning to keep me here?' Jonquil asked angrily.

'Until he's paid up. Don't worry – no one's going to hurt you. We'll have a meal sent in from the restaurant round the corner and there's a lovely room ready for you – it's not as though we've locked you in the cellar or anything.'

Nadine got to her feet. 'Why don't I show you to your room?'

she suggested. Jonquil followed her along a corridor and into a thickly carpeted bedroom done out in shades of peach.

'It has its own bathroom,' Nadine told her. 'I've put a toothbrush and toothpaste in there and some toiletries. If there's anything you need that I've forgotten, just ask.'

'I thought you were a friend of Jasper's,' Jonquil accused her. 'What are you doing mixed up in this?'

'I *am* a friend of Jasper's and you ought to be damn grateful I'm here.' She sat down on the bed before continuing, 'He's lucky he hasn't been beaten to a pulp and left in a back alley somewhere – he's had enough warnings. Mr B only uses violence as a last resort, but he's almost lost patience. This is Jasper's final chance to get hold of the money, but don't worry – they won't hurt you. They'll let you go tomorrow, whatever happens.'

'Am I supposed to find the idea of my brother being beaten to a pulp reassuring?'

'No, of course not, but Jasper's been a fool. I warned him over and over again not to play the tables – there's only one winner in the end – but he wouldn't listen.'

'But you work there,' Jonquil accused her.

'Yes, but that doesn't mean I think gambling's a smart thing to do.'

'Are you . . . are you in a relationship with Mr B?'

Nadine got up from the bed and began to fiddle with her hair in the dressing-table mirror.

'We're seeing each other, yes.'

'How can you, when you know what he's capable of?'

She turned to face Jonquil, a defiant expression in her dark eyes. 'He's a very generous man and he's always been OK with me. Usually I don't get involved with his business dealings and, if I hadn't been fond of Jasper, I wouldn't have had anything to do with this. I've pulled out all the stops to keep him from being hurt, but I've done everything I can, now.'

She went towards the door then paused with her hand on the handle. 'Hogg was watching Jasper's apartment to see if he had a girlfriend they could put the frighteners on. When he found out who you were, they decided you'd do. They came up with the idea of kidnapping you but I offered to get you here, rather than having Hogg drag you into the car by brute force and frightening you half to death. So don't you look down your nose at me – I'd much rather have nothing to do with any of this.'

'I'm sorry,' said Jonquil. 'I'm just completely out of my depth. Couldn't you help me get out of here, and I'll find Jasper and get him to disappear until we've somehow managed to find the money?'

Nadine shook her head. 'Sorry, no. Mr B would know it was me who'd helped you and I'm not getting on the wrong side of him. It's down to Jasper now – it's his stupid mess, after all.'

She left the room saying, 'Come and have a drink whenever you're ready.'

When Jasper returned to his apartment in the late afternoon he found Hogg parked outside. Resisting the temptation to drive off again, he got out of the car and walked over to the other man.

'I'm surprised you haven't broken in and made yourself comfortable while you were waiting,' he said, his hand tightening on the hammer handle he'd taken to carrying in his overcoat pocket. He didn't fancy his chances against someone with the build of a pit bull, but he wasn't about to go down without a fight.

Without saying a word, Hogg showed him the photo.

Jasper felt the blood draining from his face as he looked at it, then a red flash of fury exploded across his brain and he reached through the open car window, hooked his hands in the other man's collar and half-dragged him out.

'If you've hurt her, I'll fucking kill you,' he roared. He was barely able to get the words out for the rage that consumed him. 'Where is she, you bastard?'

Hogg's shoulders were too broad to pass through the gap and he struggled frantically to escape the punishing grip twisting his collar and cutting off his air supply.

At last he managed to wrench free, shoved Jasper away, and sank back into his seat. He was panting for breath, his face an unhealthy shade of magenta and his eyes popping wildly out from under his single eyebrow.

As Jasper regained his balance and tried to grab him again, Hogg hastily pressed the button to close the window until there was only an inch left open.

'I'll call round to collect the money at eleven tomorrow morning,' he wheezed. 'Don't do anything stupid like calling the police, because Mr B has a contact there and he'll know immediately if you report it; then it'll be worse for your sister.'

He put the car into gear and drove off at speed. Jasper raced back to his BMW, planning to follow him, but the other man had a good start and by the time Jasper reached the main road, the grey car had vanished.

Sick with fear, he took the steps up to his apartment two at a time, burst in and began to rummage through his papers for Gavin's work number. Luckily the other man was in.

'That offer you made – the money for the new software development – is it still open?' he demanded, cutting across Gavin's cheerful greeting.

'As far as I know it is, but I'd have to check with Simpson,' he said, sounding disconcerted.

'This is the deal. I'll get you a copy of the disc by first thing tomorrow and I want fifteen thousand pounds in cash when I hand it over. Go and see Simpson and phone me back. I'm at home. And Gavin, there's no negotiation on this. Those are the terms – take it or leave it.'

'All right,' Gavin sounded puzzled. 'But don't you want the job as well?'

'Fuck the job. Just go and talk to Simpson.'

'I think he's in a meeting.'

'Then get him out of the bloody meeting! If you don't get back to me within ten minutes, I'll take the offer elsewhere.'

'OK, OK, no need to get ratty,' Gavin grumbled. 'I'll go and speak to him.'

It was undoubtedly the strangest evening Jonquil had ever spent in her life. At around seven, she emerged from her room, deciding that the more she knew about what was going on, the better chance she'd have of escaping.

'Hi,' said Nadine, as she went into the sitting room to find the three of them watching a video of a film that hadn't even

196

had a cinema release yet. 'Do you want a drink?'

'A glass of wine, please,' she said, hoping it might help steady her nerves. Hogg was back and she forced herself to speak to him. 'Did you find Jasper?'

'I found him, all right – he half-strangled me to death when I showed him the photo,' complained Hogg, rubbing his throat. 'Your brother wants to watch that temper of his.'

Usually sickened by violence of any kind, Jonquil felt a surge of savage satisfaction at the thought.

'Don't worry, sweetheart, he's probably in an off-licence with a stocking over his face right at this moment,' commented Mr B.

'Mind you, he'll have to do at least half a dozen to make fifteen grand,' said Hogg reflectively. 'If not more.'

'Do you want to see the restaurant menu, Jonquil?' Nadine interjected, glaring at them. About to refuse, Jonquil decided that the appearance of being resigned to her situation might make it easier for her to escape and took the proffered menu. She couldn't be bothered to read it properly and ordered at random.

Nadine jotted down their orders and went over to the phone. 'And get a load of chips to go with that,' Mr B called after her. 'We don't want any more of that potatoes *dauphinoise* crap.'

'They were bleedin' 'orrible,' agreed Hogg.

Although she could barely bring herself to speak to Mr B, Jonquil wanted a look around to see if a way out presented itself – there must be a fire escape or something.

She forced a smile on her face and said, 'This is a beautiful penthouse – and what a great view.'

'I can open all those windows and it's like being on a boat on the river,' he informed her proudly, putting his arm around her waist and guiding her over to them. 'Do you want the tour?'

'Yes – if it's not too much trouble,' she said pulling free, thinking that if he touched her again she might not be able to stop herself thumping him.

'It's no trouble,' he said expansively. 'Right this way.'

But the tour made it clear that the only way out was through the front door. That, or leaping off the terrace into the Thames a frighteningly long way below. When she asked Mr B whether there was a fire escape, trying to sound as if her question was prompted solely by innocent curiosity, he burst out laughing.

'Sure – do you want to see it?'

She nodded and he pushed open the door to what was obviously the master bedroom. It was dominated by a huge bed covered in a fake fur throw – or at least, Jonquil hoped it was fake.

A pair of handcuffs were attached to the bedstead, the wall opposite was one vast mirror and another mirror had been fixed to the ceiling directly overhead, all indicating that Mr B took his bedtime pleasures seriously.

'Great, huh?' he asked as she stopped just inside the threshold. He draped a heavy arm around her shoulders and she stepped quickly away from him.

'Mm,' she said faintly; the way he kept touching her was making her feel ill.

'There's the fire escape,' he told her, indicating the window and giving her hip an annoying squeeze. 'If you were thinking of escaping in the dead of night, you'd have to come tiptoeing through here – although I suppose I'd better lock you in your room, when we turn in,' he added.

Thinking that she'd never formed part of such a bizarre quartet in her life, Jonquil took her place at the antique refectory table for dinner. Nadine passed round the foil cartons holding their gourmet dinners and Mr B poured champagne for himself and the two women while Hogg had a beer.

Mr B was an expansive host and kept urging Jonquil to drink her champagne, of which she only took the occasional sip. She picked at her meal while he kept up a flow of conversation, with Nadine interjecting the occasional admiring comment and Hogg munching steadily away across the table.

'This is nice, isn't it?' commented Mr B, as he helped himself to another pile of chips. 'We ought to entertain more often, Nadine, sweetheart. Perhaps Jonquil would like to come to our Christmas party, once we've got this little bit of business behind us.'

Thinking that if she had anything to do with it, he'd be spending Christmas behind bars, Jonquil didn't reply.

It was when she went back to her room to use the bathroom

after dinner, that she spotted the key on the outside of her bedroom door. The sight triggered off a memory of a childhood game she and Jasper used to play.

A thoughtful expression on her face, she went back to join the others, praying they'd go to bed early.

Then she'd make her escape.

Saskia ate dinner alone in the hotel restaurant. It had been a hectic day and she hadn't got back until after nine. As she ate she thought about Jasper and then found herself crossing and uncrossing her legs as carnal heat suffused her loins.

If only he were here with her and they could go up to her room. She'd mentally devised an erotic scenario which she thought he'd get off on as much as she would, but she still needed a couple of props which she hadn't been able to find.

She could feel a fluttering in her female core and her clit was throbbing hungrily and pressing against the damp crotch of her panties. As soon as she was alone she'd have to pleasure herself or she'd explode.

She was having coffee while trying to read through some notes when she became aware that a man at another table was staring at her. He had glossy brown hair, an expensive suit and the type of brutish handsomeness that reminded her of Terry, the escort. He was sitting with a sexy-looking redhead in a low-cut black dress, who was displaying a vast acreage of tanned cleavage. He rose to his feet and came over.

'Me and my friend thought you looked a bit lonesome and wondered if you'd like to join us for a drink.'

'No thank you,' she said icily, but the redhead came over too and sat down next to her.

'You're very beautiful,' she said in a husky voice. Her cleavage was mesmerising and Saskia found herself wondering if her naked breasts would be as full and firm as they looked, or whether they owed their luscious contours to a bra.

She had large hazel eyes and a sulky pouting mouth painted a glossy coral. Saskia suddenly had a mental image of her taking her companion's manhood between her luscious lips and sucking it until he—

She became belatedly aware that the man was speaking to

her in a low, insinuating tone of voice.

'. . . get together and have some fun,' he ended.

Having missed the beginning of what he'd said, she murmured, 'Sorry – what was that?'

'I was suggesting that the three of us should take a bottle of champagne up to our room and have some fun.'

Saskia let her gaze wander over him, wondering if she'd understood him correctly. Was he seriously suggesting a threesome? By the lascivious expression on his face, it appeared he was. She considered it for a moment. She wasn't averse to going both ways, if the woman was attractive enough – it wouldn't be the first time. The man looked fit and athletic and they were obviously offering a night of what promised to be hot no-strings sex. Maybe it was just what she needed.

'All right,' she said, 'but I decide what happens – OK?'

The woman licked her lips and smiled seductively. 'I'm Mel and this is Ed.'

'I'll get the champagne,' the man told them. 'You two go up – but don't start without me.'

Mel, it seemed, had other ideas and once they were alone in the lift, she wound her hand in Saskia's blonde hair and kissed her full on the mouth, her musky perfume wreathing itself around them both. In their opulently appointed room, she smiled provocatively.

'Shall I undress?'

'Just the frock, for now.'

Beneath the skintight dress, Mel was alluringly attired in a black basque which laced down the front. Her fox-red fleece wasn't veiled by any panties and was exotically framed by ribbon suspenders which were holding up sheer black stockings.

She turned her back on Saskia to toss her dress onto a chair and displayed the curvaceous moons of her pale buttocks. Saskia swallowed, immediately in the grip of a surge of excitement which left her breathless. Already, the permutations of how they might pass the next few hours were crowding into her mind, jostling for prominence as she considered them all.

She went over to the mirror to unpin her hair from its sleek chignon, then discarded her saffron wool suit and black silk shirt. Underneath she was wearing a cream silk camisole with matching panties and a suspender belt.

She approached Mel who drew her into a seductive embrace, her full breasts pushing arousingly against Saskia's own. Slowly, Saskia unlaced the basque to reveal ripe breasts with prominent nipples like rosehips. It was obvious that they didn't need any support because they remained high and firm as the basque fell apart on either side of them.

They sank onto the bed together while Saskia delved between the other woman's legs, wanting to gauge both her level of excitement and receptiveness to the intimate caress.

Mel's vulva was coated by copious amounts of dewy moisture and, judging by the way she parted her thighs in salacious invitation, she was ready to explore all the carnal highways and byways on offer.

Saskia stroked the slick folds of her labia, sliding two fingers high up inside her and feeling the other woman's internal muscles clenching around them. She located the plump triangle of her clit and stroked it, provoking a sigh of pleasure in response.

The door opened and Ed came in carrying the wine in one hand and three glasses in the other. He grinned at the lewd tableau that met his eyes and said, 'I thought I told you not to start without me. Someone's going to be punished for this.'

He busied himself filling the glasses, shrugged off his jacket and settled into an armchair to watch. It had been a while since Saskia had been with a woman and she enjoyed refamiliarising herself with soft female curves and smooth skin, so different from a male body.

She took one of Mel's hard nipples between her lips and flicked her tongue against it, then sucked softly, her fingers continuing to stroke her clit. Mel moaned and her head fell back on the pillow, her eyes closing. Her breathing was ragged and Saskia could tell she was about to come. She squeezed the slippery nub and rubbed it rhythmically between her finger and thumb, just the way she liked to do to herself.

'Aaah – oh yes, yes,' moaned Mel, then her voluptuous body shuddered and she cried out as she came.

Saskia rose gracefully from the bed and went to help herself to a drink. Ed pulled her onto his lap and fondled her breasts through the silk of her camisole as she sipped her champagne. She could feel the hard ridge of his manhood under her bottom and rubbed herself on it, bearing down so it would stimulate her sex through her panties.

'How are you going to punish us?' she murmured in his ear, as Mel got off the bed, allowing them both a glimpse of her coral quim as she swung her legs to the floor. Saskia was interested to see what he'd come up with and was quite prepared to veto his suggestions if they didn't meet with her approval.

'Who made the first move?' he asked.

'Mel.'

'Then I think she deserves a spanking.'

As the sight of Mel's luscious orbs had roused in Saskia a desire to administer just that for the pleasure of watching them become splodged with pink, she nodded. 'I think so, too, but first I want you to bring me off with your mouth.'

She rose from his lap and peeled her panties down her long legs, then went to sit in the armchair opposite him, thighs widely splayed. He sat between them while Mel came and perched on the arm of the chair and began to caress Saskia's honey-skinned breasts with a slender hand.

Ed's tongue was long and muscular. He plunged it into Saskia's vulva and began to lick out every fold and furrow, stabbing arousingly at her clit from time to time and sending hot tingling excitement coursing through her veins.

Warm moisture gathered and trickled out of her, making the chintz seat of the chair beneath her damp and sticky. Ed located the whorled entrance to her hidden inner chamber, swirled his tongue around it and then thrust it into her as far as it would go.

She gasped and then was silenced as Mel's mouth came down on hers and they kissed endlessly, the redhead's hands still moving over her breasts.

Ed was skilled in the use of his lips and tongue, sucking, nibbling and lapping away with a will. Saskia felt a wave of heat washing over her, then she convulsed into a heady climax which crested and crashed around her in a series of ecstatic spasms.

Ed sat back on his heels, his fleshy face shiny with her juices, before getting to his feet and pouring more wine.

'Bend over the back of the chair,' Saskia directed Mel. She obeyed, her curvaceous hemispheres thrust provocatively towards the two of them.

'Legs wider apart,' directed Ed, slipping his heavy leather belt free and winding the buckle end around his hand. Saskia didn't like the look of it – she enjoyed using one of her own supple belts on Terry, but she never put any real force behind the blows. This one looked as if it would leave painful weals.

'*I'm* spanking her,' she said determinedly. 'You can screw her afterwards while I watch.'

He dropped the belt with some reluctance and sat on the end of the bed. The plump leaves of Mel's sex were clearly displayed, the swollen nub of her clitoris protruding, a thin trickle of female honey already running down her inner thighs and soaking into her stocking-tops.

Saskia fondled the succulent globes, running her fingers down the cleft between them and circling the tiny furled bud of her anus. She pinched Mel's clit, provoking a squeal of surprise, then stepped back and raised her hand. She brought it down briskly, making a satisfying cracking noise.

She heard Ed gulp as she slapped her again, working her way gradually downwards, observing the pink marks she left with salacious satisfaction. Mel's buttocks bounced and the occasional cry escaped her, but it was obvious from the way she was grinding her mound against the back of the chair that she was getting off on it as much as the other two.

Saskia smacked her lewdly across her vulva, feeling the heat and wetness of the other woman's sex against her hand. Glancing behind her, she saw that Ed had removed his trousers and was holding his massive erection.

She moved away and he advanced on Mel, saying to Saskia as he positioned himself, 'When I've fucked her, I'm going to tan your gorgeous little hide with my belt and then fuck you until you beg for mercy.'

Saskia's green eyes narrowed. Being beaten with a belt wasn't her idea of exciting – dishing it out was one thing but she didn't like being on the receiving end. She suddenly decided that she didn't want him to fuck her either – she wanted Jasper to. She'd had her fun, but now she was ready to leave.

Coming to a swift decision, she decided to check out and drive back to London. She'd phone Jasper and tell him she was on her way, perhaps murmuring a few deliciously obscene suggestions so he'd be hot and ready for her.

Ed drove into Mel, bending over her and squeezing her breasts as he pistoned in and out, his buttocks flexing. Unobserved by the other two, Saskia slipped into her clothes and then picked up the belt.

Winding it around her hand, she took aim and lashed him across the backside with it. He let out a yell and swore, but he was too far gone to disengage himself from Mel and exact revenge.

Smiling to herself, Saskia strode across the room and let herself out.

Chapter Seventeen

By midnight, when no one was showing any sign of going to bed, Jonquil couldn't stand it a minute longer. Particularly as Mr B had been getting increasingly amorous with Nadine, openly fondling her in a way Jonquil found repulsive. Hogg was snoring gently away in his chair and she was dreading the others leaving him like that when they went to bed.

'Do you mind if I turn in?' she said, getting to her feet and pushing her chair back so its legs scraped noisily on the stone floor, making Hogg jerk awake and rub his eyes.

Mr B whispered something in Nadine's ear. Her dark eyes flashed angrily, then without a word she got up and stalked out of the room, just as Hogg stumbled to his feet, mumbled, 'G'dnight,' and lurched towards the bedrooms.

'I was asking Nadine if she minded if you joined us in bed,' Mr B leered as soon as he and Jonquil were alone. 'She took the huff, which is a bit disappointing, but there's no reason why you and me can't have ourselves a little party, is there?'

He rose to his feet and tried to take her in his arms, but backed away when she hissed, 'I'd throw myself into the Thames rather than have you touch me,' then turned on her heel and strode from the room.

He followed her saying, 'Your loss, sweetheart.' She slammed the door of her bedroom behind her and then waited, holding her breath, for him to lock her in. As soon as the key had turned she sank to her knees and pressed her eye to the keyhole. She let out an exultant sigh when she saw that he'd left the key in the lock.

When she let herself into Jasper's apartment, Saskia could barely breathe for the grip of the sexual excitement she found herself in.

'Jasper!' she called, but was greeted by unwelcome silence. She saw at once through the open door of the bedroom that his bed hadn't been slept in, but the light on his answering machine was flashing.

Thinking it might give her a clue as to his whereabouts, she pressed the playback button and then listened in bewilderment as Jonquil's voice floated out of the machine. At first she could barely make sense of the message, but then slowly, the implications of it sank in.

Jasper gambled, he owed money and someone was threatening him. Jonquil was urging him to make a clean breast of it to her, Saskia, telling him that secrets within a relationship led to disaster.

She could scarcely believe what she was hearing. How could he have been such a fool? The desire which had threatened to consume her only moments before ebbed inexorably away, to be replaced by sickening anxiety.

Where was he? Had the people he owed money to hurt him? And why hadn't he come to her for help? Her head spinning, she sank onto the sofa, wondering what to do next.

Jonquil forced herself to wait an hour before acting, then she tore a sheet out of her notebook and pushed it under the door directly beneath the keyhole, so only a corner was left on her side. Taking one of the wire coat-hangers from the wardrobe, she straightened the hook and inserted it into the lock.

It seemed to make a deafeningly loud metallic noise as she worked it against the end of the key, trying to dislodge it and make it fall onto the paper.

There was a strong chance that it would bounce off, or that when she tried to pull the paper back, there wouldn't be enough of a gap under the door to allow it through.

Her hands were sweating and she wiped them on her trousers before trying again. At last, the key fell to the floor with a subdued clunk and, holding her breath, she began to slide the paper towards her. It was with a feeling of exultation that she saw the key come into view. Grabbing it with trembling fingers, she unlocked the door.

All was still silent as she tiptoed along the corridor. Just one last hurdle to clear. Would the front door be double locked so she'd be unable to open it without a key?

There was a heavy chain in position and she undid that first. That left just a yale and a mortice lock. Almost sick with nerves, she turned the yale lock and then the door handle. It opened.

Barely able to believe it, she slid through the door then sped along the corridor to the lift and pressed the button, glancing nervously over her shoulder. Once at ground level, she ran through the foyer and headed for the main road.

She was in luck. Within five minutes she managed to flag down a cab and gave her brother's address, before sinking back in her seat. When they arrived she asked the driver to wait. She rang Jasper's bell and felt almost faint with relief when she heard someone on the other side of the door.

'Who is it?' she heard Saskia call.

'It's Jonquil. Is Jasper there?' she replied urgently.

The door opened to reveal Saskia looking completely distraught, with her usually immaculate hair starting to come loose from its pins.

'He isn't here. Have the people he owes money to got him?' she demanded. 'I heard your message on his machine – I only arrived myself a few minutes ago, and I haven't a clue where he is.'

Struggling not to panic at the thought of where he could be and what he might be doing to get his hands on the money, Jonquil tried to decide what to do next. It occurred to her that he might have gone to Boyd to ask to borrow it – yes, that was the most likely scenario.

'He may be at Boyd's,' she said. 'I'll go there.'

'I'll come with you.'

'No, you stay here in case he comes home. Ring me if you hear from him.'

She turned and hurried back down the stairs. Despite their quarrel she knew Boyd would help her in such a desperate situation. Getting back into the cab she gave the driver his address.

* * *

Getting the key to Boyd's apartment from Saskia's house had been the easy part. It was the waiting that was the difficult bit. Jasper knew he needed to leave it until at least two a.m. before letting himself in and copying the disc, so that if Boyd was there, he'd be sound asleep.

He hoped fervently that Boyd *wasn't* there, but there was no way of finding out for sure. He phoned the apartment from a call box a couple of times and got no reply, but that didn't mean that Boyd was definitely out, or that he wouldn't be back later.

Too wound up to stay in, Jasper had gone out in the early evening and proceeded to drive aimlessly round. It was undoubtedly the longest evening of his life, but at last, just after two a.m., he parked outside the apartment block and pulled on a pair of supple leather gloves. With the collar of his bomber jacket turned right up to conceal as much of his face as possible, he let himself into the building.

When he reached the door to Boyd's apartment he hesitated, and after a swift look around pressed his ear to it to see if he could hear anything, but he couldn't.

His mouth dry, his breathing ragged, he slipped the first key into the lock and turned it, praying it wouldn't make any noise. The second key stuck briefly and he withdrew it before trying again.

Thankfully it turned at the second attempt and he was able to push the door open a couple of inches and pause to listen. When nothing but the ticking of a clock greeted him, he took out the small but powerful torch he'd bought earlier and switched it on.

Slowly, he made his way along the hall and with his heart banging frantically away in his ribcage, he pushed open the office door and then closed it silently behind him.

He lifted the painting concealing the wall safe down and placed it carefully on the carpet, then punched in the right number and eased open the safe door. He began to sift hastily through the contents, pausing to dash away the sweat trickling down his forehead.

Where was the damn thing? He hadn't allowed himself to

even consider the possibility that the right disc might not be there, that Boyd might have left it at work.

When at last he found it, he had to bite his lip to stop himself letting out a moan of thankfulness, then moved silently over to the computer and switched it on.

He was just hovering over the keyboard having tapped in the password, when a faint noise from the door made him whirl round and the next second the light snapped on, dazzling him.

'Hello, Jasper,' said Boyd's voice from just inside the door. 'To what do I owe the pleasure of this nocturnal visit?'

At the sight of him standing there wearing just a pair of jeans and with a silver candlestick held almost casually by his side, Jasper felt his legs giving way and collapsed into a chair, covering his face with his hands.

'Are you going to explain exactly why you're burgling my apartment *before* I call the police, or shall we wait until they get here and you can tell us all together?' said Boyd, making no attempt to conceal the contempt in his voice.

He put the candlestick down, leant against the door frame and folded his arms as he continued, 'Although I think I can guess – presumably you're planning to sell my new software to the highest bidder. How Jonquil came to have a brother who could do something so despicable is beyond me.'

Jasper looked up, his face agonised. 'You don't understand,' he croaked. 'I'm doing this for Jonquil.'

'If you think I'll believe for one minute that she put you up to this, you're out of your mind,' scoffed Boyd. 'You're even more pathetic than I thought – your sister's never had a dishonest impulse in her life.'

'No, I mean she's been kidnapped,' said Jasper wretchedly, 'and it's all my fault.'

'What are you talking about?' demanded Boyd, taking a step towards him.

'I . . . I used to gamble and I got into debt then couldn't pay it off, so they've abducted her and if I don't get the money by eleven tomorrow they're going to hurt her.' The words came tumbling out haltingly.

'*What?*' thundered Boyd, the single word echoing around the room. 'Who's abducted her? ' He grabbed the front of

Jasper's jacket and hauled him to his feet. 'Tell me!'

'A man called Hogg's got her. He came round this afternoon and showed me a photo of her with a knife pressed to her throat. I tell you, I damn near throttled him on the spot, but he managed to get away. I tried to follow him but he lost me.'

'Did you call the police?'

'No, Hogg told me he has a contact there and he'd get to hear of it at once if I reported it. He said . . . he said it would be the worse for her if the police got involved.'

'He was probably bluffing, but you're right – we can't take the risk. Do you know where he lives?'

'No, and anyway he's working for a man called Mr B who's apparently bought my debt.'

Boyd glanced at his watch. 'Will the casino still be open?'

'Yes.'

'Right. We'll go there and choke Mr B's name and address out of the manager or whoever's in charge, then take him with us so he can't phone and warn the bastard or this Hogg character.'

Boyd left the room and Jasper levered himself out of the chair and followed him. He stood in the doorway of the bedroom and watched Boyd pull a sweater over his head, then thrust his feet into a pair of shoes.

'I'll never forgive myself if anything happens to her,' Jasper said brokenly.

'That makes two of us.' From the grim set of his face, Jasper knew the other man wasn't joking. 'How much do you owe?' Boyd wanted to know.

'Fifteen grand.'

'If we don't manage to find her tonight, I'll go to the bank first thing tomorrow and get the money for you to hand over. We can call the police after we get her safely back.'

Just as Jonquil was paying the driver she saw two figures emerging from Boyd's building. It felt like a miracle as she realised who they were.

'Boyd!' she called weakly. He stopped abruptly and looked over his shoulder.

'Jonquil,' he said hoarsely, racing towards her and gathering her into his arms. 'Are you all right? Did they hurt you?'

'I'm fine,' she reassured him, 'but I've never needed a drink so badly in my life.'

Dawn was breaking by the time Jasper got back to his apartment. It had been a long night and he was exhausted. He'd told the police the whole story, except for his attempt to steal the software which, for Jonquil's sake, Boyd had insisted he kept to himself.

Although they were going to charge Mr B and Hogg with abduction, Boyd had said that on the following day he was going to the casino and would pay Jasper's debt. When Jasper had protested, Boyd had silenced him with a gesture.

'Don't imagine for one moment I'm doing it for you,' he'd said coldly. 'I'm doing it to make sure that your unbelievable stupidity doesn't rebound on Jonquil again. My guess is that if the money isn't paid, someone else will come crawling out of the woodwork somewhere down the line demanding it, and I don't want her looking over her shoulder and living in fear.'

Jasper had felt flayed by the searing contempt in his voice and had known without a shadow of a doubt that he'd never gamble again.

Things were going to be different from now on. He'd get the first job he could and work like a slave until he'd paid off the debt in monthly instalments.

He let himself into his apartment, dreading the confrontation with Saskia, aware that now she knew what a loser he was it would be over between them. Through the open door, he saw her fall of ice-blonde hair on his pillow and went swiftly into his bedroom. Her eyes fluttered open, her long lashes casting tiny crescent shadows over her pale skin.

'Jasper – why didn't you tell me?' she asked, sitting up and pulling the quilt higher so it hid the swell of her creamy breasts.

'I was scared of losing you,' he muttered.

'You needn't have been. We all do stupid things from time to time.'

'You mean it's not over?'

211

'No – but you obviously need taking in hand,' she told him briskly. 'I think you should consider joining Gamblers Anonymous.'

'There's no need. Knowing that I've put my sister in danger because of my reckless behaviour has made me feel so ashamed of myself that I think I'd throw up if I ever tried to place another bet.' He hesitated before continuing, 'There's something else you don't know.'

'What?'

'I lost my job.'

'You *do* need taking in hand. You'd better move in with me – that way you won't have to find the rent and you'll be able to pay Boyd back quicker.'

She allowed the quilt to slip down to her waist and lay languorously back on the pillows. 'Get undressed,' she commanded.

It was early afternoon when Jonquil woke up in Boyd's bed. She noticed that she was wearing one of his shirts but had no memory of putting it on, or in fact going to bed after the police had eventually left. Had they made love? No; she would have remembered.

She felt like a sleepwalker as she got slowly out of bed and then made her way to the sitting room where he was reading a newspaper which he immediately threw to the floor when he saw her.

'How are you feeling?' he asked.

'Dazed,' she admitted. 'Have I missed anything?'

'I've been to the casino and paid the money to a slimy character called Jake. I made it very clear to him that if your brother was ever allowed to set foot on the premises again, it would be his turn to be looking over his shoulder. Just after I got back, the police rang – they have Mr B in custody along with Hogg and the woman. They want you to go along to make a statement later.'

'I hope they don't charge Nadine – she did her best to help both Jasper and me.'

'Right now, I'm more concerned about us. We need to have a serious talk.' He looked so grim that Jonquil quailed. 'I'm

212

not married to Julie. I'm not divorced from Julie. I've never been married to Julie.'

Incredulity swept through her. 'But . . . but what about the announcement of your engagement to her in the paper?'

'You never gave me the chance to explain. When I went up to London to see her just after you graduated, it was because she was having man trouble. She was always been very insecure because of her unhappy childhood, but at last she fell for someone, but he was being slow about committing himself. Too slow for Julie.'

Boyd lowered himself onto the arm of the chair, facing Jonquil as he went on, 'Her plan was that I should appear on the scene and pay her a lot of attention to make him jealous. It worked, but she felt he needed just a final push to get him to ask her to marry him. She didn't discuss it with me, just placed the announcement in the paper herself. When she showed it to me, I was as shocked as you must have been.'

Jonquil heard what he was saying, but somehow all the words jumbled together in her brain and she couldn't quite make sense of them. She shook her head, trying to clear it.

'It's true,' he insisted, misinterpreting the gesture. 'I was furious and bawled her out in no uncertain terms, telling her that she should have consulted me first. I phoned you, but your hall of residence told me that you'd packed up and left. I tried to get your home address out of both the university and your hall of residence, but they wouldn't give them to me.'

He rose to his feet and towered over her, his face set. 'Why did you run away like that? Why didn't you wait for me to come back and explain?' he demanded.

'I . . . I thought you really were going to marry Julie,' she faltered. 'She was so flirtatious with you and so possessive, that when I saw the announcement I thought it must be true, so I ran away.' She paused, then the memory of seeing them together outside his office building flooded back. 'I saw you with her this week,' she accused him. 'You kissed her.'

'She married the man she fell for and they're still happily together, seven years later – I'm godfather to their son, Felix. She came up to town to have lunch with me and to tell me that she's pregnant again. When she told me I kissed her – I didn't

213

know that you were watching and would put the wrong interpretation on it.'

'Why have you never told me any of this before?' she whispered.

'I was angry with you because you hadn't trusted me. After we got back together again in Spain, I thought you'd realised you'd made a mistake. I knew that I'd made the worst mistake of my life by putting her before you, that time. But I was in the habit of looking out for her, because no one else ever had and it was a hard habit to break.'

'I kept waiting for you to mention her, or to see some evidence that she was still in your life, but eventually I came to the conclusion that you must have got divorced at some stage,' she explained. 'When I saw you together again, I thought you were still married, but that she lived in the country somewhere.'

He advanced on her with such a determined expression on his face that she shrank back against the sofa cushions.

'W . . . what are you doing?' she quavered, as he scooped her up into his arms and stood her on her feet.

'Make an educated guess,' he said affably. He moved behind her and slid his hands under the shirt, moving them upwards until they covered her bare breasts. He weighed them in his hands then caressed the nipples, tugging on them gently until they hardened into swollen points. He stroked her belly and hips, holding her against him so she could feel the ramrod hard column of his phallus pressing into her back.

He lifted her onto the table and covered her mound with the palm of his hand. Pressing downwards, he rubbed it in a seductive circular movement. He pushed her thighs widely apart, then with the utmost delicacy parted her outer sex-lips with his hands, holding her open and studying her as if she were a rare flower.

Jonquil could feel warm moisture gathering just inside her velvety channel and the blood rushing to her sex organs as he devoured her most intimate parts with his eyes.

She felt a sudden tickling sensation on her inner thighs and realised her female dew had overflowed and was trickling onto the smooth wooden surface of the table.

Still Boyd studied her, then slowly he traced the contours

of her inner labia with his forefinger, drawing it between them and dabbling in the sticky moisture he discovered there.

Her flood of moisture obviously excited him because he inhaled sharply and began to stroke the swiftly fattening bud of her clitoris. She closed her eyes as he slipped two fingers of his other hand inside her and commenced an ecstatic exploration of her slick, welcoming sex.

Of its own volition, her bottom began to rotate on the table top as she felt herself climbing higher and higher without ever gaining the release she sought. The tantalising frustration of trembling on the brink made her desperate and she began to grind her vulva against his hand.

She found she was holding her breath. From somewhere, she heard the loud ticking of a clock filling the silence and then he quickened the rhythmic stroking of his forefinger.

The result was immediate: a jagged jolt of excitement like low-voltage electricity zapped through her and she caught her lower lip between her teeth in an attempt to hold back the cry that threatened to escape.

She held the edge of the table with both hands as a faint film of perspiration formed between her breasts and her breathing became ragged and strained. She felt the surge of heat a few seconds before she climaxed, wetly and wonderfully.

She dragged his zip down, freed his shaft and guided it clumsily to her entrance. Nothing had ever felt as good as his swollen member forging its way inside her, stretching her, filling her, pleasuring her.

She wound her legs around him and he lifted her from the table, his hands under her bottom, and held her as she rose and fell on his rearing manhood.

It was an urgent, desperate coupling as they came together in a frantic race for satisfaction. He buried his face in her cleavage as he came, holding her hard against him until they subsided against each other and he lowered her to the floor. They both collapsed onto the soft, thick carpet and lay in each other's arms.

'That wasn't bad, to start with,' he said a few minutes later, reaching for her again. 'But we've got a lot of catching up to do.'

Dangerous Desires

J. J. DUKE

*In response to his command, Nadine began
to undress. She was wearing her working
clothes, a black skirt and a white silk blouse.
As she unzipped the skirt she tried to keep
her mind in neutral. She didn't do this kind
of thing. As far as she could remember, she
had never gone to bed with a man only
hours after she'd met him . . .*

There's something about painter John
Sewell that Nadine Davies can't resist.
Though she's bowled over by his looks
and his talent, she knows he's arrogant
and unfaithful. It can't be love and it's
nothing like friendship. He makes her
feel emotions she's never felt before.

And there's another man, too. A man
like Sewell who makes her do things
she'd never dreamed of – and she
adores it. She's under their spell, in
thrall to their dangerous desires . . .

0 7472 5093 6

Vermilion Gates

Lucinda Chester

Rob trailed a finger over Rowena's knee, letting it drift upwards. She slapped his hand. 'Get off me,' she hissed, 'or I'll have you for sexual harassment.' Nevertheless, part of her wanted him to carry on and stroke the soft white skin above her lacy stocking-tops . . .

Rowena Fletcher's not having much fun these days. She's a stressed-out female executive with a workload more jealous than any lover and no time, in any case, to track one down.

Then she is referred to Vermilion Gates, a discreet clinic in the Sussex countryside which specialises in relaxation therapy. There, in the expert hands of trained professionals, Rowena discovers there's more than one way to relieve her personal stress . . .

0 7472 5210 6

If you enjoyed this book here is a selection of other bestselling Adult Fiction titles from Headline Liaison